MIDNIGHT CAPTIVE

Book 2 of the

Bonded By Blood

Vampire Chronicles

ARIAL BURNZ

MIDNIGHT CAPTIVE
Book 2 of the Bonded By Blood Vampire Chronicles

March 2013

Published by
Mystical Press
Rancho Cucamonga, CA 91701
www.MysticalPress.com

Copyright © 2013 by G.C. Henderson
Edited by AJ Nuest
Cover design by Arial Burnz

ISBN 10: 1482796104
ISBN 13: 978-1482796100

Printed in the United States of America

This book is a work of fiction and any resemblance to persons—living,
dead, undead or magical—or places, events or locales is purely
coincidental. The characters are productions of the authors' imagination
and used fictitiously.

MIDNIGHT CAPTIVE

Book 2 of the

Bonded By Blood

Vampire Chronicles

ARIAL BURNZ

Dear Sandy,
Thank you so
much for your support! I
hope you enjoy the series!
All my best!
Arial Burnz

MYSTICAL PRESS—RANCHO CUCAMONGA, CA

"An intricately crafted vampire series that will leave you *spellbound* and *thirsting* for the next book!"
~Paige Thomas, Author of *Starstruck*

"Starting with a promise, this book provides a visionary tale of *love*, *strength*, *lust*, *hate*, *loyalty*, *abandonment issues* and *vengeance*, all woven together seamlessly to create far more than just another *vampire* story."
—M. Sembera, author of *The Rennillia Series*

Writing as Arial Burnz

Bonded By Blood Vampire Chronicles:
Midnight Conquest—Book 1
Midnight Captive—Book 2

Writing as Christine Davies (children's books)

Where Art Thou Unicorn?

Buy Arial's books on Amazon!

DEDICATION

To the air that feeds my fire
To the waters that cool my soul
To my romance novel hero
And the man who makes me whole
I love you, DeWayne!

Under different circumstances, she'd be very taken with this man. And she still couldn't help wondering where she'd seen his face.

Throwing his cloak back over his shoulders, he revealed a broad chest that rippled under the thin material of his black shirt as he reached across his hip for his sword.

Cailin blanched. Not many men carried swords on their person in the port city of Leith—daggers were the weapon of choice and easier to conceal—and those that did rarely matched the craftsmanship of this blade. This was not a cheap, decorative sword. *Out of one mess and into another.* She swallowed her fear and stood her ground.

"I suggest a wager." He winked.

"I am not a gambling woman."

Tilting his head back, he laughed and Cailin clenched her jaw, her cheeks blooming with heat again. Amusement twinkling in his eyes, he ignored her comment. "A challenge. If you win, I shall let you walk free."

"And if you win?"

The amusement in his eyes transformed into smoldering desire. "I shall have to take you in hand and see you submit..." His eyes raked her body. "To the proper authority." He folded his arms in front of him, the blade of his sword sweeping up and standing erect from his fist.

Cailin's breath left her in a rush and fire surged through her body—from the fluttering in her stomach to the tingling in her toes. She did not miss his twofold meaning, and drew a deep, steadying breath, biting her tongue; though keeping her tongue proved more difficult to manage. "We shall see about this, *sir.*"

ACKNOWLEDGMENTS

Again, I could not be where I am with my writing career if it wasn't for my husband and romance novel hero, DeWayne. Not only has he given me the support and freedom to pursue my dreams, he's been an invaluable partner in helping me brainstorm my plots and iron out the many wonderful layers I have created in the tales I so enjoy sharing with the world. With you, I can do anything, my darling!

Thank you to my editor and best friend AJ Nuest for lending me her time, love and support and giving me that second pair of critical eyes needed to ensure everything falls into place. She always makes my writing better! Any mistakes or errors are my responsibility, not hers. You have been my faithful writing partner, and now business partner, through thick and thin, and I am eternally grateful. *Mwah!*

Hugs, kisses and special kudos go to my test readers, especially Lindsey Beckwith and Millie Losee. Your detailed feedback was so valuable and made *Captive* a better book!!!

A special mention goes to Ron Reil—geologist, blacksmith, engineer, rancher and fireman. He was kind enough to answer my endless questions about how silver could be incorporated into melee weapons. He also introduced me to the amazing *Wootz* blades that are mentioned in this book. I encourage you to research "wootz steel" in your favorite search engine. Don't forget to stop by Ron's website to see the wealth of information he has about forging weapons and tell him Arial sent you! He can be found in cyberspace at RonReil.abana.org.

As the Scottish poet Robert Burns said in his 1785 poem, "The best-laid schemes o' mice an' men gang aft agley." Or more commonly heard: "The best-laid plans of mice and men go oft awry." I planned this book until I thought I could plan no more, crafted an extensive outline, hammered out the details and laid out my final storyline. Yet when I sat before the computer to finally pen the prose you hold in your hands...I was stumped. My characters seemed wooden, they refused to speak to me, and my story would not progress. I owe the completion of this story to Alan Watt and his fabulous book *The 90-Day Novel: Unlocking the Story Within.* You can't have a body without a heart pumping life into it...and that's exactly what Alan's book taught me: to give my characters heart and motivation. I enthusiastically encourage anyone who writes to explore Alan's book. He can be found at LAWritersLab.com. Thank you, Alan!!

And finally, a heartfelt 'thank you' goes out to my fans. Because of the above, this book took much longer than I expected. I promise not to put a forecasted date on another project for fear of fostering frustration when I am unable to meet the said deadline. As an author, editor, cover artist and now audio book recording artist...on top of the repairs/remodel we're doing at home...I have a lot on my plate. Deadlines are unpredictable with so many variables. I appreciate your encouragement and patience. After nearly a two-year wait, at last I present...MIDNIGHT CAPTIVE. Enjoy!

Arial Burnz
February 2013

PROLOGUE

Stonehenge, England—1530

Cordelia Lynn Harley stood beside one of the stone sentinels in the monolithic circle. Eyeing the ancient cragged surface, she traced her finger along a crack while she waited. She scanned the horizon for any sign of the prophetess and, again, saw none. The new moon above, like a silver claw in the black sky, lent little illumination to the landscape. Her immortal eyes beheld only far-stretching flatlands of fields and grass dotted with sheep and cattle.

"Thank you for coming on such short notice."

Cordelia started and spun to face Malloren Rune. "I still do not understand how you can sneak up on me, being mortal."

The prophetess smiled under the glow of the lantern she held, her brown eyes sparkling with mischief. "You weren't paying attention, *Vamsyrian.*

I'm sure your mind was exploring the possibilities of the news I have for you."

Cordelia's heart hammered and she followed Malloren to one of the fallen stones of the monument. The prophetess sat on the sleeping giant, setting the lantern beside her. Cordelia knelt in breathless anticipation with her hands clenched on her lap. "You found the second sign?"

"That I did."

Cordelia near collapsed from the wave of relief. "'Tis just as you foretold and everything is falling into place. What *is* the second sign?"

"That cannot be revealed until certain events take place. First, you must deliver an important item for me." The prophetess patted the stone, encouraging Cordelia to sit.

Though disappointed at the delay, Cordelia became excited over the new task. "An item?"

"Indeed. One that will spark a chain of events to move the prophecy along and ensure the second sign can be fulfilled." Malloren produced a small leather pouch a hand's width across and three fingers deep.

A wire-and-wax seal secured the flap closure. Cordelia recognized the seal of the *Tzava Ha'or*— The Army of Light. "What is the item?"

The prophetess curled a finger under Cordelia's chin to draw her gaze. "Listen to me, dear one."

The grave expression on Malloren's face made Cordelia shiver.

"You must not open this pouch or you will undo all we are working toward. Do you understand?"

"Yes." She swallowed.

Malloren presented a folded piece of parchment. "You will take this pouch to the location detailed on this map."

Cordelia set the pouch on her lap and pried open the edges of the paper.

"You must be at that designated location just after nightfall three days hence. Not one day sooner or later. A man will be waiting for you. The pouch is for him to open and none other. He has further instructions inside."

Cordelia met the intense gaze of the prophetess and nodded. "Why are *you* not delivering the pouch?"

"Because I cannot wipe his memory of our encounter. Your abilities as a Vamsyrian are why you must deliver the pouch. Give him the satchel and leave no trace of your face or my instructions to meet you in his mind. He should wake up with the satchel in his hand and my instructions to guide him." She pursed her lips in disapproval. "And you must not wait for him to open the pouch. You deliver it and leave. You will meet me here again on the first full moon after the summer solstice."

"'Tis almost a year hence! Why—?"

3

"During that time, certain events will take place to advance the prophecy so we may perform the second sign. Besides, you will have other errands to run."

Cordelia dropped her jaw at the enormity of her mentor's previous statement. "*We* will perform the sign?"

Malloren kissed the top of Cordelia's head. "Yes, child…we will."

CHAPTER ONE

Leith, Scotland—June 1531

The cold steel of the blade pressed so hard against Cailin MacDougal's throat, she couldn't swallow the lump forming there—nor could she be sure her eyes watered from fear or her attacker. He smelled atrocious! His body odor and bad breath hovered around her like a fog, and she struggled to breathe. Grand appreciation filled the stranger's blood-shot eyes as they raked over her face and neckline, the corners of his mouth forming an evil grin. "Oh, ye shall be a tasty treat for ol' Jasper before I hand ye over!"

Cailin cursed over falling for the trap. She had heard of this happening—a young child asking for assistance, luring unsuspecting yet helpful strangers into alleyways, only to be jumped by someone waiting to rob them of their goods...sometimes worse. Where the young lad she followed had gone

5

to now was hardly her concern. The chance that this Jasper might be working for Angus Campbell—which was a constant fear of her family's—pressed upon her as acutely as his knife pressed against her throat.

She tried to squirm out of Jasper's grasp—his one beefy hand holding her wrists behind her—only to be pressed harder into the barrels against the back, hidden corner of the alley. With the sharp edge against her skin, the dread over falling into the hands of her father's enemy, and the frustration of her attacker stepping on her skirts, effectively pinning her in place—Cailin's mind swirled. She fought the images of Angus feeding from her mother Davina in the dark cell he'd taken them to, his taunting eyes, Davina's blood on his smiling lips. She willed her emotions into submission. If she didn't calm down, she would never be able to concentrate on escaping and would suffer the same fate as her mother.

Jasper removed the knife from her throat to caress her cheek and she breathed easier, finally able to swallow and find her voice. "Sir, you have my purse. If you would just—"

He grabbed her throat. "Be still, ducks."

Heat rose in Cailin's cheeks when he trailed the blade to her neckline, cutting through her material. How she allowed this lout to pin her in such a confining position was beyond her, and she would never forget such a stupid mistake. This was what she deserved for underestimating him in his slovenly appearance. Admittedly, her skirts made hand-to-hand combat most difficult, so she allowed herself some forgiveness. Training in a gown would be next on her agenda, but until then, she still had this situation to manage. If she could just get her hands on her daggers, hidden within the folds of her dress! She ventured one last glance down the narrow passage. No one had yet come running up the alley, so evidently her initial cry for help went unheard. She was on her own.

There! The idiot shifted to straddle her leg, no longer pinning her, and rubbed his erection against her hip. Ignoring the blush that heated her face, she seized the long-awaited opportunity to pivot her weight, push him away and bring her knee up between his legs, gladly making contact with his offending member. Jasper collapsed to his knees, howling. Hiking her skirts, Cailin kicked the dagger from his hand, brought her foot back and swiped it across his jaw. He curled into an infantile position, groaning and clutching his groin. Cailin dusted her hands in triumph. Not wanting to make the same mistake twice, she pulled at least one of her daggers out at the ready. Shaking her head at his pitiful display, she crouched beside him and searched his vest for her pouch.

A deep, rumbling laugh echoed against the brick walls and she contemplated the raven-haired figure standing at the entrance of the alleyway, a long dark cloak concealing his rather large frame. "And just who is robbing whom?"

Pale-green eyes assessed her as he sauntered forward, crossing his arms. Something seemed vaguely familiar about this man. A delightful shiver tickled over her skin when his eyes fell upon her breasts and the smile melted from his mouth.

He swallowed hard. "If you do not close your bodice, my dear, I cannot be held responsible for my actions."

His deep voice flowed over her body like warm water from the Mediterranean Sea. Cailin glanced down at her bodice—the top of her bosoms flushed pink and rounded above her torn neckline. She narrowed her eyes at him. "Your *actions* may lead you to join this poor soul on the ground."

With the knife clutched in her left hand—giving her a little more courage than she should probably dare—she searched the robber with her other hand while keeping her eyes trained on the intruder. Jasper stirred as she retrieved her belongings and she diverted her attention just enough to deal him another blow to his jaw, causing him to slump into unconsciousness.

She tucked the purse into her dress pocket. Standing, she raised an eyebrow, the corner of her mouth lifting in a smirk, and faced the wide-eyed and slack-jawed handsome stranger.

At a quick intake of breath, he stepped before her and stole his arm around her waist in one motion. Pressing her against the full form of his hard body, he pushed her breasts even more over her torn neckline.

"Unless you wish to keep your private jewels intact," she warned, "I suggest you keep your distance, sir." With her dagger at his groin, she tilted the silver-plated blade up to make her point.

His body stiffened against her and fear flickered across his eyes. Taking one step back, he peered down at the dagger between them and fingered the cut she sliced in his breeches. He hitched his breath and offered a respectful nod, retreating. But the sneer returned to his lips. "I see the lady is handy with a blade." He studied the dagger before his eyes roamed her body and he crossed his arms again. "And how is it a gentile maid such as yourself came to be so experienced at close combat with such expertly crafted weapons? Mind you, I use the terms 'lady' and 'gentile' with much reluctance." He snickered.

Cailin narrowed her eyes. "Obviously you underestimate my skills."

"Obviously." When Cailin tried to step past him, he countered to block her exit. "You also dodged my question."

She clenched her jaw at his arrogance. "Aye, 'tis unbecoming of a *lady* to have such extensive training, but I have likely seen more tutelage in this area than you could hope to dream of, *sir.*"

Cailin resisted the urge to sigh at the rich laughter that rumbled from his chest and, at the same time, she wanted to punch him square in the jaw.

"Do I detect a challenge, my dear?" His eyes near sparkled at the prospect.

Oh, why do men always have to prove themselves? "Nay, dear sir, 'tis a simple fact I pass along to you for your own good. Now, if you will excuse me."

Another bout of laughter poured from him. "As a good citizen, I cannot let you pass without extracting some justice for this poor soul you have robbed and rendered unconscious."

It was Cailin's turn to laugh. "Good citizen? With the crime that riddles this port? Surely you jest at dispensing justice."

"Precisely why I can only assume a woman wandering such dangerous streets alone can only be up to ill intent." He grinned.

Cailin stepped left, as did he. She stepped right, only to meet his expansive presence again. Not wishing any further delays, she half-heartedly swiped her dagger at him to feign him off, which he dodged effectively. She stepped back and drew her other dagger from the specially tailored belt crafted for her weapons. With it positioned low on her waist, the leather-and-steel sheaths lay against her hips and hidden amongst the folds of her gown. Narrow crossbars made it easy to withdraw the silver-plated Wootz blades, which she twirled in her hands before facing him, poised and ready. She reveled in a certain measure of satisfaction at seeing a dumbfounded expression replace his cocky demeanor. "Please step aside, sir, so that I may pass. Do not force me to do something you may regret."

A fire blazed in his green eyes, which gleamed like opals at her challenge, and that sensuous mouth curled into a smirk. Jasper moaned and the bonnie intruder stepped forward to give the man on the ground a quick jab to the jaw, knocking him silent again. He stepped back and resumed his arrogant position.

Under different circumstances, she'd be very taken with this man. And she still couldn't help wondering where she'd seen his face.

Throwing his cloak back over his shoulders, he revealed a broad chest that rippled under the thin material of his black shirt as he reached across his hip for his sword.

Cailin blanched. Not many men carried swords on their person in the port city of Leith—daggers were the weapon of choice and easier to conceal— and those that did rarely matched the craftsmanship of this blade. This was not a cheap, decorative sword. *Out of one mess and into another.* She swallowed her fear and stood her ground.

"I suggest a wager." He winked.

"I am not a gambling woman."

Tilting his head back, he laughed and Cailin clenched her jaw, her cheeks blooming with heat again. Amusement twinkling in his eyes, he ignored her comment. "A challenge. If you win, I shall let you walk free."

"And if *you* win?"

The amusement in his eyes transformed into smoldering desire. "I shall have to take you in hand and see you submit…" His eyes raked her body. "To the proper authority." He folded his arms in front of him, the blade of his sword sweeping up and standing erect from his fist.

Cailin's breath left her in a rush and fire surged through her body—from the fluttering in her stomach to the tingling in her toes. She did not miss his twofold meaning, and drew a deep, steadying breath, biting her tongue; though keeping her tongue proved more difficult to manage. "We shall see about this, *sir.*"

With a chuckle, he advanced. Cailin had the upper hand with two blades and extensive training. Twirling her arms and bending at the waist, she parried his thrust, continued through her movement and landed a sound kick to his side, sending him sprawling into the barrels. Once the loud clatter of boxes and debris settled, he shook his head. Her opponent gazed at her with large eyes while she widened her stance and readied her blades.

His brow furrowed and he rose to his feet, adjusting his shirt and positioning his sword. "Shall we try that again?"

"I can repeat that if you are a glutton for punishment, but I think you are fool."

He laughed. With a sweep of his sword, he forced Cailin to switch her stance to block his blade. To her dismay, he also pushed her off balance and wound his arms around her, pinning her hands behind her back. She faced him, chest against chest, seething at the advantage he had taken.

"'Tis dangerous you are with those blades." He wrested the daggers from her and tossed them aside. "Now, how do you suppose we should settle this matter?"

She grumbled. "He tried to rob me. I defended myself and you interfered. What is there to settle?"

"You must understand, from my perspective, I saw quite the opposite."

Cailin wriggled, making a concerted effort to free herself, but gained no purchase against him. Huffing in defeat, she said, "I care not what you *think* you saw. He trapped me and I was forced to defend myself." She wiggled again and stopped when his arousal pressed against her belly. Heat stole into her cheeks and she gazed into his sea-green eyes, growing stormy with desire.

Before Cailin could utter another word, his mouth descended upon hers, capturing a seeking kiss. Surely her lack of will to resist was due to the ordeal she'd just experienced. But the flutter in her stomach told her she enjoyed this man's touch far too much to blame exhaustion. The daydreams of her first kiss with her promised groom—what the experience would be like, how she would respond—all vanished like smoke on the wind. She never imagined this hungry, carnal reality. When his tongue teased along the crease of her lips, she opened her mouth to him, inviting a new swirl of quivers down her spine as their tongues danced. A primal heat stole into her belly and sank to settle between her legs, which wobbled and threatened to give way.

"Cailin MacDougal!"

As if a bucket of cold water had been thrown in her face, Cailin stumbled back, sputtering and struggling to gain her composure. Jasper was gone and the handsome stranger stared at her with his mouth open and his cheeks red. With a purposeful stride, Davina MacDougal marched down the alley toward Cailin and the man who had so wonderfully assaulted her mouth. Cailin rolled her eyes.

"Child, I should slap that expression from your face!" Davina stood before them, huffing her frustration, then clasped Cailin in a tight embrace. "Why must you insist on venturing out alone? This is not a jesting situation. Your life is in danger every time you wander about unescorted."

"M'ma, Ranald and Will *were* right behind me, but there is something I— "

Davina held up her hand toward Cailin and turned to the man standing with his mouth open. "Well?"

He gawked at Cailin. "Mouse?"

Cailin swallowed and gaped at his face with understanding. "James Knightly," she whispered and the blood drained from her face. Well, at least this explained why he seemed so familiar. Spending a lifetime dodging the dangerous intentions of her father's clan enemy, Angus Campbell, gave Cailin no choice but to learn the necessary combat skills to defend herself—hardly the behavior her groom-to-be would want in his wife. Not knowing who he was, she showed him a side she never intended him to see. James would never have her now and the shock on his face confirmed that.

"Cailin MacDougal, do not *dare* stand there and tell me you thought you were kissing a stranger!" Davina sighed, shaking her head, and fussed with Cailin's torn neckline.

She waved off her mother's attentions. "Obviously I was a stranger to him as well! Save some of your wrath for *him*." Fighting the tears stinging the backs of her eyes, Cailin pushed past her mother and retrieved her daggers, returning them to the sheaths at her hips. She faced her mother, prepared for the onslaught of scolding, only to find a sly smile on James's face. It had been seven years since she'd last seen James Knightly and her memories of him did not match the towering and imposing man before her.

"Come," Davina prompted and led the way out of the alley.

Cailin started to follow her mother, then doubled back to snatch her forgotten bundle, which she'd dropped when Jasper jumped her. Doing so landed her back into James's embrace as they collided from her sudden change in direction.

"'Tis thrice you've ended in my arms." A wolfish grin curved the corner of his full lips and Cailin near swooned. "I could fast get accustomed to this."

A flutter tickled her belly at the hum of his deep voice vibrating against her breast. He was sure to toss her aside once he learned more about her, though, so she fought the attraction for him tingling across her skin. "Do not hope for such chances in the future. I shall be sure to avoid them." She pushed away from the circle of his arms and picked up her package.

Cailin pivoted, marched out of the alleyway and smashed into a hard, leather breastplate.

"My apologies, Mistress Cailin," said Ranald.

She scowled at him, sick to death of the way he followed her around like a shadow. She turned her glaring eyes to his accomplice, Will, who offered a reluctant grin. James pressed his body behind Cailin and presented the parcel she'd dropped when colliding with Ranald.

"Lose something?" he whispered against her ear.

She struggled against the urge to fall back into him and snatched the package, clinging to her frustration for strength. "Only my sanity at being surrounded by brutes!"

Shoving away from the three towering men, she scampered after her mother's determined pace, James so close behind her, she swore she could feel his presence.

Davina led them around the building, down High Street and toward the docks to their destination. Saddling up beside Cailin, James matched her furious steps. "As my betrothed, I would think such close encounters would not only be unavoidable, but desired."

She bit her lip to steady it before whirling to answer. "But that is where you are mistaken, Master James. We are not betrothed, but *promised*, and that is something you and our fathers arranged when you were far too young to make such a decision. You need not worry yourself with having to be saddled with the likes me."

His brow furrowed. "And why would you speak of yourself in such a way? I may have been young, but I still believe we are a smart match." He stepped closer and trailed his fingertip along her jaw line. "Why would you not agree to a union that has not only been planned since our youth, but holds an obvious attraction betwixt the two of us?"

Cailin allowed herself the moment. How she wanted to fall into his arms and believe this could actually work. However, his inevitable rejection loomed before her and she brushed his hand away. "I am not the simple child you once knew," she whispered with regret. "Much has transpired since you went away to attend your schooling." The buried longings of happiness in marital bliss oozed from her heart and Cailin swallowed the lump forming in her throat. "Our circumstances have changed." Picking up her skirts, she glanced at the trailing guards before scuttling after her mother.

The three of them filed into the office of MacDougal & Knightly Shipping Company, the guards standing outside in their usual position at post. Davina motioned for both James and Cailin to sit down in the wooden chairs available in the room for conducting business. James hung his cloak on the hook by the door, while Cailin placed her bundle on the desk before her mother.

"I thought to bring you something to eat since you mentioned this morning you would work through the afternoon."

Davina's shoulders sagged and a sad smile turned up the corners of her mouth. "Thank you, Cailin. You make it difficult for me to be cross with you when you make kind gestures."

Kissing her mother's brow, Cailin grinned and sat down.

"I am glad that lad Brian at the stables had sense enough to come fetch me when he saw you trail after that urchin. You have heard me express my grievances over these lone ventures many times before." Her mother's voice was laced with compassion. "But for James's benefit, I will not repeat myself."

Cailin relaxed, thankful their discussion would be tabled for another time.

Davina turned her attention to the ledger before her, scratching her quill across the parchment pages. Over a decade ago, Cailin's father Broderick MacDougal—in actuality her step-father, but the only father she had ever known and dearly loved—began a small shipping company in the port city of Leith, just a few miles outside of Edinburgh. A meager beginning to be sure—especially in a town still repairing itself in the wake of devastation from the English—but in the capable hands of her father, the business grew to be a reputable establishment. Due to Broderick's inability to tend to the duties during the day, many responsibilities fell to Davina—especially since Alistair had disappeared, abandoning his partnership and his son, James. Though Broderick did what he could at night to maintain the majority of the transactions and scheduling, Cailin recalled the many times in her childhood, playing on the floor while her mother labored over the accounting and records. As an adult, Cailin realized this allowed Broderick to focus on generating business arrangements and the actual managing of the merchandise with hired help. Now, she blushed over the countless fits she pitched as a child, demanding her mother's attention.

Cailin had learned to read and write by diving into the business with her mother. She learned that MacDougal & Knightly primarily dealt with the shipping of wool, cured salmon, cheese and furs; however, Broderick frequently arranged to secure other avenues of trade for spices, dried fruits, dye-stuffs and choice cloths and embroidery. Working side-by-side with them, Cailin developed a deep respect for her parents' ingenuity, teamwork and intelligence. They were an inspiration in her preparing to be the perfect partner for James, once he claimed his partnership with her father. She cast a sidelong glance toward her promised groom, who caught her peeking at him. He winked and the room grew warm. She cleared her throat and pretended to study her mother's busy hands.

As of late, Broderick impressed her by importing fine art from Italy and used her mother's loose connection to the crown to garner an increasing demand for such items. Being a cousin to the King—though illegitimate—had its privileges, including the opportunity for her father to be awarded the meager title of Lord for his accomplishments and many favors to the King. The desk, which Cailin's mother leaned against now, was piled with contracts and accounting ledgers. Though Davina usually appeared as worn as the papers burdening the office, Cailin was pleased to see her mother in higher spirits today.

Davina turned to James with a smile. "Thank you for your patience while I finished these documents. I am relieved to see you finally home, James. Broderick and I have a special surprise for you this evening. I pray you do not have any other engagements?"

"Of course not, Lady MacDougal." James dipped his head respectfully with a grin.

"And as for you, my darling," Davina addressed Cailin as she rose from her chair. "Though I appreciate your gesture at bringing me some nourishment, I am finished for the afternoon. I have finalized some documents here to be picked up on the morrow by a client and the shipments we had scheduled for today have set sail for their destination."

James rose and grabbed his cloak. "I shall escort you both back home where you may enjoy a hot meal together."

James cast Cailin a warm smile and winked. He seemed oblivious to what had transpired between them in the alley. Nay, his behavior leaned toward a favorable demeanor. Dare she hope he was forgiving over her rash and masculine display with weapons? Turning her back to James as she adjusted her skirts, she sighed with relief. He laid a possessive hand upon the small of her back, ushering her out after her mother, and Cailin allowed the excitement over their union to bloom anew.

"'Tis good to see you back home, Master James," Ranald offered once they were on the road out of Leith.

James nodded at both the guards trailing behind. "'Tis good to be home," he said distractedly. After retrieving their mounts at the stable on High Street, James allowed the two women some distance on the road toward the MacDougal estate. Cailin's fire ignited an intense curiosity and he needed to digest his thoughts. Seven years ago, he'd left to become a defense master at one of the best *Fechtschulen*, or fencing schools, in the Kingdom of Germany—leaving behind a promised bride with doe eyes, a freckled face and a lanky figure. He had returned to find a storming bundle of independence that had his mind swirling at the thought of her wielding those silver blades. He adjusted his suddenly tightening breeches. She was indeed accurate in her description—she was not the simple child he once knew.

And the surprise on her face reminded him he was not the same person she once knew. Guilt flushed from his throat and burned his cheeks. He scrubbed his hands over his face to hide any signs of his shame. He had been seventeen and Cailin nine years of age when he proposed their union to their fathers. And though time and maturity did change a person, what had transpired over the last seven years of his life was surely more than she would have expected. But she didn't know. She couldn't know. James never told her in their letters, finding it best to keep such morbid facts to himself. He would deal with his own demons and not burden his bride.

In spite of his past, he still believed neither of them had deviated from the core of their beings. Why she thought circumstances between them had altered so much as to dissolve their union he wasn't sure…unless she'd found out what he had done. He sorely hoped not.

Oh, that he could go back and reclaim the innocence of when he first proposed the betrothal. Broderick MacDougal had raised a brow and crossed his arms over his massive chest, a stance that never failed to make James shrink in his presence. However, James had stuck out his own chest and stood his ground.

"Well?" Broderick had prodded. "Tell me why you think I should let you wed my daughter?"

James was prepared. "I realize she is still very young, so I am obviously not proposing this betrothal with an immediate union in mind."

"Of course not, James," Broderick conceded. "My concern over your proposal is more about why you think the two of you are a smart match."

Clasping his shaking hands behind his back, he cleared his throat. "In the four years I have known Cailin, I have not only been impressed with her quick wit and adventurous spirit, but she looks up to me with respect and honors my opinion, as do I of her. I think those are good qualities in a wife—trust, friendship and a passion for life."

Broderick smirked. "That tells me why you think *she* would be a good match for *you*. I ask you to further explain why *you* are a good match for *her*."

James stood not saying a word for a spell, so caught off guard by Broderick's intense demeanor. In spite of his preparations, his mind seemed an empty cavern. *Answer the question, infant!* Broderick's lips pursed, seeming to suppress a smile. James cleared his throat. "There is nothing I would not do for her, my lord, and I would be good to her. I offer her all I have to give, a safe home and children to love. I can assure you, I will do everything in my power to make her happy."

Broderick considered Alistair, who shrugged. Though James had expected his father's lack of support or indifference, it still irked him that his father seemed to care so little about his efforts to show himself a responsible man. *His opinion matters not. MacDougal's is the approval I seek.*

In the silence drawing out between them, James felt the strength of his argument fading. "I think of myself as a practical man," he dared proclaiming, hoping to impress Broderick with his confidence. "Because Cailin and I have developed a friendship and loyalty toward each other, I think it's smart to build on that and plan for a stable future for us both. You and my father are business partners and I have ambitions to captain a ship for the company. Since our families will be united for many years to come, it only seems logical to solidify the union with a marriage of families. Cailin and I have a reasonable amount of years betwixt us."

"A little full of yourself there, lad," Alistair grumbled. "Remember, Broderick here's a Lord and you're still a commoner. You had better watch yoursel—"

"Those answers will do for now, young Knightly." Broderick nodded. "We will draw up the papers for a *promise*, not a betrothal. A betrothal is too binding at this point and I want Cailin to have the final word. She will make that choice when she is of an age to do so."

Only now did James understand what Broderick had sought. The answers James provided, though satisfying for Broderick as a father, did not address the spirit of the relationship, but James had been too young to be aware. He had been too inexperienced to voice the true meaning behind his request and somehow Broderick had known all along. There had been a kinship between him and Cailin that sparked the moment they met. She was six years of age, him thirteen, when Broderick introduced his family to the Knightlys. She had carrot-red hair falling in ringlets around her face dotted with freckles. Large cerulean eyes gazed up at him when she stepped forward. He crouched to meet her height and smiled. "Well met, Cailin."

A grin spread across her face and she blushed. "Wewl met, James," her mousy little voice intoned. Cailin placed her palms on James's cheeks, her little hands cool against his skin. He laughed when she pulled at his flesh and tugged his bottom lip.

"Oh, she fancies you," Davina said through her chuckles. "The first time she met Broderick as an infant, she mauled his face. That is a rare gesture she has granted no one else."

Even now, James smiled at the memory of their first meeting. And since that day, they had spent many childhood hours together playing games, conversing about the world around them and learning about life in general. That kindred spirit they shared, that union of their souls, is what had unknowingly prompted James to request their union. He felt…at home with Cailin. There was a peace he experienced around her. Aye, they made a fine match for many reasons. He would find out why she had changed her mind and dispel her fears…even if she had learned the truth.

The road they journeyed led out of Leith toward Edinburgh, the seat of the royal house of Scotland. Halfway between was where James's future father-in-law built his home for his family. A year before James had left for *Fechtschulen*—when Alistair had disappeared—the MacDougals insisted James stay with them. The home had been a cottage only slightly larger than the one James's family kept within the city. Now that James and Cailin were older, it would hardly be appropriate for him to stay in such close quarters, so he had gone straight to the house in Leith. Greeting Broderick at the docks the night before, he'd learned from his future father-in-law that he had made considerable improvements on the MacDougal holdings, and he insisted James continue to stay with them. James respectfully declined. After dueling with Cailin in the alley, he conceded it was a wise decision not to be under the same roof. His loins stirred when he recalled the ice-blue fire in her eyes and her flush-pink breasts pushing over her torn neckline.

As they rounded a bend in the road, getting closer to the home of his in-laws, a slight anticipation rose over discovering these "considerable improvements" Broderick mentioned. The trees parted to reveal the horizon and James had to make a conscious effort to close his mouth and not gawk. Though he had helped Broderick build a gate and curtain wall about the cottage, it had been a meager attempt to provide the family privacy and a small measure of protection. He never imagined it would grow to the massive stone fortification he gaped at in the distance.

"Building more than just ships, I see," he muttered, regarding the towering curtain walls surrounding the formidable fortress.

A curious circumstance, to be sure. They were merchants. Most people of such profession chose to live within the city of Leith to be close to their business and affairs, just as James and his family had. But then his family didn't have a beautiful young daughter to keep safe. Leith was a hard place in which to live…the murder of his own mother Fiona evidenced the brutality running rampant through its streets. James pushed his grief aside and redirected his thoughts.

He appreciated any man's efforts to build from his success and respected the desire to provide the best for his family—but MacDougal had created a structure to stave off an army.

"M'ma!"

Cailin's voice interrupted James's awe-inspired trance and he kicked his hackney into action, chasing both Cailin and Davina as their jennets galloped down the road. The two guards kept pace with James. Just ahead, a cluster of colorful caravans, tents and campfires nestled beside the trees edging the bordering forest. The small and temporary establishment stood back several paces from the road. Davina yanked on the reins and leapt from her horse, running into the waiting arms of a chestnut-haired woman, the two of them spinning and laughing like children. Cailin slowed her jennet and shook her head. Turning to James, she flashed him a smile…and his breath caught in his chest.

"Friends of yours?" he asked, once he'd gathered his wits, and came along side Cailin.

"Family, actually." She pointed to the joyful pair. "'Tis my Aunt Rosselyn, my mother's sister."

James cocked an eyebrow at the gathering people. Gypsies. He knew of Rosselyn, but had never met her...nor did he know she was a Gypsy. He smirked. *What other surprises lie in wait from the MacDougals?* Jumping from his saddle, James urged Cailin's horse forward and, when they neared Davina and Rosselyn, he helped Cailin from her mount. He grinned and eyed her swaying hips as she sauntered toward her mother. Swaggering after them, he settled at the edge of the small crowd.

"Look how you have grown!" Rosselyn exclaimed and took Cailin into her arms. "I never thought it possible, but you are even more bonnie than your mother."

"Nay, no one is more beautiful than she!" Cailin protested and hugged both women.

"Tell the man to get off his horse!" The dark-haired Gypsy with a Spanish accent waved toward James and strolled forward, his raven eyebrow raised as his eyes assessed James's height.

Davina laughed. "Nicabar, allow me to introduce you to my future son-in-law, James Knightly. James, this is my sister's husband, Nicabar Mendoza."

James stepped forward and offered his hand to the stocky Spaniard.

"He is almost as tall as Broderick," he said with a hearty greeting, the two of them grasping each other by the forearms. "*Saludos*, James Knightly."

"Well met, Nicabar."

Pulling a pair of strapping young lads forward, Nicabar presented them with pride. "My sons, Andre and Dion."

James nodded at Andre, who seemed to be a tad younger than Cailin's age. The lad returned the nod. The younger Dion smiled and James clasped forearms with him as well.

"And this is Zarita." Nicabar gleamed, sweeping a thin girl into his arms. All three children had the curling ebony hair of their father. The little Zarita shared the hazel of her mother's eyes.

The various Gypsies approached and greeted the circle of friends and family. Rosselyn pulled Davina aside from the noise, but still close enough for him to hear their exchange.

"We have much to share, Davina," Rosselyn began, "but we are here for more than a family visit. I have a message to deliver from Amice to Broderick."

Davina's eyes flitted over the band of Gypsies, her smile fading. "Forgive me for not even thinking of her. Where is she?"

Rosselyn's eyes welled with tears. "She passed this last winter, Davina. I am so sorry."

Davina covered her mouth with her hand and the two women hugged, sharing their grief. Not wanting to intrude on the moment further, James advanced toward Cailin to give the sisters their privacy. Sliding up beside her, he touched her elbow to catch her attention. She twirled to face him with that heart-breaking grin. The smile faltered when she saw who addressed her, fading to a memory on her full lips.

James stepped closer and pressed his mouth to her ear. "Your smile is more radiant than a sunset over the North Sea." He pulled back to gaze into her cerulean eyes. "Pray do not let it diminish in my presence."

Her lips parted in surprise and the doe eyes of the young girl he'd once known stared up at him. The grin returned and she gave him a saucy bump with her hip. "It seems school taught you to use more than blades, Master James. Such a silver tongue you wield to coax a smile from me!"

Thankfully, she wheeled away before he could remark about what else he would coax from her with his tongue.

CHAPTER TWO

Broderick MacDougal's heart ached over the sweet sobbing of his beloved wife. "Davina! Where are you, Blossom?"

Sifting through the surrounding fog, he stepped into a clearing in the woods—the meadow between their property and the road to Leith. In the center of the clearing stood the band of Gypsies he'd traveled with when he'd first met Davina seventeen years ago. Weaving in and out of the trees bordering the space, Cailin dodged shadows...and Broderick shook his head. The faint clash of blades echoed through the forest and he squinted his eyes in speculation.

Diverting his attention back to Davina's crying, he faced the gathering group. Their backs to him, they encircled a large stone. As Broderick neared the small assembly, people parted, revealing Davina's weeping figure kneeling beside the stone, holding the limp hand of Amice, who lay upon the altar-like slab. The old Gypsy's long silver braid had been draped neatly across her chest, her body dressed in her favorite rainbow-colored garb with tattered edges, her skin pale and gray in a shroud of death. He laid a comforting hand upon his wife's shoulder and knelt at her side.

"She's gone, Rick," Davina whispered through her tears. "I am so sorry, my love."

Rosselyn, Nicabar and young people bearing their features and coloring, all stepped forward and soothed Broderick's heart with gentle hands. Grief threatened to consume him. "'Tis the natural cycle of life," he reminded himself. And yet the dull ache in his chest echoed the emptiness of those words.

Stretched out on the large canopy bed deep within the chamber of his fortress, Broderick opened his eyes. His senses returned as he stared at the stone ceiling, tears slipping over his temples and wetting his ears. "Farewell, my old friend."

Drawing a deep, calming breath to soothe the grief over the visions he received from his wife, he groped the void next to him. Davina usually lay at his side, waiting for him to awaken, but not tonight. And he understood. Guessing from the images of his dreams, she would be visiting with her sister, Rosselyn. Since the day they had met, he and Davina had shared a spiritual bond—a connection that allowed him to receive images from her as he slept during the day. Strange, to be sure, inasmuch Vamsyrians didn't dream. He'd become accustomed to a blank veil during his daytime slumber during his five-and-forty years since joining their race. But, somehow, in meeting his spiritual mate and equal, he'd not only discovered a deep love, but had been blessed with her silent communication. All she need do was concentrate on him and the issues at hand, and he would dream. The visions varied between literal and symbolic and imbued him with the spirit of the woman he could not get enough of, no matter how much time they spent together. The only real limitation was proximity. If he ventured out more than a mile or two from Davina, the images faded to nothing.

He stood, shook off the lethargy of his daytime repose and dressed. Ascending the lengthy stone staircase, he exited his underground chamber and pushed the hidden panel in the wall to reveal the entrance to their master bedchamber. Only Davina and Cailin knew of the entryway leading to the room sequestered under the foundation of their castle; the place where he slept while the sun scorched the sky and the earth kept him safe.

Greeting him—as she did every night—was the enchanting visage of his wife Davina. Her sapphire eyes gazed at him with that knowing glint, forever immortalized in the paint strokes hewn by his own hand. Closing the panel behind him, Broderick stepped into their bedchamber and sauntered to the portrait he'd painted over a decade ago. He had insisted she pose with her cinnamon curls unfurled about her. She wore a gown the same deep blue of her eyes. She'd blushed when he'd loosed the neckline and pulled the garment aside to reveal her creamy shoulders and a hint of the top curves of her lush breasts. In response to her giggling protests, he'd assured her this painting would only be in their bedchamber. A few cups of wine and several languorously passionate sessions in bed…over several delicious nights of posing…Broderick was proud to have captured the essence of the woman he worshiped. The heated blush of her skin tones from the wine and lovemaking. The desire burning in her eyes. Her lips as red as crushed strawberries and plump from his kisses. "My Blossom," he whispered.

Stretching out his senses, he searched through the castle for Davina and her spirit became a beacon, her sadness drawing him to her. After stalking through the high-ceilinged hallways of gray stone, passing the tapestries, imported furniture and artwork, he meandered down to the kitchen hearth where Davina and Rosselyn sat talking. Judging by the spiced apple aroma, he spied cups of hot cider steaming before each of them at the trestle table. Straddling the bench beside his wife, he kissed her neck as she leaned against him. "Good evening, Blossom."

She nodded and hugged his arms as he wrapped them around her.

"Good evening, Rosselyn," Broderick greeted with a gentle voice. "'Tis good to see you."

Rosselyn stared at him a moment, her mouth agape and eyes wide. Though he refrained from listening to her thoughts, her astonishment over his agelessness swirled around him like a breeze.

Davina squeezed his wrist in their silent signal, giving him permission to hear her thoughts. *I have explained all to Rosselyn. She knows the nature of what you are.*

He kissed the top of her head as a response.

Once Rosselyn cleared her throat and straightened her posture, she tried a smile. "'Tis good to see you as well, Broderick. I wish the circumstances were more joyful. How do you fare?" She slouched a bit and her hazel eyes glassed with tears.

He offered her a wilting grin. "I'm saddened at the loss of our friend, Amice, but that is all I know. Pray tell me what happened."

His wife's sister sighed and nodded. "As I told Davina, she passed this last winter. She was very insistent we make it back to you to deliver this." Rosselyn pushed a small, wooden box he hadn't noticed across the table to rest in front of him. "An amulet of some kind, I believe."

The box was simple and the size of his fist, banded with iron hardware and beaten with age and use. Opening the box, an odd, yet familiar, oppression radiate from within. The interior, including the underside of the lid, seemed lined with doeskin. He tilted the box. A thick, coin-like medallion slid to the corner. Broderick narrowed his eyes at the strange writing and symbols gouged into its surface. A leather cord laced through the ring linked to the piece, indicating it was to be worn about the neck. He reached in to pick up the amulet…and hissed as it burned his fingertips, his hand jerking back involuntarily. A wave of weakness traveled up his arm and caused his eyelids to droop. Shaking the drowsiness from his head, he pushed away the box.

Davina sat forward and scooted along the bench to give Broderick some space. Both she and Rosselyn stared at him with large eyes and raised brows.

"What did Amice tell you about this?" He glared at the box, uncomfortable with the sense his energy drained from his body. Standing up, he put some distance between him and the medallion and a measure of relief seeped into his muscles.

"Nothing. She actually handed the box to me right before she died." Crimson mottled Rosselyn's cheeks and she cast sheepish eyes at him and Davina. "In all the years we spent with her, I never learned much French. As she passed, she said a number of things in her native tongue I wish I could relay to you now. I know only that she mentioned 'family' and your name a few times. I am sorry."

"Please come to me, Rosselyn."

She glanced at Davina, who nodded with assurance, and scuffled to stand in front of Broderick.

Placing tender hands upon her shoulders, he radiated a calmness to his sister-in-law. "Please close your eyes and think to the moments you had with Amice before she died."

Rosselyn nodded and her eyes fluttered closed.

Framing her face with his palms, Broderick also closed his eyes and opened himself to the images whirling in her mind. Seeing the world as if he were Rosselyn, feeling her sadness, he saw Amice in his arms on her tiny bed in her caravan.

Age had broken her frail body and her time on this earth drew to a close. "Broderick, my son" she rasped in French. "I am sorry I could not deliver this to you myself." Amice grabbed the box from the floor of the cramped space and held it to her chest. "This is to protect your family from other Vamsyrians. The wearer of this medallion cannot be harmed by an immortal like yourself. As I understand it, there is a way to create more of these to further protect those you love, but I do not know how." Labored breaths interrupted her speech. "There is a sorceress, a keeper of secrets, named

Malloren Rune. She lives by the circle of stones in England. I believe this place is called Stanenges. *You must journey to see her if you wish to discover the secrets of the medallion. This is my gift to you, my son, to give you peace at last, to guard those close to your heart from the clan enemy, who I know must still plague you."* Amice's lips trembled and tears raced down her cheeks. *"My love to sweet Davina and Cailin. My love to you and farewell."*

She touched Rosselyn's face and said in Gaelic, "You must take this to Broderick. This is my dying wish and all that I ask of you and Nicabar."

Broderick sobbed with Rosselyn in his arms, both of them reliving the moment of the old Gypsy's passing. She had been like a mother to him, and thus he grieved. With a kiss to her brow, Broderick encouraged Rosselyn to sit at the table again. He closed the box and the oppression subsided, so he sat beside his wife once more.

"Take this," he urged and pushed the box to Davina. "The medallion inside will protect anyone who wears it against Vamsyrians."

Davina's lips parted in surprise. "You mean Angus cannot harm Cailin or myself if we wear it?"

"So it would seem. When I touched the metal, it burned my skin." He examined his fingertips, his skin still pink and tender. "The piece also drained me, making me weak. At least until I closed the lid."

Davina's face brightened at the news and she clutched the box as if she'd found a chest of gold. "Oh, Rick! This is wonderful." She turned her sapphire eyes to him, but the glee melted from her face. "Pray tell me what troubles you," she whispered with a gentle hand to his cheek.

He kissed her palm and pressed it to his heart. "I must make a short journey."

Her brow furrowed.

"Thankfully, the medallion can offer some protection while I'm away, but since we don't know its full power or use, do not trust to take chances. I suggest you and Cailin still keep to the guidelines we have set for our family." He rolled his eyes. "Though I see Cailin still needs to be told to obey such precautions." The images of his step-daughter running through the shadows of the trees in his dream came to mind and Davina nodded. Such visions usually indicated Cailin had ventured out alone again. He explained to Davina and Rosselyn what Amice had said on her deathbed. "Perhaps through this Malloren Rune we can gain a full understanding of what this medallion can do, and other insights into how to further protect you both—and anyone else in our household, for that matter—from Angus."

"'Tis several years since Angus has troubled us," Davina ventured with hope in her voice. "I pray that peace lasts long enough for your journey."

Broderick sighed an uneasy breath. "Aye, as do I." Kissing the curve of Davina's neck, he rose from the bench. "I will leave you two to your conversation." He communicated silently to Davina, *I must feed, my love.*

She nodded and grasped Rosselyn's hand affectionately. "Aye, we still have six years of catching up to do since we last saw each other."

"Again, 'tis good to see you, Rosselyn." Broderick excused himself from their presence, exiting through the back kitchen doorway. As he swaggered across the courtyard, he spied Cailin talking with Fife at the stables, and approached with his arms crossed and his eyebrow cocked in disapproval.

"Och, lassie!" the elderly stable master exclaimed. "I know that look."

Cailin frowned. "Aye, Fife. I also know it well."

"Evenin', Lord Broderick," Fife greeted pleasantly.

Broderick nodded—glancing only for a moment to the man out of courtesy—his eyes still trained on his daughter.

She huffed and pouted, crossing her arms. "Ranald and Will were right behind me, Da."

"Mmm-hmm." He opened his arms to her. "May I?"

Cailin huffed again, but nodded and stepped into his embrace. Fife chuckled and shuffled into the stables, closing the doors behind him. Though Davina and Cailin both knew the nature of Broderick's immortality, they did their best to keep such things from most of the household. His request for a hug gave the outwardly appearance of fatherly affections. And though the gesture was indeed a show of love, it was also a private agreement for Broderick to delve into Cailin's memories for the accounts of the day. The images flashed through his mind: Cailin genuinely thought Ranald and Will were right behind her—as they always were—when she followed the young boy into the alleyway; a man named Jasper had jumped her unawares; Cailin's apprehensions about his connection to Angus; her exchange with James; Davina confronting Will and Ranald at the stables and finding they were conversing with prostitutes when they lost sight of Cailin; the arrival of the Gypsies; and other benign happenings up until this moment.

Kissing the top of Cailin's head, he encouraged her to walk beside him, his arm still about her shoulders. When he was sure they were out of earshot from Fife or anyone else, he said, "I know you have had such encounters in Leith before and they have not amounted to any connection to Campbell. But based on your exchange with this Jasper, I would have to agree with you about Angus's possible involvement." They stopped and faced each other and Broderick sighed. "I'm glad you're safe and I'm proud of your ability to protect yourself." He chucked her under the chin and she frowned.

"I truly wish it didn't have to be this way," she complained.

Guilt washed over him and he nodded. "I know, little one." He embraced her and her frustration swirled around him in a heavy haze. He had apologized to her many times over the years and though another was pointless, he offered one anyway. "Cailin, please know—"

"Unnecessary," she whispered, the warmth of her breath seeping through the linen of his shirt and over his heart.

He nodded again. "Then I also do not need to remind you—"

"To be more careful," she finished. "Aye, Da."

They'd been through this countless times. Pushing her back to peer into her sorrowful eyes, he cocked an eyebrow. "So you let a stranger kiss you?"

Cailin rolled her eyes and shoved away, marching ahead of him. "You *know* it was James."

"But *you* did not know that during the time he kissed you," he countered, striding after her.

She whirled, a disapproving scowl on her mouth and hands on her hips. "I am not going to discuss this with you."

He crossed his arms and maintained a reflecting scowl of disapproval. "I'm glad you fancy him, but you still didn't know who he was when you fell victim to his charms. How do—"

She huffed and turned away, stomping toward the gate. "Why is everyone scolding me? *He's* the one who took liberties with that kiss. Why is *he* not being reprimanded for kissing a stranger when he has a promised bride waiting for him?"

"Do not change the subject, little one. I am addressing—"

"Nay, you are not. I am *not* going to discuss this with you!"

Broderick caught up with her, pulling her into his arms again. She resisted, but he refused to let her go. "Forgive me for being so protective."

Her protests eventually melted into returning the hug.

"I am finding it difficult to accept that you're…well…"

She chuckled and peered up at him. "A woman?"

Broderick frowned.

She laughed. "Off with you now," she said, pulling him down to her height so she could plant a kiss upon his cheek.

He gave her one last parting hug, pushed open the gate and waved over his shoulder. Once the gate thundered close behind him, he dashed down the road and followed it into Leith. *A woman? When had that happened?* He shook the idea from his mind.

Fog coming off the Firth of Forth hung in thick banks as Broderick strolled through the streets of the dirty, port city. The stench of horse manure, the fishy residue of the docks and the oppression of the crime hung just as heavy as the moisture in the air—a perfect hunting ground for the likes of his kind. Though the summer months made the days longer, thereby the nights shorter, it was still early enough in the evening for the bustle and commotion of the ale houses. Using his acute hearing, he studied the sounds for any indications of mayhem—gasps, screams, struggling, grunts, etc. He gravitated toward the busier sections, hiding in the shadows.

"I got *some* pride in meself!" a raspy female voice protested. "This 'ere ain't the place for it."

Broderick winced at the distinct slap of a hand against flesh. "Ye do it where I tell ye to, whore!" a man grumbled in response.

After dashing across the street, Broderick slinked through the darkened byway and toward the voices in the alcove ahead. A familiar discomfort pierced his gums as his mouth watered and fangs extended, pushing against his upper lip. The rustling of clothes, thumping that indicated a struggle, and a muffled cry guided him the rest of the way. As

ARIAL BURNZ

anticipated, he found a man cornering a woman, his hand clamped over her mouth as his other hand fumbled with their clothes to get at what he wanted. The doxy's eyes grew wide when Broderick approached and grabbed the man off her.

"Oy! What—"

Broderick silenced him with a punch to the gut, knocking the wind from him. Rick turned to the woman, snatched her by the nape, and pressed his palm to her forehead. She slumped into unconsciousness in his arms. He set her gingerly on the ground, willing her to forget him. Spinning toward the lout kneeling and nursing his breath back into his lungs, Broderick heaved him up by the lapels and propped him against the wall. The man's mouth opened and closed like a fish, gaping and struggling for sustenance. Broderick turned the man's head to the side, exposing his neck, and sank his fangs into the tender flesh, drinking deep the warm flow of sweet blood filling his mouth. The man he now knew as Gavand ceased struggling, went limp and sighed.

When he had his fill, Broderick reined in the *Hunger* and pulled away from his victim before taking his life. Years of practice made the task of stopping in the middle of feeding so much easier than it had been when he first learned to control the urges. Vamsyrians seemed, by nature, to desire the kill, and those first few years were impossible for him to stop. Though he had always fed from thieves, murderers and thugs, those deaths would forever weigh upon his soul, as did the souls he had condemned to madness when he made a feeble attempt at trying to reform such criminals. Implanting horrific visions to scare them into changing their ways had only served to drive them mad. A fact Angus Campbell had brought to his attention those many years ago at Stewart Glen, where Broderick met Davina.

Shaking off the past, he focused on the now. Gavand moaned, still in Broderick's grasp, and he pressed his palm to the man's forehead, willing the experience to vanish from his mind and render him unconscious. Gavand slumped to the ground. Broderick turned to the woman—Nan by the accounts of Gavand's memories. Relocating her to another place was useless. She lived with Gavand and though she did sell herself for money or favors, theirs was a mutual arrangement. Broderick fed from her, then sliced open his thumb to smear his healing immortal blood on the wound at her neck. He did the same to Gavand, then shook his head and left them both in the alcove between the two buildings at the docks.

James stood in the parlor of MacDougal Castle, waiting. The fire crackled and popped in the hearth, ticking his nerves and increasing the mounting tension. He pulled the missive from his breast pocket and needlessly scrutinized the words once again.

Please come at once to discuss the matters concerning your future.

—Broderick MacDougal

He replaced the paper and paced. Though Davina had prepared him earlier today for their meeting this eve, the wording in the note had him wonder if something was amiss. Had Cailin convinced her parents to dissolve the union? Had his little skirmish in the alley with his betrothed cause them second thoughts? *How was I to know who she was?* James wiped his face and grumbled.

The door swung open. "Greetings Lady Dav—" He stopped himself. "My pardons to you. I thought you were the lady of the manor."

The woman of similar build and color to Lady Davina chuckled. "Aye, yer not the first to make that mistake, laddie."

Cailin trailed in after the older woman, a tight grin on her face and a tray with a pitcher and mug in her hands. "Master James, I'd like you to meet my handmaid, Margeret."

James nodded. "Greetings Margeret. Greetings Cailin."

Margeret stood in the doorway, beaming proudly at Cailin as she set the tray on the center table. Cailin stood by, her eyes locked to James's. Margeret cleared her throat and Cailin gasped.

"Some refreshments of small beer, Master James?" she offered and blushed.

He crossed his arms, sizing up this docile and formal woman...such a contrast to the dagger-toting hellion in the alleyway. "I thank you very kindly, Cailin." He reached for the pitcher, but Margeret cleared her throat...quite loudly.

Cailin gasped again and shooed his hands away. "Allow me, Master James," she twittered and poured the common drink from the earthen vessel into the mug before pushing the tray toward him.

"Something amiss, my ladies?" James eyed them both with suspicion.

Cailin and Margeret both frowned and exchanged glances. "Naught is amiss, lad," Margeret assured him. "What troubles ye?"

This did not bode well. "Nothing, save for the unusual behavior coming from you both." James peered into the mug. "Have you poisoned my drink, I wonder?"

Cailin covered her mouth, laughing. "Nay, James," she said through her chortles and peeked at Margeret's disapproving scowl. Gaining her composure, Cailin clasped her hands behind her back and resumed her dutiful posture. "'Tis our own home brew and fine for the likes of a common drink."

He clenched his jaw and narrowed his eyes at Margeret. "Is it now?"

The women exchanged glances again before nodding.

Cailin frowned. "'Tis obvious something does bothers you, Master James."

He remained standing with his arms crossed. "Aye, *Mistress* Cailin. Care to explain the sudden change in disposition?"

Her lips parted and she glimpsed over her shoulder at Margeret, who shrugged. "Come again?"

"I'm uncertain why you feel the need to assert the appearance of a dutiful servant. 'Tis unseemly of you."

"Dutiful ser—" Her eyebrows and full lips leveled in a straight line and she clenched her fists before stomping to him. In one swift movement, she dumped the contents of his mug over his head and slammed it to the table. "Enjoy your libations."

"Cailin MacDougal!" Margeret huffed after Cailin's retreating figure.

The two women left James to stew in the weak beer dripping down his face and into the collar of his linen shirt. Obviously, Margeret was in charge of *schooling* Cailin in the matters of manners and maintaining a household. At her age, Cailin should be well versed enough to handle such tasks. But why did Margeret seemed so strict and untrusting of Cailin's actions? Furthermore, why did Cailin feel the need to be someone she was not? He'd find out soon enough, to be sure. He plopped onto the bench and licked the brew dribbling over his lips. "'Tis actually quite tasty," he mused with a frown.

Broderick MacDougal entered, his wife Davina trailing behind with a small scroll of parchment in her hand. She closed the door as Broderick advanced, cocking an eyebrow at James, who scrambled to his feet. Davina gasped and scuttled toward him, pushing past her husband and snatching the cloth from the tray Cailin had brought in. Fussing over him, she wiped his face and shoulders. "Cailin's foul temper, no doubt?"

He stilled Davina's hands. "I'm not so sure I didn't deserve her wrath. I believe I insulted her by calling her a…dutiful servant." His face grew warm and Davina smirked, retreating to a cushioned chair in the corner of the room.

James stared a moment at the man before him. Almost a decade had passed since he'd last seen Broderick and it seemed as if no time had gone by. *The years have been kind.* Davina, in all her grace and exotic beauty, appeared as he had expected—hair streaked with gray, attractive age lines around her eyes and mouth, which bespoke of years of laughter and smiles. Gaining his composure, James stepped forward in greeting. "Well met, Lord and Lady MacDougal."

"What folly, lad! Why the formality?" His future father-in-law grasped him into a fierce hug and the two slapped each other's backs in their embrace. Stepping back, Broderick assessed the front of his shirt, now wet with the beer. Humor twisted MacDougal's mouth into a grin. "I take full responsibility for spoiling Cailin and apologize in advance for what you will be inheriting in the union." Waving to the bench, the large and imposing man encouraged James to sit, yet Broderick remained standing, hands on his hips. "However, 'tis nothing she wilna do for you if you win her heart, lad." He winked. "Forgive me for the late call, but I'm leaving my family on the morrow for a short journey, and we have much about which to speak." As if in afterthought, Broderick poured James a fresh mug of beer.

"Thank you, sir, and think nothing of the late hour. Your family has been a blessing to me and I wouldn't be where I am today if not for your generosity."

Broderick nodded thoughtfully. Crossing his arms, he narrowed assessing eyes on James. "'Tis a long time you've been away, lad. You've had the opportunity to see a world most men of our status can only dream of, and did very well for yourself for someone of your age. Five-and-twenty is it?"

James nodded.

"Congratulations are in order for your attainment of Grandmaster at the *Fechtschullen*—a title, I understand, that is granted to few and awarded by the Emperor himself?"

James dipped his head and an uncharacteristic lump formed in his throat at the overwhelming pride on MacDougal's face. He swallowed and coughed into his fist to remove the uncomfortable sensation. "I could do no less, sir, since you were the one to provide for my schooling. I'm glad my efforts pleased you."

"Pleased me?" Broderick shook his head and chuckled, a deep rumble that moved through the room like thunder. "They surpassed my expectations, lad."

James didn't trust himself to do anything more than nod and smile.

"Having conquered the world and returned to your humble beginnings, how do you feel about the path chosen for your life?"

The image of Cailin's fire-blue eyes and heaving bosom came to mind and the corner of his mouth turned up in appreciation. However, the frown returned when he recalled the docile lass who poured his beer, and how her mood flipped as easily as the mug she dumped over his head. He said truthfully, "Though I am uncertain about a few facets of my life, I am eager to embark upon such a path."

MacDougal raised a fiery brow and narrowed his eyes once more, myriad emotions seeming to cross his countenance as he searched James's face. James speculated a mixture of uncertainty or disapproval, even frightening sparks of anger in his emerald eyes, but Broderick's squint soon melted into a roguish grin that spread his mouth wide. That rumbling chuckle thundered another round about the room. "Glad to hear it, lad. You still have ambitions to captain a ship?"

James nodded.

"*Very* glad to hear that!" Broderick took the rolled parchment presented by his wife and handed it to James. "Open it."

He broke the wax seal and unrolled the stiff paper, contemplating the curves and swirls of the words scratched onto the document.

Broderick chuckled. "'Twould be a waste of a good ship if you had changed your mind."

Excitement swelled in James's chest. "These are the papers for my appointment as captain!"

"Aye. She's still at the shipyard waiting to be christened and launched. We thought to do so at the betrothal celebration. What say you?"

Again, James did not trust himself to speak. His head bobbed and he smiled his agreement.

"Wonderful." Broderick nodded, then he and Davina shuffled to a dark-wood cabinet against the far wall. She opened the doors carved with delicate scroll work and extracted a crafted mahogany box with a fine luster finish. He withdrew a sword that arrested the breath in James's chest. She placed the box onto the center table—away from the spilled beer—and retreated a few steps while Broderick faced James. "A captain and Grandmaster swordsman is incomplete without sterling blades at his side. We had these weapons commissioned for you as soon as we received your letter of appointment." Broderick presented the sword, horizontal.

James reached forward with tentative fingers, his lips parted in awe. "Broderick...Lady Davina... You shouldn't have—"

"Hush, lad," his gentle tone encouraged. "You have more than earned it." James still hesitated and Broderick leaned in, lowering his voice. "You do me the honor as I will never have a son of my own but, as you know, you have been so to me."

James searched Broderick's face and found a compassion he once ached to see from his own father, Alistair. His father be damned. James didn't want anything from him. Broderick was more of a parent to him than Alistair could ever hope to be. MacDougal's brow creased with sadness, prompting James to smile in an effort to lighten the tension.

"Aye, Broderick...Lady Davina. Thank you." He bowed to each in turn. With a deep breath, he grasped the sword in his right hand, the scabbard in his left, unsheathing the weapon. The narrow blade swirled with light-and-dark folded patterns along the polished edge. Fading from the swirling metal patterns and to the center of the blade, gleamed a thick layer of shining metal. James swallowed in an effort to find his voice. "Is this actually a *Wootz* blade?" he breathed in awe.

Broderick's eyebrows rose and he glanced at Davina's surprised expression before nodding. "I am impressed you know about Wootz steel."

"We had heard about these swords at *Fechtschulen*—blades stronger and sharper than any steel known to man. I even saw such a blade cut a piece of silk dropped onto its edge and would not have believed such a thing had I not witnessed it myself." James's eyes worshiped the weapon. "And now I *own* one?" He studied the shining metal plated along the blade. "Is that silver forged across the surface?"

Broderick crossed his arms and grinned. "Aye." He winked knowingly at his wife, who grinned with pride.

The weight of the weapon settled comfortably in James's palm, the grip molding to his hand as if it were crafted with him in mind. Intricate Celtic knots and images etched the silver surface closer to the hilt.

James remembered to breathe.

He gawked at the thumbnail-sized sapphire in the lion-claw setting in the pommel. "A man could get used to carrying a blade like this," he whispered, near forgetting he wasn't alone. Snapping out of his love-induced trance, he smiled at MacDougal. "'Tis lighter than the swords I trained with."

"Aye, that blade will slice through moonbeams." Broderick laughed.

James stepped back and twirled the weapon through the open space, the blade whistling through the air. "I have no doubt about that, sir!"

Broderick opened the mahogany box and presented two stilettos—matching the sword's craftsmanship and style. They were also forged of the swirling metal and silver plating.

A twinge of uncertainty pricked his heart and James replaced the sword in its sheath. Setting the fine weapon upon the table, he faced Broderick. "Sir, I do not mean to seem ungrateful, but would care to tell me what you're asking of me?"

MacDougal raised an eyebrow. "This is the future you planned for yourself. You have achieved great things, James. I dote on those close to me and those who deserve it."

Hrmm. "You are also a man with purpose."

Davina's fingertips covered her suppressed smile. Broderick's steel gaze locked with James for a long stretch of time before he swaggered to the table and pushed the open mahogany box aside. "I see you find it troublesome accepting gifts."

Instead of the disappointment James expected on MacDougal's face, mischief brewed in his emerald eyes.

So, he is testing me. James crossed his arms, rising to the challenge. "I have not had the benefit of being around here for nigh on a decade, growing up instead away from my homeland and countrymen; supported by your generosity, of course. The Holy Roman Empire is excellent training ground for a young man coming into his own, especially at one of the best *Fechtschullen* in the Kingdom of Germany. As a result, I am no stranger to death...or taking the life of a man." He paced, arms still crossed, pushing his guilt aside. "I come home to find the woman I am promised to living in a fortress that rivals the king's and she is well-versed in hand-to-hand combat, with tailor-made sheaths and dueling knives...of silver-plated Wootz blades, no less." He picked one of the stilettos out of the finely-crafted box, twirling the impressive dagger in his fingers. "And now I am gifted with equally brilliant weapons." Placing the knife back into its velvet-cushioned home, he faced his future father-in-law. "I am in debt to you for treating me as a son, supporting my tutoring, for the lessons life has taught me, and for the way you continue to bless me with gifts as well as the hand of your beautiful daughter and her handsome dowry—none of which is deserving of my station. You say you leave on the morrow and this conversation could not wait. I know for a fact you do not journey away from home without your family." He shrugged. "I would venture to say you are asking me to watch over them while you are gone, an honor I humbly accept." He bowed to Davina. "But…it appears to me they do not need my protection. The real question I have for you, Broderick, is what am I protecting them *from* that I would need silver-plated blades?" *How is that for your test, old man?*

Broderick threw back his head and his rich laughter filled the room. Davina's face gleamed from her bright smile.

James cocked an eyebrow and placed his hands upon his hips.

"Though I have certain advantages you are about to find out, I have impressed even myself in allowing you to wed my daughter, lad." Broderick bowed before a confused James Knightly. "Again, you have exceeded my expectations. Please sit down. You will need the support." He stepped before his wife and took her in hand. Broderick kissed her cheek and ushered her to the entrance of the parlor. "Would you please have Cailin bring in some of our strongest wine for her betrothed?"

Davina curtsied and attempted to leave, but Broderick pulled her into his arms for a hungry kiss that caught James off-guard and gawking. Davina's face blushed deep crimson and she smiled apologetically to James before smacking her husband's shoulder. She scampered down the hall and Broderick closed the door with a grin.

James cleared his throat and sat. Returning to the matter at hand, he wondered about the *support* Broderick had referred to. *What the hell is this man about?*

Broderick chuckled. "If you would but give me a moment, I will explain."

His breath caught short. MacDougal's statement almost sounded as if he heard James speak instead of think. Or had he said his thoughts aloud and not realized it? *Coincidental,* he thought and settled in to listen.

"Nay, not coincidental at all, young Knightly." Broderick leveled a piercing gaze, that mischief storming in his eyes. "I would prefer you had some stronger libation at your disposal before I deliver my news, though, so be patient young buck."

Not giving James much time to be stunned, Cailin stomped into the room with two chalices in one hand and a lead pitcher in the other. Broderick held up his hand, stopping his daughter in her determined tracks. "Lass, don't make me reprimand you in front your future husband," her father's voice was soft and bordering deadly. "Your sour mood will spoil our best vintage."

Her simmering blue eyes, still glassy with unshed tears, wandered to the unoccupied side of the room, a calming breath pushing the delightful curve of her bosom to swell deliciously over her neckline. Irritation seemed to emanate from her pores and James teetered between sympathy and desire. With a forced smile plastered to her full lips, she slammed a cup before James, poured the rich, burgundy liquid to the rim, and set the pitcher and extra chalice before him. *There's the hellion from the alley!*

All the while, she afforded him a generous view of her cleavage and he had to restrain from adjusting his suddenly tightening breeches.

"Will there be anything else, Master James?" Her husky voice oozed annoyance.

Broderick chuckled. "Thank you, Cailin."

She cast her father another irritated frown from under her brow and sauntered from the room.

Aye, lass, you can ride my aching— James darted his eyes to a disapproving father.

Broderick scowled. "Very wise of you to stop that train of thought, lad."

James guzzled the smooth wine and poured himself another cup.

MacDougal laughed.

"Though I am not sure I want to hear the answer, how is it you know what I am thinking? Do my actions betray me so much?"

Broderick's eyes squinted with warning. "Your gaze did not leave her neckline from the moment she walked through the door, so aye...you are very obvious." He sat before James across the table. "Truly, I am glad you find Cailin attractive. Now that both of you have reached the proper age..." He frowned and sighed. "I personally feel such attraction makes the marriage bed that much sweeter, outside of the other qualities you pointed out when you asked for this union." He studied the wood grain on the table surface, a pondering expression creasing his brow. "How I know your thoughts, however, has nothing to do with your actions." Broderick's eyes locked with James's. "I adore you as a son, so I impart to you a great secret that will explain many things about this family, about your experiences with us to date." His brows drew together and his green eyes pierced James with such intensity, he held his breath. "Understand that the safety of my family comes first, so you guard this secret with your life...or I will end it."

The unwavering steel in his emerald gaze lent no doubt MacDougal meant what he said and James gulped another mouthful of wine. "Aye, sir, you have my word."

"I'm confident I do, James." Broderick leaned forward. "I am of a race of immortals called Vamsyrians."

James raised his brows. "Immortals? Meaning you cannot die?"

"'Tis more than just long life, but aye, 'tis part of immortality and explains why I haven't aged since you departed to attend your schooling."

He nodded and studied Broderick's face. *And here I thought he had aged well.*

Broderick chortled. "'Tis a benefit, to be sure."

"And this explains why you know what I'm thinking? Can you actually hear my thoughts?"

"As if you were speaking them aloud. However, as a courtesy to my family and those close to us, I have made a…limited vow of silence, for lack of a better phrase. I can make the effort not to hear thoughts, although emotions tend to linger around some people like a scent." He chuckled. "With others, it's more like an odor."

The corner of James's mouth turned up in appreciation at the jest, but the gravity of the issue weighed down his humor. "What other benefits or facets does immortality hold for you?" He should be protesting the very idea, but the fact that

Broderick could hear the thoughts in his mind allowed his curiosity to reign.

"I have the strength of, say, twenty men or more. I heal incredibly fast and can heal others."

"Heal?"

Broderick nodded and grabbed the spare cup Cailin had brought in and set it before him. Grabbing a steel dagger from his belt, he dragged the blade across his palm, slicing it open. The blood from the cut hardly had the chance to drip into the chalice before the wound closed …as if the blade had never touched his skin.

James's jaw went slack and he grabbed Broderick's hand to examine his palm. Neither a scar nor a mark gave any evidence of what James had witnessed. Broderick seized James's hand and made a small incision in the fleshy part of his palm. Hissing, James tried to pull away, but Broderick tipped the cup, dripping his blood onto the cut…which also vanished as if it had never been. No pain. No marks. After wiping the blood clean with the cloth on the table, he released James's hand.

"'Tis not possible," James whispered as he smoothed his thumb over his skin, back and forth as if that would conjure the cut again or reveal some trace of it. "Fascinating!"

Another chortle from Broderick drew James's eyes. MacDougal raised an eyebrow and sneered. "I thought you might find this information of interest with that inquisitive mind of yours."

James nodded and grinned, relenting to the appeal of the situation. "I must ask…how old *are* you?"

"I was born the fourth day in April of the fourteen-hundred-and-fiftieth year of our Lord."

James frowned in concentration, then went slack-jawed once again. "'Tis one-and-eighty years you are?"

Broderick gave a solemn nod.

"Are Cailin and Davina also immortal?"

Broderick shook his head. "Nay, they are mortal as you are. And, in truth, Cailin is not my daughter. Davina was a widow and with child when her husband died. Cailin was but eight months old when I met them."

"I never did understand what Davina meant when she referred to Cailin touching your face when she first met you. I thought that an odd thing to say of one's daughter." James's mind swam in a whirl of confusion and wonder, only to have a sobering thought jar him back to the situation at hand. "Why are you imparting such information to me and how does it relate to my future?"

"'Tis a smart lad you are. Quick to nail the point." Broderick's appreciative grin faded and he rose to pace the length of the room. "Wedding my daughter Cailin will mean protecting her."

"Of course, sir."

Broderick stopped and regarded James. "From another Vamsyrian."

James nodded and sipped his wine, waiting for Broderick to proceed.

"His name is Angus Campbell." MacDougal resumed pacing. "Our clans have been at war since my youth. I shall not go into the details of our history at this moment, except to stress this." Standing before James, Broderick leveled his crystal-green gaze at him, a blending of sorrow and anger in his immortal eyes. "For reasons I have yet to truly understand, Angus's way to me is through those I love."

James raised an eyebrow and crossed his arms. "What exactly do I need to do?"

"You need to try to kill me."

He downed the last of his wine and smiled. "My pleasure."

Cailin paced the length of her bedchamber, fists clenched so hard her short nails pressed into her palms. With her face flushed and the backs of her eyes stinging from tears, the world closing in around her.

"That darn temper of yours, lass," Margeret admonished with kindness softening her voice.

"Aye, Maggie! He is infuriating, though! Why can I not maintain my composure in front of him?"

"If yer encounter with him in the alley is any indication of what kind of man he is, and based on his brash behavior in the parlor…" Margeret shook her head and rubbed her chin. "The lad will be a handful, no doubt."

"Oh heavens, the alley!" She groaned and plopped onto the settee at the foot of her bed with a grunt. Inhaling deep, she closed her eyes in an effort to calm her thumping heart. Even with her eyes closed, tears slipped down her cheeks. "He won't marry me, Maggie," she whispered.

Margeret rushed to Cailin's side and wrapped a warm arm around her. "Nay, lass! Doncha be sayin' such things."

She would ruin her chances of marriage if she continued to allow her emotions to reign free. "What man wants a rebellious woman for a wife?" Cailin wiped her cheeks with her sleeve. "I never should have learned to fight."

"What choice did ye have, sweetness?" Margeret kissed the top of Cailin's head. "Angus Campbell forced the hand of yer entire family, he did."

"'Tis what James was sent off to school to learn, though," Cailin argued. "'Tis not my place to learn such things." *If I hadn't learned to use a blade, I never would have*— Cailin pushed those thoughts from her mind.

"Oh, lassie," Margeret cooed. "This is the life ye have and 'tis no worth in frettin' about it now." She pulled back and dabbed at Cailin's tears with the kerchief she pulled from her sleeve. "Yer a bonnie lass and he's a grand fool if he fails to see yer generous heart and giving spirit. Bide a wee bit on yer temper, Cailin."

Cailin nodded. "Thank you, Maggie." She stared at the flames in the hearth through her tears, grateful for Margeret's consoling efforts, which allowed her to grow indifferent. Aye, indifference...a good place to be. It quieted her soul enough to find rest, to crawl into the cave of her spirit and recover to rise another day.

CHAPTER THREE

A grunt rushed from James's throat as his back slammed to the mat, Broderick standing over him with a smile and outstretched hand. "Do you understand now?" He helped James to his feet. "Since I can hear your thoughts, I can anticipate your moves, so regardless of how skilled you are at the sword or knife, your approach has nothing to do with speed or ability."

Rotating his shoulder to work through the pain, James frowned. Broderick had taken him into an armor and weapons room of sorts, similar to his training grounds at *Fechtschulen*, complete with padded mats and sawdust-filled figures tied to wooden posts. He had applied everything he learned becoming a Grandmaster at swordplay and, at Broderick's encouragement, came at him with all he had. Broderick had bested him no matter what he did. "Then how can I possibly win any advantage over Campbell if he knows my every move?"

"*That* is the trick, lad." Broderick picked up the steel blades James had dropped on the ground. "Part of your defense is to have your strategy well planned and so rehearsed as to be second nature, therefore there is no thinking—only instinct and reflex." Stepping forward, Broderick sheathed James's daggers in his belt and adjusted them. "Arrange thus for easy reach." He began circling James. "The second part of your defense is to take a non-aggressive approach. Do not attack."

James scrunched his brows and planted his fists upon his hips.

"Since you know his immortal speed will always best you, do not advance. Maintain a passive demeanor and reason with him."

"Is Campbell a reasonable enemy?"

"When he chooses to be, but certainly not with me." Broderick stopped before James with his arms crossed—a most commanding figure. "The point is if you remain passive, it is very likely he will have no reason to approach you with aggression or speed. He will be the cat to your mouse." He stalked around James again. "Circling you and—" James started at the sudden presence of MacDougal's voice close to his ear. "Stepping in to keep you off guard."

Heart pounding, James inhaled deep to soothe his nerves. "I understand your meaning."

Broderick faced him again. "Allow him to do so. It will be to your advantage. If he comes in close, you will have your opportunity to strike."

"But again, if he knows my thoughts—"

"That is the next part of your defense." MacDougal rubbed his chin as if in thought. "Teaching your mind to create a mental barrier is the best skill, but unfortunately this I cannot teach you tonight. With the limited time I have with you now, I had to do what I could to prepare you for what may happen while I am gone, and these small measures of defense are better than having none at all. The way you came at me before will surely get you killed. I have bought you some time. Though...not much." He frowned and turned away from James.

"Broderick...what are you not telling me?"

Peering askance over his shoulder, MacDougal whispered almost distractedly, "I can never prepare you for the attack of a Vamsyrian, son." He faced James. "The full onslaught of one such as I is truly staggering to a mortal. If you witness such an assault, pray you are not the target. It is why I must leave on the morrow."

"Where are you going, sir?"

James blanched to see tears well in Broderick's eyes. "To chase after a hope that I have finally found a way to protect those I love." He cleared his throat and slapped James on the back. "Come, lad."

Nodding his head toward the door, Broderick led James to return to the parlor and poured him another cup of wine. Leaning against the table, James drank and pondered what had transpired over the last two hours.

Broderick's voice pulled him from his thoughts. "I want you to work with Cailin during my absence."

"Cailin?"

"Aye, she has learned how to guard her thoughts to some degree. Mayhap she can give you at least a foundation on which to start. Of course, you cannot know if you are successful until I return so I may judge, but there is a measure of practice you can still begin. We have prepared a chamber for you, so I would like to you stay here where my family will need you." Broderick inclined forward. "The chamber is on the far side of the castle…away from Cailin's chamber. I trust you will behave until after the wedding?"

MacDougal raised a warning brow and James chuckled. "Aye, my lord, I will do my best to keep my hands…and thoughts…to myself."

"Very good."

"How long will you be gone, my lord?"

A muscle ticked along Broderick's jaw line before he responded. "Too long for my taste, lad, but I hope not more than a week's time. Angus has not shown any sign of activity or made any attempts on the family in almost five years, so it is our hope all will remain quiet until after I return."

"As is my hope."

Nodding and crossing his arms, Broderick settled his rump against the edge of the table beside James and regarded him with sorrow in his eyes. "I know this is not news you will cherish, and I do not wish to be the one to deliver it, but…Alistair has returned to Leith."

James clenched his jaw and turned about to pour another cup of wine, occupying his hands with the benign task. He did not relish a judgmental encounter with his father. "How long has he been thus?" He gulped a mouthful of the soothing vintage.

"Three months." Broderick paused, his words floating upon the air. "Though he comes and goes for a few days at a time. You may have noticed some signs of his presence at the cottage in Leith, even though Cailin has taken it upon herself to keep the house in order during your absence."

James nodded and gripped the cup. "What does he want?"

"I know not, lad. He has not spoken to me at length—"

"Can you not divine his thoughts?" James snapped unexpectedly, shocking even himself.

Broderick sighed. "'Tis a strange pattern to his thoughts, James, unlike anything I've encountered. Your father knows what I am, so I've wondered if he has also learned some skill at blocking his thoughts while he disappeared to…only God knows where he went. Though in my opportunities to probe his mind, I have not discerned any sign of Angus. Still, I am suspicious that Angus may have made some contact with him, knowing he was connected to this family. I urge you to be cautious. He is your father and I cannot keep you from him, but I request you do not see him until I return."

James released a derisive snort. "I've no wish to visit with the vile worm. Have no fear there. I will only go back to the cottage on the morrow to collect my belongings."

Broderick nodded and James was glad he didn't push the topic. Back when Fiona was murdered, Broderick tried to ease James's pain by convincing him Alistair's heart couldn't bear the loss of his wife and his father needed time to heal. Even now, James could not understand how a father could leave his only son behind without a backward glance, without any effort to inquire after his welfare. Though the MacDougals were far from strangers and were close to his family as friends and business partners, Alistair had not even made arrangements with them to watch over James. The MacDougals did that of their own accord. Mayhap they were close enough for Alistair to assume they would be there for James. *Close enough to know what Broderick was.*

"Forgive me for not sharing what I am with you sooner," Broderick replied.

James cast a sideways glare and pushed away from the table. "That is damned annoying, MacDougal."

Broderick threw his head back and that rumbling laughter filled the room once more. "Aye, lad, so I have been told."

"Well, I agree with Lady Davina, if that *is* who enforced such a…vow of silence, as you called it."

Broderick nodded, his eyes gleaming with amusement.

"Then I trust you will stay out of my thoughts?"

Broderick dipped his head in agreement.

James could no longer suppress his grin. "And I understand why you did not share such a secret with me until now. I was young, impulsive and reckless. I'm glad you ushered me off to learn my way and release my anger through fencing."

MacDougal stepped forward and clasped James by the forearm in mutual accord, drawing him into another fatherly embrace. "Stay the night, lad." He ushered James out of the parlor and up the stairs to the first level. "I shall have Will and Ranald accompany you to the cottage on the morrow to help you collect your things."

"Will I see you before you set out?" James asked as they turned down the corridor toward the bedchambers.

"'Tis another thing that goes along with immortality." They stopped in front of a chamber door. "I cannot come out during the day."

James inclined his head. In all the time he'd known Broderick, he had never put much thought to the fact that he had indeed only seen him after sundown. "Pray tell me to what purpose?"

"Press upon me another time to go into greater detail. However, the answer to your previous question is aye, I'll leave shortly after sundown and won't depart before saying my farewells."

James knew Broderick said the last for James's comfort and the corner of his mouth tugged up in appreciation. "Aye, my lord. Rest well."

Davina looked up from brushing a woolen vest as Broderick stepped into the room, a thoughtful gleam in his eyes and an easy smile upon his lips.

"How did he fare?" She set the brush on the settee at the foot of their bed and crossed the room to greet him.

"The lad did well. Better than I expected." Gifting her with a lingering kiss, Broderick patted her bottom before slipping into the wardrobe and emerging with his satchel. "A few strong cups of wine did well to stiffen his courage."

Davina laughed and her eyes followed his large form as he glided with purpose around the room, packing for his journey. Returning to the settee, she settled in, content to drink in his presence while she had the chance. They would soon be apart.

As he turned to put the last few belongings in his satchel, a furrow formed on his brow.

"What troubles you, my love?"

"James still holds much anger in his heart for Alistair and I cannot blame him."

She nodded. "He is young. He may only need time at home in peace before he can settle his heart."

"Mayhap you are correct." Broderick closed his satchel and knelt before Davina. "What concerns me more is what Alistair's intentions might be. As I've mentioned, I couldn't hear his thoughts on the two occasions I encountered him. They faded in and out and I could only catch a word or two. I wonder if he may have been taught to block them, but is not yet skilled at it. And yet…"

"And yet?"

"Even when you and Cailin were learning to do the same, the patterns were not like this. This is something…I know not, Davina. And I like it even less."

She framed his face with her hands, pressing a kiss to his full lips. "Don't let this stop you from going. We need this. Since James became a Grandmaster and you have given him the silver weapons, I do feel better about you making this trip."

Broderick frowned. "Aye, I agree, but only by a margin. The sooner I get back, the better I will feel." His eyes wandered to the window. "I can't help but suspect there's more to this. That I'm being lured away."

Though Broderick made an agreement of privacy regarding her thoughts, emotions were like scents carried on the wind to him. Inside, Davina agreed with his suspicions, but she did her best to mask those misgivings. "This is a profound opportunity to finally find an effective way to protect us."

His gaze met hers and her heart ached at their intensity. "What good will this protection be if he strikes while I'm gone?" His voice was but a whisper.

She swallowed the lump in her throat. "We cannot run forever, my love."

Broderick nodded. He trailed a fingertip down her cheek. "'Tis many years since I have been away from your side."

Tears pierced her eyes and she blinked the pain away. "You will be preoccupied with the swiftness of your journey, and I know you'll make haste to be away no more than necessary."

"That I vow." Broderick sealed his words with a possessive kiss.

Davina melted into the arms of her husband, marveling at the fire he still stoked in her spirit after almost two decades together. Sliding his hands down her back to cup her bottom, he lifted her from the settee. Her skirts bunched around her waist as she wrapped her legs around him and he carried her to the bed. With eager hands, they stripped each other of their garments and nestled into the warmth of the covers and their arms. Davina sighed at the familiarity of Broderick's naked skin against her body, at the thrill of his erection against her belly, the hard planes of his chest and rippled stomach under her fingertips. She opened her thighs and grasped his cock to guide him into her, his tip wet and slick against her trembling quim. With slow, methodic pulses, Broderick eased into her and she savored each inch of him as he entered, delighted in the protection she experienced from his weight atop her.

"These miles will keep you from my dreams," he whispered against her ear. "And these days will be a black void. I want the taste of you on my soul."

Though Broderick meant he intended to make love to her for as long as possible this last night, she wanted to leave a more profound memory upon her beloved husband's being. Placing her hands upon his cheeks, she met his gaze. "I *want* you to taste my soul, Broderick." She held her breath for a moment before whispering, "Feed from me." He would be able to see and know everything she had experienced in her life since the day of her birth. All Vamsyrians gleaned this of everyone they fed from. Her soul would be laid bare to him in a way they had yet to experience.

Broderick's lips parted and his eyes widened. His body stopped moving and Davina swore his breath ceased.

"I know in seventeen years I've never asked that of you, but..."

"Blossom," he breathed. The corner of his mouth turned up in a half-smile and he kissed her with such tenderness, she almost wept. "You have me at a loss for words."

"If this is not something you want—"

"Oh, Davina." Broderick captured her mouth, devouring her and stealing her breath, leaving her dizzy. Finally breaking their kiss, he brushed a stray curl from her brow. "I have ached to taste the sweet nectar of you since I first saw you in my dreams. And to do so while we make love is a joining, I am told, like no other."

"In all the years since you crossed over, you have never done such a thing with anyone else?"

"Nay, Blossom. Before you, I never thought to find someone as precious to share such a special act of joining. Considering the harsh way you were introduced into my world, I never thought me feeding from you was something you wanted to experience."

Guilt darkened her heart. Until this moment, a small part of her still had not accepted Broderick for everything he was.

"Now, my love," he soothed, kissing her brow. "Do not have any regrets. Believe me when I say you are worth the wait." His comforting lips caressed her temple. His warm tongue darted out to taste her tear. Breathing across her cheek, his mouth hovered over hers, his eyes gazing at her with a love that melted any remaining shame she had regarding time lost at sharing this moment. Davina opened her mouth to her husband, inviting him in, and his tongue penetrated her lips at the same rhythm his cock penetrated her quim. Deep, slow, agonizingly sensuous and pushing her to the edge of madness.

Wrapping her legs around his hips, she dug her heels into his backside, pulling him into her. She groaned as his hands cupped her bottom, angling her entrance up to bury himself to the hilt. Every stroke pushed her higher and she shivered as his long, iron shaft pumped into the depth of her being. His mouth licked, suckled and kissed from her lips, across her jaw line and down to her throat. Her eyes flicked open and she clutched Broderick to her as she gazed with unseeing eyes over his shoulder. A dancing fire of fear and excitement flickered in her belly. She opened her heart, letting the love and arousal coursing through her body swirl around her so Broderick could absorb her soul.

Her orgasm came as swiftly as the piercing of his fangs, but lingered with the sweet euphoria of his feeding, driving her climax to a height of unknown territory. Her head dropping back, she closed her eyes and fell into an ecstasy that rippled throughout her limbs and focused on two throbbing points of her body—her throat and the hot, wet center between her legs where Broderick pumped his own orgasm.

After what seemed like hours, the shuddering waves of both their bodies subsided. Davina opened her eyes to find herself straddling Broderick's powerful thighs as he knelt in the center of their bed. Disoriented and delirious—even drunk from the experience—she heaved thirsty breaths as Broderick licked her blood from his lips. The silver, glowing core faded from his eyes hooded with passion. A tear slipped down his cheek and he buried his face in her hair, hiding from her…and she knew why. Through the impressions on Davina's blood, Broderick saw—for the first time—the true extent of the abuse she had suffered at the hands of her dead husband Ian, and she winced from the old wound. So much time had passed since she allowed herself to recall the memories, she did not think about them resurfacing in the act of Broderick's feeding.

"I tried to keep you from seeing and experiencing what transferred through your blood," he rasped, grief abrading his voice.

"You *did*, my love." She stroked his hair and hugged him tight for reassurance. "I just now allowed myself to remember the past, but that was my doing." She pulled back to gaze into his eyes. "You have given me so much joy over the years, I am happy to say I had forgotten the past." She smiled. "Thank you for such a gift."

"'Tis your gift I hold in sharing your blood. The gift of your life, your sweet childhood memories, and understanding the true depth of the love you hold for me in your heart."

The corner of Davina's mouth tugged as she resisted smiling at her beloved, and she pushed a rebellious strand of hair from his cheek. "Are you aware that you wax very poetic when you are melancholy?"

Broderick grinned and smacked her bare bottom, causing his wife to yelp and giggle. "Do I, now?" His delicious rumble of laughter vibrated between them and Davina squealed as they fell backward onto the bed.

Her husband slanted his mouth over hers, chuckling, and Davina tingled at the coppery taste of her blood, her face flushing with the forbidden pleasure. Broderick swelled inside her and rocked his hips to another rhythmic dance of lovemaking that carried them into the night.

After a solid night's sleep and a hearty breakfast in the castle kitchens, James set off with Ranald and Will to the house in Leith. He halted as he opened the door to the cottage. Alistair sat by the hearth– head down, as if sleeping. "Wait outside for me, lads," James instructed Will and Ranald. They both eyed Alistair, hesitating, only doing as James asked when he nodded, indicating all was well. They settled outside and he closed the front door.

Alistair started in the chair, cast weary eyes around the room and stumbled to his feet when his eyes landed on his son. "Well, 'tis right friendly of you to finally come home," he slurred, hands fumbling about his person to seemingly make his appearance presentable.

"The same can be said of you." James avoided his father's gaze, clenching his jaw as he picked around the cottage, gathering his belongings. Since his return, he had not spent much time unpacking or getting settled in…and he was glad for it.

Alistair stood in the center of the front living area, blocking James from taking his saddlebags to the door. "You only just arrived."

"And now I'm leaving." James stepped around his father. Placing his bags along the wall, he navigated past Alistair to his room to fill his satchel with the last of his clothing.

Alistair waited in the doorway to the small chamber. "Where are you going?"

Not taking his eyes from packing, James said, "Staying with the MacDougals. Broderick will be out of town for a few days, so I will be looking after his family."

The silence from his father unnerved him, so he chanced a glance in Alistair's direction. Eyes blood-shot and glassy with unshed tears, he regarded James with a trace of joy…perhaps even hope. "How have you been, lad?"

He shook his head in disbelief. "You ask me this now. After you disappeared for almost eight years. Only now do you finally care about my wellbeing." He faced his father and curled his hands into fists to quell his anger.

Alistair stuck his chest out and gripped the door frame. "I have been a good father to you and if you'll let me explain myself, you'll understand why I left and why I'm back here to help you. I—"

James stood nose-to-nose with Alistair. "A good father? You left without a word. You drowned yourself in drink and then disappeared! How is that being a good father? You felt sorry for yourself instead of seeing to the family you had left."

"She was my life, James!" Alistair protested. "I felt I could not—"

"I miss her, too! I wanted to grieve with you as well, but you shut me out and walked away! You cannot expect to come back into my life, now that you've accepted her death and are ready to move on."

"I haven't accepted her death, lad. I'm here to avenge it! You don't—"

Grabbing his now-filled satchel, James pushed past his father. "Nay, father," he growled. "Those men who killed her are long gone."

Shuffling after James into the main room again, Alistair pleaded, "Nay, James. You don't understand the truth behind what those men did, what they wanted."

James whirled and pointed a rigid finger into his father's chest. "Enough! It's taken me years to recover from her death, from you walking out of my life. And now you want to dig up graves and reopen old wounds. I've made a new life for myself and it doesn't include you."

For a long moment, they both stared at each other, James's breath ragged and his hands shaking. Pulling a small bottle out of his coat pocket, Alistair popped the cork and took a swig. He followed James's glare down to the bottle, then raised it and said in a gravelly voice, "I thank *you* for this, lad. Helps with the pain, among other benefits. You should try it. I gained it from a physician in Germania after I went to see you at school. A new elixir he created."

James grabbed the bottle and sniffed its contents, detecting the scent of brandy, spices and some other familiar essence. He searched his memories. What *was* that smell? He knew it. "Laud...laudanum," he recalled. Two of his fencing mates used it frequently after matches for pain. One had died from consuming too much.

Alistair snatched it back and gulped another swig, a sadness dragging his face into a frown. "Even then, you wouldn't listen to the truth about your mother."

James closed his eyes, willing the long-forgotten ache to recede. He had been glad to see his father, thinking he had traveled all that way to Germania to apologize for leaving, to tell James how proud he was he was going to school. Instead, Alistair did what he always did best—made James feel he didn't deserve any good fortune that came his way, made sure James knew anything good was because of him. Alistair felt inferior to his own son and the only way to make himself feel better or accomplished was to browbeat him. Yet in spite of this, while it was happening, James allowed Alistair to feed him the poison against Broderick. It took him years to filter out the doubt and suspicion Alistair had planted in his mind.

James shoved his father away, sloshing the bottle in Alistair's hand. "'Tis nothing but a liar you are! No truth ever comes out of your mouth. You blame Broderick for being the father you never could be. You blame me for being the man you wish you were."

His father clenched his jaw, his body trembling and his mouth distorting into a grimace. Tears welled in Alistair's eyes before his obvious anger ebbed and he nodded with resignation. "'Tis undeserving I am of your forgiveness, James." He tentatively stepped forward. "But I hope to make it up to you. I'm making efforts to free myself from the past and finally put this all behind me, and I want you to be part of a better life I have planned."

Humility wasn't a character trait his father had ever exemplified, a man who never seemed to be pleased with anything James did. Who was this stranger standing before him, ill in appearance and contrite, such a contrast to the judgmental taskmaster of his youth? In light of this "plan" to avenge Fiona's death, James had the answer. Alistair had gone mad. Or he was up to his usual lies and false appearances.

He shook his head and turned to the entrance. "Godspeed, father. Enjoy this *better* life you have planned. I want no part of it." Grabbing his satchel and saddlebags, he left and closed the door to his past.

"Ouch!" Cailin sat in an armchair before the hearth, her embroidery in her lap, sucking on her fingertip…for at least the hundredth time since she had hurried to the parlor to wait for James.

He had come back to the castle and sequestered himself away in his chamber for the last several hours. A few of the servants reported him in a black mood, so everyone had allowed him to be alone. This gave Cailin the opportunity to ensure she had tucked away her daggers—strapped to her hips out of habit—and fumble through her needle projects to find one that seemed far enough along to show *some* evidence she did wifely duties. That proved to be more difficult than anticipated. She'd been sure she had spent hours embroidering many projects only to find one or two no more than a third finished. Hurrying to the parlor, she had made haste to stoke the fire and sat with her skirts arranged in what she hoped was a pleasing manner. And then she waited. And waited.

And waited.

Her nerves were frazzled, her fingers sore from the many times she'd stuck herself, and little spots of blood dotted her fabric. She dropped her hands to her lap, leaned against the back of the chair and closed her eyes with a sigh. After a moment's peace, she resumed working on the embroidery.

A familiar, but almost forgotten, chirping twittered off the stone walls of the parlor and she resisted the urge to grin. She struggled to keep her eyes on her needlepoint and not look at James, who surely stood at the parlor door to her left, out of her direct line of sight. He twittered again and Cailin responded…licking her lips and sucking in just enough air at the corner of her mouth to make the sound that so resembled the squeak of a mouse or squirrel.

James swaggered into the room, crossing his arms, and Cailin's stomach quivered.

"Still my little mouse," he drawled. "You remembered."

She let her full smile emerge. "Of course I remember. That little noise always let me know you were on to my hiding place. It said you were close and coming for me."

"I did it to give you the chance to run and find a new place to hide." He chuckled. "You were always so easy to find, my little mouse. Mayhap you wanted me to find you."

Cailin giggled. "You never failed to give me a sweet sucket when you caught up with me." She still enjoyed the candied citrus peels, though now she used them more to sweeten her breath than as a treat. "Of course I wanted you to find me." Rising from her chair, she placed her embroidery on the cushion and faced him.

James considered the pile of cloth and raised a brow. She glanced at her seat and caught her breath when she saw the spots of blood. As casually as her shaking hands could muster, she bent over and bundled the fabric into her basket on the floor, ignoring the embarrassment heating her cheeks, and pushed the project under the side table.

Upon hearing James emit what could only be described as a growl, she straightened and whirled to face him, but collided with his solid frame. He caught her in his arms. Clutching his shirt, she swooned as the hard muscles of his chest flexed under her fingers and her breath quickened. She regarded his face and her heart stopped at the desire storming in the depths of his eyes.

"Hrmmm. As I said, I could fast get accustomed to you being in my arms. Tell me, Mouse," he whispered, "how do you think you have changed so much that I no longer wish to have you as my wife?"

Cailin opened her mouth to speak, but no words formed. Her tongue seemed frozen and the room lacked the air to breathe.

James touched his lips to her forehead for a lingering caress and she sighed, the tension melting from her body. His warm breath on her skin sent tingles across her scalp. He feathered his mouth to her temple for another kiss, to her cheek for another, and his lips sought hers...hovering, his half-hooded eyes gazing into hers before he pressed in, fusing their mouths together. Wet, warm and desperate, the kiss deepened, coaxing a moan from her throat. She inhaled deep, loving the scent of him, so indescribably him. His teeth nibbled at her lower lip, teasing her mouth open to enjoy the sensation of his feasting and allowing his tongue to sweep in for a taste. Following instinct, she mimicked his actions, their tongues dueling as they parried back and forth, in and out.

"Cailin," he breathed, breaking their kiss only a moment before delving in for more, his arms pulling her harder against him.

Lacing her fingers in his hair, she clung to this moment and the euphoria she never wanted to end. Light-headed, breathless, her knees trembling, her stomach fluttering with the flock of a thousand butterflies—

"Ahem!"

Cailin jumped out of James's arms and whipped around to face a scowling Margeret.

"I was told, Master James, that you were to be behavin' yerself whilst you were here." She uncrossed her arms and planted her fists on her hips. "Seems I cannot be leavin' you two alone." She marched to a chair in the corner of the room and plopped down, wriggling her rump into the seat, glaring eyes watchful.

Cailin avoided his face and brushed her palms against her skirts. "Would you care for some drink, Master James?" Without waiting for his answer, she scampered to the trestle table and poured a mug of small beer from the pitcher she had brought in anticipation of his arrival.

"Nay," he quipped. "I had plenty in my chambers."

"Oh." She smoothed her hands over her skirts again. "Mayhap I can bring you something to eat from the kitchens. I believe—"

"Nay." James's brow creased and he paced the length of the room in a slow and deliberate stride, a thoughtful frown marring his features.

Cailin glared at Margeret, who glared back. The presence of her handmaid obviously put James into a foul mood. How to get him out of it, Cailin was at a loss and she gritted her teeth again, clasping her hands behind her back to still her rising frustration.

James faced Cailin, his eyebrows a straight line over his jade eyes. "Have I been gone so long, we no longer know each other?"

"You *have* been away for over seven years," she answered tentatively. "Surely, you have gone through some transformation of your own."

"Aye, that I have." He resumed pacing, his right arm crossed over his chest, supporting his left elbow as he absently pinched and tugged his bottom lip.

"I can assure you, *I* have changed much."

He stopped and placed his hands upon his hips. "Aye, *that* you have. You are not what you pretend to be. You are definitely not what I expected."

His sweet kisses seemed to indicate otherwise, yet here he stood scolding her. Cailin squeezed her fists, still behind her back. "Am I no longer pleasing to you, Master James?" She had tried to make her voice even and unemotional, however, she internally grumbled at how her words grated and displayed her anger clearly.

The corner of his mouth turned up. "I see the lass I knew as a child."

He is mocking me! She inhaled deeply, not allowing herself to be goaded. "I do not know what you mean. I am indeed a mature woman and have spent the last several years learning my duties as a wife."

She paced. *Though my combat training may have been a higher priority, I think I've managed both well.* "I know such things as running a household, embroidery, maintaining the dairy, organizing—"

"And who was that woman I encountered in the alley?" He tapped his foot and scowled.

"You caught me unawares! That was a woman defending herself against a thief!" Tears stung the backs of her eyes.

"Stop pretending to be something you are not, Cailin! I do not—"

She ran from the parlor and scampered up the stairs toward her chamber.

"Cailin!" James's voice faded behind her and she burst into her room with Margeret in her wake.

Closing the chamber door, Margeret scolded, "Child, why did you run? You need to face that man—"

"I don't trust myself to keep my anger in check!" Cailin paced. "You saw how easily I am incited to wrath. How am I going to be this dutiful wife he is expecting me to be? You heard him. He hated that woman he met in the alley. 'Tis who I am and he hates me!"

"Oh, he does not hate you, child!"

Cailin stomped into her wardrobe and donned her cloak.

"Where are you going?" Margeret blocked her from leaving the room.

"I wish to go for a ride. You know it clears my head." She tried to push past Margeret, but she side-stepped to block Cailin's exit.

"Nay! Look out the window! Dusk is upon us. Your rides are never short ventures."

Cailin relented and flopped onto her bed, growling. "Enough! I will stay inside, but leave me to work myself through this." She pouted. "Mayhap I may even find a short rest. Wake me when my father has risen." She tossed her cloak to the settee and lay rigidly on the bed while Margeret exited the chamber with a frown.

Huffing out a ragged breath, Cailin stared at the ceiling with her fingers entwined across her belly. Her heart thudded in her ears. She inhaled and exhaled deeply to calm her spirit. *I'm a fool. I cannot do a simple thing such as control my temper. What is so difficult about this?*

She turned to her side and hugged her pillow.

It would be so much easier if I had never learned to defend myself. I should have trusted Da, and eventually James, to protect me. There was no need for me to have learned to fight.

She turned onto her back and squeezed her eyes shut against the memories of the man falling to the ground, his blood— She groaned and curled into a ball.

If Da had never come into our lives, if he and my mother had never fallen in love, Angus would not target us.

Shaking her head, she turned to her other side. *Nay. Angus will target anyone in Broderick's life. It's Angus who is the cause of all my woes. If he wasn't such a coward and faced Da one-on-one, then those he loved would not be in danger.*

She flipped onto her back again.

Oh I wish I could be the one to drive my dagger into Angus's heart! No matter how skilled I am with the blades or how I can prevent him from hearing my thoughts, he's still immortal. He'll have such an advantage over me. Nay, I cannot blame the man I call father for this life. It's because of Da I know the face of true love. I see it in their marriage. Such a love, the eternal devotion he shares with my mother, is worth dying for. It's the kind of love I crave, one I believe I can have with James…if I could just be disciplined enough to be the woman he needs me to be…the woman I need to be for myself.

Hugging her knees to her chest, Cailin wept at the helplessness overwhelming her.

Though the hours were short, Broderick refused to leave without making sweet love to Davina one last time. She had been snuggled to his side, waiting for him to awaken, and he had slipped into the bliss of her warmth. Reluctant to leave her arms, he grudgingly encouraged them to dress, and then asked her to gather Cailin and Margeret in the parlor. He would meet them there with James to say his farewells, after he had a brief word and gave further instructions to his future son-in-law.

"Broderick."

He stopped at the door of their chamber and glanced over his shoulder.

"Mayhap you should wait until you return to let James know about Fiona."

"Nay, Blossom. If he does encounter Alistair, I want the lad to know the truth."

She sighed. "Aye, my love."

Broderick made his speech to James brief and the lad took the news well. Afterward, he escorted James to the parlor. Davina handed Broderick his satchel, which he slung over his shoulder and across his chest to hang at his hip. With his arm around her, he faced the small group of people he loved. "As you know, I don't like to venture anywhere without those dearest to my heart. However, on this occasion, I fear the dangers in bringing you with me outweigh the benefits. I know not where this journey will lead, who will be awaiting me other than this prophetess or what the outcome will be. My only consolation is I'm leaving a very powerful amulet of protection behind along with the superior skills of both my future son-in-law and the precious girl I am privileged to call my daughter by name." He focused on Cailin. "Use the walls of this fortress, little one. During the day, they are a haven. At night, you will have the amulet." He embraced his daughter. Nodding to Davina, Broderick stepped back as she came forward with the small box Rosselyn delivered from Amice. Cailin opened the box and Broderick stood behind her, lifting her hair from the back of her neck. "Put on this amulet, wear it close to your skin, and *never* take it off. Do you understand me, Cailin?"

She nodded, reached into the box and tied the ends of the leather cord together behind her neck. Davina placed the box onto the trestle table along the parlor wall.

"Conceal it wherever you need to so it will protect you from Vamsyrians at all times."

Cailin obeyed with a wide-eyed expression, tucking the amulet into her bodice.

"It is my greatest hope I learn how to make more of these so you all might wear them and, at last, be safe from my enemy." He faced James. "Though I will be gone only a few days, I want you practicing those routines I demonstrated for you. And Cailin…I want you to teach him what you know about blocking your thoughts and some of the moves you have perfected."

Cailin's eyes grew even wider and she shook her head, and then scratched her temple, indicating she wanted Broderick to read her thoughts. He nodded, but heard nothing of her mind. Her eyes pleaded with Broderick and he frowned. "Cailin, I cannot—" His breath hitched with dawning realization. "Take off the amulet for a moment, child, and hand it to your mother."

Cailin slipped the medallion over her head and handed it to Davina.

"Try again," he encouraged.

Do not ask me to engage in combat with James, Da! He abhors such behavior in a woman, especially of his betrothed.

Broderick shook his head. *You are mistaken, Cailin. We do not have time to discuss this. Trust me when I say this should not vex you so.* "Put the amulet back on, Cailin."

She grumbled, but obeyed.

"Now try to say something else to me with your thoughts." Broderick waited and again heard nothing. "If you just communicated your mind to me, I did not hear it. It appears this amulet also prevents Vamsyrians from hearing thoughts. Well, that will be another way you will all gain some privacy against my gifts."

Chuckles and subdued laughter floated about them.

"I will make haste and not tarry so that I might be back with this treasured information as soon as possible. Until then, stay close and within these walls."

Several heads bobbed in agreement.

Davina strolled with Broderick to the main gate while James and Cailin lingered by the front entrance. Broderick pulled Davina into his arms. "Eternally yours," he whispered into her hair.

"Together forever," she responded and her tears seeped through the material of his shirt, warming his skin.

Savoring Davina's lips, he kissed her one last time, then whirled around and avoided looking back as he pushed through the gate. He would be traveling on foot using his immortal speed, as a horse could never run as fast or for as long as he. Thunder rumbled in the distance and he scanned the black sky, void of stars. Moisture tainted the air and he groaned. As if in response, the showers began. Though the rain wouldn't slow him down, he did not relish running in it. In hopes of protecting Davina, he dashed through the pelting drops, leaving the fortress and the very breath of his soul behind him.

CHAPTER FOUR

His new stilettos at his side, sweat dripping off his brows, James stood on the mat with his eyes focused on a decorative sword hanging on the wall across the room. The Training Room—as Broderick named it—appeared different during the day, a dull light from the overcast sky coming through the oriel windows and illuminating the canvas-padded mats strewn about the wooden floor. A few cabinets and boards with blunt-edged weapons hanging on pegs covered the wall opposite the windows. The daylight showed off the splendor of the room decorated with various shields, weapons and paintings of battle scenes, something James wasn't able to fully enjoy the night he sparred with Broderick.

Hands relaxed at his hips, he employed the technique he learned at *Fechtschulen* to gradually work through the next exercise. Moving slowly, he grabbed the daggers, slid them out of their sheaths, elbowed his invisible opponent behind him and spun to stab his phantom chest. James shook his head and replaced the daggers. *Sloppy. Again.*

He repeated the movement several times at a slower pace to ensure he was comfortable with each step in the execution. Once he performed the maneuver smoothly and with ease, he increased his speed. On occasion, he'd drop a weapon, curse himself and start again. The point of the exercises this morning were to complete as many of the movements Broderick had taught him without having to think about what to do.

Grab the daggers. Elbow opponent. Spin and pivot. Stab through the heart. Grab. Elbow. Spin. Stab. Grab. Elbow. Spin. Stab.

And then to accomplish the moves while thinking of something else.

Grab. Elbow. Spin. Stab. Why must she...grab...always run...elbow...when our exchanges...spin...turn into heated...stab...arguments? Grab...she has always been...elbow...one to speak her mind...spin...and now I see...stab...her holding back...grab...and hiding behind...elbow...this façade...spin...of the dutiful wife...stab. What I would like to do is GRAB her by the ELBOW, SPIN her around and STAB her with my—

"Good morrow, James."

Cailin's sultry voice floated about the air as she sauntered into the room...wearing a pair of form-fitting, tan breeches...that showed every...single...curve of her slender legs, and hips sweet enough to grab onto!

"I see you have been working hard on your routines." She smiled that heart-breaking grin and James sighed.

He nodded and dropped his jaw to the floor when Cailin swiveled that perfectly curved backside toward him, bent over and placed something on the bench before her. His mouth watered and the blood in his body rushed so suddenly to his groin it ached. *For the love of God!* Turning his back to her, he stomped across the room and quickly donned his shirt, leaving it hanging loose to cover his erection straining against his breeches, demanding to bury itself to the hilt inside that luscious and surely creamy temptation.

He clenched his jaw and cursed his body's fierce reaction. "Your father allows you to wear such revealing garments?" He winced at how his harsh words grated his ears, and most likely hers. He spun to face her again and groaned inwardly at her wounded expression.

"I...my...mother made them for me...to do the training with my father. My skirts would get in the way, you see, and..." She shrugged and her fingers fumbled with the hem of the loose linen shirt she wore. "I never wear them outside of this room. Should I change?"

Difficult question to answer! His groin screamed, "NAY!" His head screamed, "AYE!" His groin won the argument. "Nay, Cailin. Never change. I mean, all is well. You just caught me by surprise." He swallowed and cleared his throat, stepping toward her, a little uncertain on his feet.

A deep red mottled her cheeks and her lips parted with a tiny gasp—those full lips, growing flush with realization, begging James to taste them. She must have understood what the site of her in those breeches did to him, for she backed toward the door. "Perhaps I should—"

James stood before her in two strides, grabbing her shoulders. "Nay...please." He eased his hold on her when she shrank from him, and he caressed her cheek with the backs of his fingers. Thankfully, she visibly relaxed from his gesture. He was being ridiculous and offered her a boyish smile. "I promise...I shall do my best to behave. We have much to go over and I cannot let something such as wardrobe interfere with learning to protect you. 'Tis my duty as your husband and I will not fail." He winked at her. "Come, Mouse. Show me how to wield my new weapons."

A small frown tainted her grin, but she nodded and dropped to her knees on the mat before him, and his breath hitched at the innocently provocative position in which she just placed herself.

"Come sit with me first," she said, patting the mat in front of her, her head moving just a few inches toward his groin.

James dropped to his knees and groaned.

"Are you already sore?" She giggled as she pulled her long, cinnamon curls back with a leather tie.

He didn't trust himself to speak and waited for her to continue.

"The first defense against a Vamsyrian is to create a mental barrier for your thoughts, like a curtain wall about a castle." She closed her eyes and breathed deep, her breasts pushing against the material of her shirt.

Good Lord in heaven, she has no chemise or undergarment! This woman is sure to be my undoing. Has MacDougal never noticed this? As a father, he should be—

"Deep, calming breaths help you relax and will allow you to apply your mind to the task." She opened her eyes. "I will do my best to explain the method I use, based on what my father learned from his Gypsy friend Amice...and I have made my own modifications to suit my imaginings. Perhaps through this, we can explore your imagination to find out what methods work best for you."

He clenched his jaw when his cock twitched. Clearing his throat, he nodded. "Aye."

"Wonderful. Now close your eyes and breathe deeply through your nose."

James did as she instructed, grateful for the moment her tempting visage no longer dominated his senses. The deep breath did seem to calm him.

"Now blow your breath out through your mouth."

He did thus.

"Another deep breath through your nose." Cailin's voice, just a whisper, was now at his left. "And blow out through your mouth." Her soft voice to his right. Apparently, she had stood and was circling as she instructed him. Her delicate hands touched his lower back and pulled on his shoulder. "Be sure to sit straight for easier breathing." The scent of citrus wafted through his senses. *She must have a sucket in her mouth.* "And let your shoulders relax." Her fingertips pushed on the tops of his shoulders, her voice in front of him now. He opened his eyes just enough to see where she was…bent forward before him, giving him a perfect view of the creamy, round mounds of her breasts. She lowered herself to her knees and James closed his eyes. In the darkness of his private world, those perfect breasts remained branded on his eyesight.

"Now that you have relaxed your body and slowed your breathing," her sultry voice caressed his ears, "you are in a position to explore your imagination, to develop a picture for the purpose of creating your barrier."

The side of his mouth turned up. "And just what picture should I develop for my barrier? Anything at all?"

"Well, when you think of a barrier, what comes to mind?"

Your clothing. "Hard...stone. A masonry stone wall, perhaps."

"Very good, James." She seemed genuinely pleased with him. "So, using that picture, can you imagine building a wall in your mind, one stone block at a time?"

This was a good distraction, excellent for getting his mind off of her lush curves and white skin. He nodded. "I can see a field with masons stacking these large stone blocks to create the wall."

"Excellent! Imagine them building that wall. Imagine that wall blocking out anything and everything and that it is surrounding your mind."

He lost himself in the imagery for a few moments, building the stone wall block by block.

"You may open your eyes now."

James did and Cailin's red hair and cerulean eyes came into view. Her grin lit up her face like the sun and she tucked a curled strand of hair behind her ear. He adored those freckles dotting her pert little nose.

"Just before you rest each night, use that image, build that wall in your mind and imagine that wall never coming down once it has been built."

"'Tis all there is to it?"

"Aye, but it does prove difficult to maintain when you engage in fighting. You have to keep that image of the built wall around your mind at all times." She rose from the mat and ambled to the bench. After picking up her knife belt, she strapped her daggers to her hips, gathering the material of her shirt around her…providing more definition to her tiny waist and slender form. James licked his lips, his mouth gone dry, as her petite breasts peaked against the cream-colored muslin, her nipples brushing the fabric, perhaps in response…

"…do not want to get stabbed now, do we?" Cailin's voice faded into his private fantasies.

"Hmmm?" *Apply yourself, lad!*

"I said…we should switch our blades for the training weapons. We do not want to get stabbed now, do we?" Cailin pulled her blades from her belt and set them on the wooden table against the wall beneath the peg board. She grabbed two blunt-edged daggers from a peg.

"Of course!" James followed suit, replacing his stilettos for the crudely-formed daggers. "They are quite similar in weight."

"Aye. My father had the blacksmith make the effort to get the weight very close to our weapons.

It does no good to learn with a different weight. I am sure you know the dynamic is different."

He could not help grinning. "Of course."

"So, what routines did my father show you?"

"Ah! Well…here." He turned Cailin and stepped in front of her, showing her his back. "Let us propose that you are Angus and standing behind me." He went through the motions gradually…*grab, elbow, spin, stab*…Cailin dodging the slow-moving knife when it came around.

"Very good. I know of that routine. There is another variation on that one, easy to pick up." She stood in front of him now, putting her back to him, and James ensured their bodies did not touch. "When you grab your daggers," she demonstrated, "and after you elbow his stomach, spin in the other direction." She twirled thus. "And stab either in the back or side…depending on what he gives you." She bent over as she reached around…and brushed her tender bottom against his erection.

James gritted his teeth and searched the ceiling, counting the wood beams, nails, anything his eyes could find.

"Forgive me!" Cailin gasped. "Did I jab you?"

"Nay," he assured her and sought her eyes. Those cerulean eyes. "All is well. Why do you ask?"

She raised a brow and cocked her head. "You looked as if you were in pain. I thought…"

"Nay, I was…preparing myself just in case."

"I can assure you, James, I have enough control over my weapons not to touch you."

"I am sure you do." He winked.

She frowned and eyed him with suspicion, but jutted her chin forward. "You try now."

They switched positions, James in front of Cailin, and he moved through the motions she had just demonstrated. When he bent over and reached around for the strike, Cailin laid her hand upon his back and shoved. He kept his ground though, and she laughed.

"Very good, James!"

He faced her and chuckled, caught up in her gaiety.

"I expected to catch you off balance and you did splendidly!"

"Your father did not waste his money on sending me to school, then?"

"He shall be pleased with my report." She covered her mouth as she giggled. Straightening her posture, she waved her hand for him to face her. "Come. We shall do it quickly now."

They sped through the routine several times, fumbling on occasion, but working through the mishaps and perfecting the moves. James demonstrated the two other routines Broderick had shown him and they worked through those. Cailin had excellent advice and impressed James with her command of close-combat engagement. The more they danced through the routines, the more comfortable they were with their bodies touching...and the more Cailin aroused James.

"'Tis one more routine I would like to show you." She grabbed his shoulders, positioning him in front of her.

At his height, towering over her small frame, James was gifted with another delightful view of her cleavage. A rivulet of perspiration trailed down the sweet valley between her breasts and he imagined capturing it on his tongue.

"Now, standing thus, you have just approached me." She dropped her arms to her sides, causing her breasts to jut forward and James's cock to twitch. "Stepping in toward him is not something he will expect." Cailin stepped forward, pulling her dagger from her sheath, and placing her foot between his feet. Such a lunge pressed her thigh between his knees and her breasts against his chest...and his impulses surged and overruled his reasoning. He caught Cailin by her waist and she snapped her head up in surprise, full lips parted and eyes wide. James dipped forward and captured her mouth with his, the sweet taste of orange on her tongue. His hands slid down to cup her bottom. With ease, he lifted her against his body and she wrapped her legs about his waist as he carried her to the table and shoved the weapons aside.

"James," she pleaded between kisses. "What if...We should..."

His breath ragged and his mind swirling, he could not get enough of tasting her. "Aye, Cailin, I know...but..." He ground his cock against the heat between her legs, his groin throbbing for release. When she squeezed her legs tighter, drawing him harder against her, he groaned into her mouth. His hands fumbled with her belt, unbuckling the leather and giving him free reign to explore her damp skin. His palms smoothed over her back, along her ribs and Cailin gasped when he cupped her breast and pinched her nipple.

"Nay, James." She pushed his shoulder. Her eyes implored him, her chest heaving. "We cannot...though God knows I ache to..."

He nodded, panting, and touched his forehead to hers. "Aye...aye..." God, how he did *not* want to pull away from her.

"Cailin?" Margeret's voice echoed down the corridor.

Cailin practically leapt from the table, shoving James back and putting some distance between them. She snatched her dagger belt and hurriedly fastened it around her waist. James grumbled when Margeret poked her head through the doorway and assessed the situation. Her eyes darted between Cailin and James several times before settling on Cailin. She stepped into the room with a tray in her hands, balancing an earthen pitcher and two mugs. The handmaid set the tray down upon the table where Cailin's sweet bottom had just been. "Have I interrupted something?"

"Nay, Maggie!" Cailin had her blunt weapons in hand, ready to do battle. "I was just showing James a new maneuver."

Margeret narrowed suspicious eyes at James and he crossed his arms. "And just what is the meaning of that expression?" he growled.

Margeret gasped. "Watch that tongue of yours, Master James!" She stalked forward, pointing her finger in his face. "It is my station to watch over Mistress Cailin."

"And you suppose I have ill intentions upon my *wife*?" he retorted.

"She is not your wife yet, laddie! And you best not be forgettin' that."

"'Tis only a few—"

Cailin stepped between them. "Maggie, I assure you, James has behaved himself perfectly." She marched Margeret to the bench and sat her down. Grabbing the two drying cloths from the bench, Cailin then marched over to James. "We have been working very hard to prepare for the worst, have we not, James?" She handed him a cloth and proceeded to blot the sweat from her face. "'Tis hard work sparring, and you know how I loathe to do it, Maggie, but it cannot be avoided."

Oh, Lord in heaven, 'tis the dutiful wife stealing my Mouse!

"I know, child." Margeret pouted and nodded her head.

And Maggie must be the one feeding this rubbish to her!

Cailin poured small beer into the two mugs. "'Tis kind of you to bring some drink, Maggie." She pivoted and held a mug out to James. "Would you like something—"

"Nay, I do not."

Tight-lipped, Cailin placed the mugs on the tray and faced him with her hands clasped before her. "Might I ask why your mood has soured so suddenly?"

"'Tis pretending to be something you absolutely are not, *Mistress* Cailin."

Flames roared in her midnight-blue eyes and she clenched her jaw, though several moments passed before she opened her mouth again. "And what exactly are you implying, *Master* James."

He tipped his head back and let the sardonic laughter pour from him. "I am not *implying* anything, *Mistress* Cailin. I am stating quite plainly that you are not this dutiful wife you pretend to be. You—"

"She most certainly is, laddie!" Margeret defended and stomped forward, her finger pointed at him again.

He leveled his eyes at her and she shrank. "Maggie, you had better stand down with that finger of yours or I shall—"

"Do not dare to threaten Maggie, James!" Cailin took one step forward and opened her mouth, but as she had done in their last heated exchange, she whirled and ran from the room.

"Oh, no you don't!" James threw the drying cloth to the floor and ran after her. Far down the hall, her chamber door slammed. *How the hell did she get down there so quickly!*

Davina stepped into his path, almost colliding with him, and he slid to a halt. She gasped and put her hand to her breast, breathing a few gulps of air. "I'm sorry to interrupt you, but your father is at the front gate."

"My father?" *Blast!* His eyes darted between Davina and Cailin's chamber door before he heaved a sigh of resignation. "Aye, I'll see to him. Thank you."

"Broderick has already warned me not to trust your father, James." Her brow furrowed. "Do not let him through that gate, do you understand me?"

"Very clearly, my lady. I want him in this home less than you do, I can assure you." He nodded to Davina and grabbed his sword before he hurried down the steps with a grumble and fastened the weapon to his hips.

Cailin finished changing into her riding habit and stormed out of her room on the verge of crying. She swiped at the tears, refusing to give into their needling demand for release.

Margeret trailed after her. "Cailin, you cannot let that man bother you so much."

"Maggie, now is not the time to reprimand me about my temper." She continued through the castle, dodging servants and navigating through hallways until she burst through the door to the back courtyard. She didn't care if Maggie was behind her or not. Stomping across the yard, she entered the stables. She grumbled while snagging her saddle off its stand, hefted it into the stall of her horse and threw it over the mare's back.

"Easy there, lassie." Fife the stable master stepped into the stall with Cailin and stayed her hand. "Let me do that for ye before she nicks ye."

Cailin turned and started pacing.

"And ye best be taking that outside the stall before she nicks *me*." His voice was firm but compassionate.

"Sorry, Fife." She did as he requested, the winds taken out of the sails of her anger. "I wish I could control my temper better," she muttered.

"Temper?" Fife toddled to the other side of Cailin's mare, Blossom—a name she chose due to her fondness of father's pet name for her mother.

"Nay, 'tis just a passionate nature ye have, just like yer mum."

Cailin smiled and rested her forearms on the stall ledge, propping her chin on the backs of her hands. Fife had been caring for their horseflesh since before she was born, having once worked for her grandmother, Lilias, who passed away four winters ago. He was ever patient with the animals and with her, the man always possessing a gentle spirit.

Patting her mare's flank, he led her out of the stall and into the yard. "She be ready for ye, lassie. Be easy with her, now."

Standing on her tiptoes, she pecked a kiss on his cheek. "As always, thank you, Fife."

He chuckled. "Ooo, Mary will flog me if she sees me gettin' a kiss from such a bonnie lass."

Cailin couldn't stop the laughter from bubbling out of her mouth. As she mounted Blossom and arranged her skirts for riding, Ranald and Will stalked toward her. "Good day, sirs." She cocked a brow and her knees hugged her mare. The back gate was just being opened, allowing Libby and her marketing cart through.

"Now then, Mistress Cailin," Ranald scolded with his arms crossed. Will mirrored his stance and frown of disapproval. "You know riding alone is not encouraged."

"Then you had better get your horses saddled quickly if you wish to catch me." She winked and kicked her heels into Blossom's side, her laughter echoing around the courtyard as she dashed through the back gate. Looking over her shoulder, she giggled at them scrambling into the stables, hollering at Fife to help them get saddled. She shook her head and slowed her pace. She'd not venture too far ahead so they could still see her in the distance.

"Now you listen to me, lad!" Alistair growled, pointing his finger into James's chest.

James mustered every bit of control he had left after dealing with Cailin. His father was on the brink of getting his jaw knocked from his head. "Trying to get me to turn on the MacDougals is hardly the path to choose in reconciling with me, father, and I'm not going to stand here and listen to your lies."

"I'm not lying to you! You weren't told everything about the murder of your mother, James." Alistair ground his teeth as James sighed. "Broderick MacDougal killed your mother!"

"Now that is a lie straight from the pit of hell!" James boomed at Alistair.

"'Tis the truth, as surely as if he cut her throat with his own hands!"

"*Angus Campbell* is responsible for Mum's death!" Though it had been a blow to James yesterday when Broderick filled him in on the details of

Fiona's murder, he trusted Broderick's word and his account of the tragedy. Campbell had used two masked henchmen during the day to kidnap Davina and Cailin—ten years old then—from the shipping house. Alistair and Fiona had also been there. Fiona's throat had been slashed open and Alistair stabbed in the gut and left for dead. Davina and Cailin were tortured until Broderick rescued his family and Campbell escaped...again. MacDougal had returned as soon as possible to find Alistair barely hanging on to his life and used his immortal blood to heal him.

The news had slashed open old wounds, making them fresh again. James couldn't prevent the trembling in his voice. "You forget Broderick saved your life and Campbell sent those men. I know what you say about this...if we had not become involved with Broderick—"

"If he had but warned us about what Angus was capable of doing," Alistair finished with his twist of the situation. "We could have been more prepared or even had the choice of not becoming involved with him. Do you not see, lad...MacDougal was just using our family and we are but casualties in this endless war he has with Angus."

James narrowed his eyes and crossed his arms. "Strange that you use his given name, this enemy of the MacDougals. I wonder, father, how well you know our friend Campbell."

Alistair shook his head. "Son, I tell you—"

"Enough!" James drew his sword and touched the point to his father's throat. Alistair's eyes grew wide and his breath caught when the sharp point pierced his skin. "You walked away from your responsibilities to me when I needed you most and now you come back here blaming your own mistakes on the only people who ever gave a damn about me. Broderick is guilty only by association and you are nothing but a coward." He stepped back, but kept his sword leveled at Alistair's heart. "Begone! You are dead to me, Alistair Knightly. Leave this place and never return."

James stood his ground, his father glaring at him, tears threatening to spill over his lashes.

Without another word, Alistair turned and stomped over the bridge and down the pathway, away from MacDougal Castle.

Finally releasing his breath, James sheathed his sword and spun on his heels, pushed through the gate and headed back inside the fortress. Now to deal with Cailin.

CHAPTER FIVE

As he bounded up the steps to the first-level bedchambers, Margeret cleared her throat rather loudly. James stopped, clenched his fists and swiveled to face her haughty leer.

"You will not find her in her room, Master James." Her chin jutted forward and her lips formed a thin line of disapproval. "Gone for a ride to clear her head, she has."

He reined in his temper and nodded. "Thank you, Maggie." He turned to continue up the stairs when Margeret's voice arrested his progress again.

"Both of you should learn to control your tempers." Accusation laced her voice.

James whirled and stopped a breath away from Margeret, towering over her now-shrinking figure. "What Cailin needs is to stop listening to your ideas of what you envision to be the perfect and dutiful wife. She is fine just the way she is. I do not know what they taught you in Ireland growing up or what your late husband instructed you on how Scottish Highland wives should behave. Here in the Lowlands a woman is appreciated for her natural talents."

Margeret jutted her chin again, albeit a bit more hesitant, but she nodded.

James relaxed. "I mean you no disrespect, Maggie, and I know you mean well. I am not exactly at my best today."

Margeret relaxed her shoulders. "Aye, Master James. 'Tis a challenging time you've had. You know where my heart is for Cailin. I suppose I shall let the natural order of things prevail."

He chuckled. "Well, you are right not to trust her alone with me."

Maggie snickered behind her hands. "Aye, laddie, I'm glad yer honest with yerself about that, but I shall be sure you keep yer breeches on around her."

"I still won't make it easy for you!" Laughing, James pivoted back up the stairs and went to his chamber. He would give Cailin a chance to bring her temper down to a simmer. It would be best for them both if they had time to let their anger ebb.

Cailin glanced over her shoulder and chuckled at Will and Ranald's failed attempts to find her. She had grown very adept at hiding enough so they could not see her, but she could still see them. Such games she played at their expense did wonders for her on many levels. She perfected her tracking and hiding skills and this frequently distracted her from whatever troubles had plagued her enough to take a cleansing ride, thereby always lightening her mood. She pranced her mare about in a circle, stirring the mud and leaves so the guards could see her tracks, then trotted deeper into the forest. Branches and the canopy of trees above her still dripped water from the previous night's rain. Cailin frequently wiped the wetness from her cheeks. Perhaps she should find a nice hiding spot and ambush them when they ran by. She stopped and, leaning forward in the saddle, peered around a tree.

Alistair Knightly trekked through the forest at a determined pace. She slipped from the saddle and followed him at a distance. *What is he doing out here?* He wasn't welcome in her home and James had made it abundantly clear he wasn't open to receiving his father for visits either. So what would have him venturing so close to MacDougal Castle or into these woods?

She followed him to an even denser part of the forest she never before explored, not wishing to wander too far from the protection of her home. Nestled into the side of a small hill was a tiny thatched-roof cottage. Alistair rapped on the door and waited. Cailin tied Blossom to a large tree out of sight and padded closer to the small building to get a better view of who might answer the door. Alistair rapped one more time and someone grumbled from within. "Aye, give me a moment!"

Cailin narrowed her eyes. That gruff voice sounded vaguely familiar.

The door swung open and Cailin clapped her hand over her mouth to keep from gasping aloud. That man named Jasper, who had jumped her in the alley, stood in the doorway and ushered Alistair into the house. He quickly swept the area with his gaze. Cailin stayed low and Jasper slammed the door.

Checking the area with her own sweeping gaze, she scampered up to the house and positioned herself under the shuttered window. Just to be safe, she checked the small sheath in her sleeve to be sure she had her slender dagger at the ready…also forged with a thick layer of silver, as all her blades were.

"Thank you," Alistair said. "I could use a mug after the exchange I just had with my son."

"What did ye learn?" Jasper prodded.

"MacDougal is out of town."

Jasper sputtered, apparently choking on whatever drink he shared with Alistair. "Are ye sure?"

"Aye. James is staying at their castle, helping to protect the family while he is away." Alistair slurped and slammed down his mug. "You should have seen the fancy weapon he threatened to cut my throat with."

"How long will MacDougal be gone?"

"I know not and neither does James."

"We have to move quickly then." Jasper paused and gulped. "Ye need to go back and talk to yer son, find out if there is an opportunity for Cailin and Davina to be alone."

"No need for that." Alistair had a little too much confidence in his voice for Cailin's comfort. "I just ran into the Gypsies and they're preparing to celebrate the betrothal of James and Cailin. Strange enough, they're the same Gypsies who told me—"

"When?"

"Huh? Oh, last year. Remember I told you—"

"Mate." Jasper sighed. "Let's not get distracted when yer revenge is finally at hand. When are they celebrating the betrothal?"

"Right you are. On the morrow, in the afternoon. And it will be at the Gypsy camp, in the open. They will surely have guards, though."

"Bah!" Jasper exclaimed. "We just need to create a diversion to get everyone's attention off of Davina and Cailin. Once we do that, we grab 'em." A loud slapping caused Cailin to start. "Good work, Alistair. Angus will reward ye greatly."

Cailin's heart hammered against her ribs. She had lingered far too long. Guarding her steps carefully, she padded away from the cottage and navigated through the trees and wet leaves back to Blossom. She checked behind her and was relieved she was neither discovered nor followed, and swung up into the saddle.

Kicking her horse into a gallop, she headed toward the castle. *Angus has been planning another capture, but for how long? And Alistair…what has caused him to betray us like this? I have to get back and tell James what his father—* She yanked on the reins and looked through the trees, now closed behind her to conceal the cottage.

This was a rare opportunity she could not pass up. Pulling the amulet from her bodice, she ran her fingertip over the grooved surface of the strange markings. "So, Angus. If you wish to bundle me off again, you shall have more than you bargained for." She tucked the amulet under her chemise and turned her horse toward Jasper's cottage.

After a few yards, though, she slowed to a halt. "Nay, I cannot just barge into that hut and state, 'I am here. Take me to Angus!' They will think I am setting them up for a trap." She shook her head. *I must make them think they have succeeded with their plan.* She nodded, satisfied with her idea. "Come and get me, you bastard," she hissed. "I am truly ready for you!"

Cailin dug her heels into Blossom's side to return toward the castle and prepare for her capture on the morrow.

Margeret shook her head as she helped Cailin lace the back of her bodice. "I do not understand why you refuse to wear the other gown." She peered over Cailin's shoulder to glower at her reflection in the looking glass.

"Enough, Maggie," Cailin scolded. "Knowing the Gypsies, there is sure to be plenty of dancing and merriment and I am not going to wear one of my better gowns. Not only will it get soiled with mud and sweat, but it will restrict my movements and my breath as well. I would like to enjoy this afternoon rather than end it by fainting into oblivion." *Nor am I going to confine myself to a gown in which I cannot move freely enough to fight Angus.*

The gown she wore was confining enough as it was, though she did choose one that did not require layers of underskirts. Instead, her cream-colored chemise draped to the floor and peeked through the front opening of the dark-green brocade outer skirt. The bodice of the same green brocade hugged her ribcage and waist before dipping into a "V" in front. Margeret tied forest-green ribbons, blousing the sleeves at her elbows first, then at her wrists, in a practical arrangement that was also attractive.

Cailin tugged at the slits in the gown sleeves to pull portions of the chemise through for the accenting contrast of the two fabrics. The entire ensemble was trimmed in ivory ribbon, lace and embroidery all done by her mother's delicate hands. She eyed the perfect stitches with envy. *Once Angus is dead, I will have plenty of time to perfect my skills.*

"What troubles you child?" Margeret leaned around Cailin with a furrowed brow.

She plastered a smile to her mouth and faced her handmaid. "Nothing, Maggie."

Adjusting the chemise collar along the bodice's neckline, Maggie attempted to cover Cailin's cleavage. "'Tis quite all right to have apprehensions about such a memorable event."

You have no idea, my dear sweet friend. Cailin frowned and pulled her bosom up to swell over the chemise. "Truly, I am not nervous about wedding James. I just wish Da could be here for this." *Not entirely untrue…*

"Well, that is understandable." Margeret returned the frown and yanked Cailin's chemise higher for more modesty. She nodded her final position on the matter of how much bust Cailin should be exposing. A moment after disappearing into the wardrobe, she emerged with a pair of green, glass-beaded slippers.

"Oh, Maggie," Cailin protested. "I do adore those shoes, but they refuse to stay upon my feet."

"Nonsense! You look lovely in these shoes and they complement your gown so well." Margeret knelt before Cailin and grabbed her ankle, slipped her foot into one shoe, then the other. "If you insist on wearing this moderate gown, you must at least dress it up with these slippers." She rose to her feet and planted her fists upon her hips. "Go on, skip around the room," she encouraged with a few waves of her hands.

Cailin sighed and grabbed handfuls of her skirts, obeying her handmaid. To her surprise, the slippers did not fall off. "Oh, very well."

Guiding Cailin to the tapestry-covered stool, Maggie encouraged Cailin to sit before the looking glass. She proceeded to comb through Cailin's auburn tresses that hung down her back. Margeret had just finished working out the tangles and split the hair into sections for braiding when a knock vibrated the chamber door. "I shall tend to that," her handmaid announced and padded to greet the visitor. Cailin yanked her chemise back down to expose her bust. To her reflection, she nodded *her* final position on the matter.

"Is my lady dressed?" James's deep voice swept through the room like a warm breeze. Cailin's heart staccatoed in her breast.

"Aye, you may see her if you wish." Margeret stepped aside, allowing James to enter the room.

Cailin stood and had to stop herself from gawking. Dark-brown hose hugged his muscular thighs above knee-high black boots formed over his calves, making her mouth water. Midnight-blue sleeves, bloused and laced at his shoulders, protruded from the matching brown brocade vest. Save for the cod piece at his groin—which Cailin found herself staring at a bit too long—and the billowing sleeves, his outfit left little to the imagination of his excellent and wondrously fit form. His baldric was slung over his right shoulder and hung diagonally across his chest, the sword her father presented him nestled at his trim hip. He looked magnificent. Her eyes finally met his. The roguish grin on his face told her he enjoyed her open admiration of his outfit.

Cailin cleared her throat. "Give us a moment, would you, Maggie?"

"My pleasure," she said, and sat herself upon the settee at the foot of Cailin's bed.

She tore her eyes away from James and glared at her handmaid. "We are hardly going to consummate our marriage in the few moments I am requesting. Please step out of the room."

"I most certainly will not!"

Cailin marched over to Margeret and shooed her out of the chamber all the while saying, "James and

I are to be wed in a just a few months. Even if he did toss my skirts, we are to be wed anyway! What difference does—"

"A pox on that mouth of yours, child!" She stood in the hallway, pointing that scolding finger. "We taught you better than—" Cailin closed and latched the door.

James dashed to Cailin and snatched her up, his hands on her bottom and wrapping her legs around his waist as he carried her giggling to the bed. She screeched when she lost her shoe.

"I can guarantee," his deep, husky voice promised as he nuzzled her neck, "that I can most certainly toss your skirts and consummate our marriage in just moments!"

Playfully beating his shoulder, she spoke through her laughter. "Behave, you rogue! She is going to break that door down if you do not cease your wonderful ravishing of my person."

He pulled back and his eyes raked over her face and rested upon her neckline. Her belly fluttered wildly. "You look sweet enough to eat," he growled and nibbled hot kisses over her swelling bosom.

An aching surged between her thighs and she made every effort to stifle her groans. His lips left a fiery wet trail over her fevered skin as he worked his way back to her neck. When his tongue seared a path over the shell of her ear, she gasped, clutching his shoulders and squeezing her legs around him.

"Cailin," he breathed, sending more waves of heat across her body. "God's blood, I love the way you respond to me!" His mouth sought hers, capturing her in a kiss that stole her breath. Grinding his erection against her mound, his groans mingled with her panting.

With every sweep of his tongue, every piece of her flesh he devoured with his mouth and hands, Cailin slipped deeper into passion…and deeper into despair. This was what she wanted—these breathtaking moments of amorous attention. This was what she craved and needed for her soul.

But…Angus Campbell.

Hovering in the blackness at the edge of their lives, her father's enemy would haunt them, terrorize their happiness and shatter their dreams of having a family. She did not want their children living in the shadow of fear that had darkened her childhood. Cailin savored the taste of James's sweet mouth. Burned the memory of his arms around her into her soul. If she died in the efforts to free their lives of Campbell's menace, she would at least take these treasures with her to the grave.

As much as she did not want him to stop, she pushed at his shoulders. "James," she protested between his kisses. "My darling, please."

His lust-clouded eyes gazed at her, hooded and so very delicious. "I know, Mouse." He kissed her again, leaving her thirsting for more. "I am

134

speaking to your parents…we wed as soon as humanly possible."

He seized her mouth in one more seeking kiss and groaned aloud as he pushed up off her body. Grabbing her hand, he helped her to her feet then bowed before her, the image of a perfect gentleman. The way his mouth made love to her palm, however, was very much the rogue who ravished her just seconds before. Her legs would surely collapse beneath her.

When he straightened from his bow, she stepped closer. "James, I…" She had asked for this time to communicate her heart to him, and yet the words would not come forth. How could she possibly express, in such a short span, the respect and love she held toward him? Since they met when she was but a child, that connection had deepened and, through the years, she cherished his opinion and their friendship. Now, standing before her, the man he had become made her grow weak in his arms and turned her into a puddle at his feet with just a kiss. However, if she did not survive this reckless venture, pouring her heart out to James would not be fair to him. She couldn't bare her soul and make promises she may never be able to keep.

His palm cradled her cheek and he pressed his lips to her brow. "What is it, Mouse?"

"I…am…wondering if our wedding night will be as lovely as this." Though a true statement, guilt plagued her for not speaking her mind, in spite of her convictions to save him pain.

James wrapped her in his arms with a seductive chuckle that made her tremble. "Oh, my little Mouse, this is only but a taste of what is yet to come." He gazed at her with desire storming in his sea-green eyes. "I can promise you that."

He cocked an eyebrow, ever the rogue.

Margeret cast darting glances of disapproval at Cailin as they strolled down the road toward the Gypsy camp. Cailin did her best to ignore them, though her cheeks still burned with embarrassment. She and James had received a royal scolding when they finally opened her bedchamber door.

Maggie had indeed listened in on their encounter. Her handmaid confessed she had been two beats away from fetching Davina. "I care not how soon you are to be wed," she berated them both. "Cailin will reach the marriage bed with her maidenhead intact!"

Cailin had groaned with mortification while James only chuckled at her declarations, enflaming Margeret's anger even more. This had made Cailin's hairstyling session a painful experience. Maggie grumbled the entire episode, yanking and twisting Cailin's cinnamon hair into her coiffure and hairnet.

Now Cailin diverted her eyes to James's profile as a distraction from her handmaid's venomous glares.

Servants bustled up and down the path, nodding and smiling. "Mistress Davina," James asked, humor lighting his voice. "Did you lend your entire household to the Gypsies?"

Davina chuckled. "Nigh on that! They insisted on hosting these festivities with or without my assistance, and I could not, in good conscience, put the entire chore upon their shoulders."

Davina's handmaid, Elizabyth, chuckled and whispered in Davina's ear.

Cailin's mother nodded. Looking around as if to see if any but their group was listening, she leaned in conspiratorially. "Truth be told, I did not trust the Gypsy cuisine to be grand enough for such a celebration for my sweet Cailin and dashing James." James chortled and Cailin blushed with protests, but Davina waved her off. "Though baked hedgehog is a tasty venture for the tongue—"

Most present expressed groans of disapproval.

"You see! I urge you to try it! It's really very tasty." More groans and Davina rolled her eyes heavenward. "In any manner, as you all have proved, I didn't think everyone would be so inclined to such an adventure for the palate. And in all honesty, the Gypsies were more centered on the events and decorations. They were more than accepting of our hospitality to provide the feast for the occasion." Cailin's mother considered the train of servants and pursed her lips. "Perhaps I did get a bit extreme?"

Trailing behind the small group and chuckling at Davina's assessment of her involvement, Ranald and Will conversed with each other and the three other armed escorts, chatting about the anticipated festivities.

Cailin's rising anticipation, however, traveled more along the vein of fear and uncertainty. Could she go through with her plan? She barely had the chance to strap a silver-plated dagger to her thigh and her small sleeve sheath to her forearm. The blades she usually fastened to her hips were left in her room at Margeret's insistence. Protesting otherwise might have raised some suspicions and Cailin reasoned Jasper and Alistair would most assuredly confiscate them anyway. Armed only with these small weapons, she would indeed be at their mercy and very naked without her usual personal protection. What would she do if they found them? What would she do when she finally faced Angus?

Her desire to see through her original plan and her determination to die than rather continue to live in fear, forced the apprehensions out of her mind. It was now or never, so she might as well enjoy the evening while she had the chance. She fingered the amulet tucked into her bodice for courage.

James wrapped his arm around her shoulder and hugged her close. "What is that furrow upon thy lovely brow?" His hot breath against her ear sent shivers of desire through her body.

She snaked her arm about his waist and held tight. "These shoes are surely to be the death of me," she lied.

He chuckled. "I will always be here to catch you if you fall."

She gazed up into his adoring eyes and swallowed the lump forming in her throat. "I have no doubts, my love."

Rows of trestle tables—with a head table at the forefront of the arrangement—were the focal point of the Gypsy camp. From dove, chicken and duck, to wild boar, veal and lamb, the aroma of meats and mounds of vegetables permeated the air. The Gypsies hadn't eaten this well since Broderick and Davina shared their wedding feast with Rosselyn and Nicabar during their dual wedding…or so were the comments floating around the mixed company. Wine and ale flowed freely, trenchers piled with food filled everyone's bellies, and laughter echoed about the surrounding forest throughout the afternoon.

James stood and raised his goblet above his head, garnering the attention of the gathered guests. When the throng quieted, he nodded his thanks. "A well-deserved cheer and a rousing *huzzah* to Clan MacDougal!" Frivolity ensued, thundering through his chest, and he nodded to his future mother-in-law on the seat to his left. After the crowd indulged a moment longer, he waved for their silence. "Broderick and Davina have given me more than any man deserves, and more than just taking me into their fold. They secured my future with a ship to command, and I look forward to her christening once Broderick has returned. But more importantly…" He gazed down at the woman seated to his right and lost himself for a moment in her cerulean eyes. Grasping Cailin's hand, he encouraged her to stand at his side. "More importantly," he repeated, "the most beautiful woman in all the world to claim as my own." He kissed her knuckles and the cheers and encouragement rose to a deafening level.

James groaned when his cock twitched in response to the taste of her skin. Cailin's brow creased and, what he presumed was worry, glassed her eyes. He caressed her cheek and leaned in to whisper in her ear. "What is it, Mouse?"

She shook her head and touched her lips to his cheek. "All is well," she said, but even through the noise, he thought he heard her voice crack.

The guests pounded in unison on the tabletops, urging the couple to kiss. Laughing at the boisterous crowd, James swept Cailin into his embrace and fused his mouth shamefully to hers in a kiss that made him glad he wore his cod piece. His heart pounded at the warmth of her body pressed against his.

Margeret pounded uselessly on his back. He released his hold on Cailin only when he was good and ready. As far as he was concerned, he'd branded her as his and no one would interfere with his attentions on her.

Though Cailin's skin glowed pink with embarrassment, passion sparkled in her eyes. Aye, the MacDougals may be disappointed with a post celebration of their union. He could not wait much longer for the betrothal ceremony at the end of the month, let alone their wedding in the winter.

Eventually the feast was cleared. Both musicians from the neighboring town of Edinburgh and the Gypsies raised instruments to provide trilling music to accompany the stomping and dancing that ensued. A grand circle formed where James and Cailin were thrown into the center and goaded to dance. James waved his arms at Cailin, getting his hands ready to perform a little routine they used to do in their youth.

Cailin gasped and put her hands over her mouth, shaking her head vigorously.

"Aye!" he yelled and laughed above the cacophony of notes and cheers. "Come, Mouse! Do it for me!"

She pursed her lips, repressing a grin, but heaved a dramatic sigh and relented. She stepped forward with obvious reluctance, shaking her head and rolling her eyes.

James chuckled and positioned his hands again. Cailin mirrored his stance, placing her palms against his. Stomping his foot to start their timing, he counted to three and they began. Laughter poured out of Cailin's mouth as they ran through a series of claps and elbow jabs, knee slapping and turns, performing the silly dance from their childhood.

Davina covered her face, guffawing, thoroughly amused with their antics. The Gypsies roared their approval, getting louder as the couple repeated the cycle of rehearsed movements. The musicians increased the tempo of the music, daring James and Cailin to keep up with the timing, faster and faster until one of her shoes slipped off and she tumbled into James's arms. The crowd erupted into applause, swarming around the panting pair, and lifted them onto their shoulders.

A scream pierced the festivities and the noise level dropped to near silence while the betrothed pair was placed on their feet once again. Cailin donned her shoe and her heart lurched in her chest. *The diversion.*

"Fire!" someone hollered from east side of the encampment. A clamor rose as people scattered and shouted orders, organizing efforts to put out the flames reaching for the darkening sky. Black smoke billowed as a tent became engulfed. Men stepped forward with blankets, beating back the inferno in an attempt to get the blaze under control. Women carried more blankets to aid the battle.

Cailin whirled as James ran to help, grabbing a blanket from the arms of her mother. Training her eyes around the crowd, Cailin searched for her captors.

"Over here!" someone screamed from the west side of the camp. "Another fire!"

Small buckets were dunked into rain barrels, gathering water to throw onto both fires. People ran in various directions, doing what they could to save the encampment from being reduced to black cinders.

And at the edge of the panic and chaos, Jasper leered.

Heart thundering in her chest, Cailin twirled and ran into a tent to grab some blankets. She emerged and handed them to the nearest person running by. She ducked back into the tent and pulled out another blanket, handing it over. This time when she disappeared into the tent, she crawled under the back flap, popping up between the tent and a caravan and out of the general flow of bodies. Panting with anticipation, she closed her eyes and tried to steady herself. *I can't do this!* Fear swarmed over her like a dark wave and sucked her under its suffocating influence.

Cailin gasped as a firm hand gripped her arm.

"What are you doing back here?" Margeret screeched.

"I'm looking for more blankets!" Cailin hissed.

"Come with me now, child!" Her handmaid's face contorted with fear. "There's no doubt something's amiss. Let us get you back to the castle."

Before they could take another step, an acrid musty odor assaulted Cailin's nose as a sack went over her head…and all went black.

CHAPTER SIX

At least two hours after the chaos began, James grabbed the bucket handed to him and threw the water on the last struggling bit of flames. They hissed and died. *Thank God it rained again last night.* "Is everyone well?" he asked, twirling around and scanning the crowd. "Did anyone get hurt?"

Many heads shook, indicating the guests were all right as they looked around to assess the aftermath.

"Cailin!" James maneuvered through the crowd of guests and Gypsies, not finding her among them. "Cailin!"

Panic-stricken, his future mother-in-law dashed between people. *"Cailin! Cailin!"* Davina's worry-laced calls turned to wails of despair. She fell to her knees in the mud, sobbing, repeatedly cursing Campbell.

Rosselyn rushed to her sister's side and enveloped her in her arms. "Margeret is nowhere about either. Perhaps she took Cailin back to the castle."

"Search the area!" James ordered. "Look for tracks! Spread out in all directions!"

Many did as he instructed, fanning out and searching the grounds.

"I need a horse! I'll check the castle." He pointed at Nicabar, who waved for him to follow. Grabbing the reins of a mount tied to a caravan, Nicabar threw the leather straps at James. He hoisted himself onto the back of the protesting animal and charged out of the camp and up the road to the castle.

"Open the gate!" The large oaken doors swung inward and he navigated to the stables. "Fife! Get my horse ready. Now!"

The old stable master nodded as James leapt from the Gypsy mount and dashed in through the kitchen entrance. Kitchen maids screeched and he held his palms out. "Cailin! Is she here?"

Wide-eyed, they shook their heads and he cursed. Taking the stairs three at a time, he bolted to his bedchamber and grabbed his saddlebags, stuffing anything inside he thought would be useful to help recover Cailin—a blanket, some drying cloths and salve for wounds which he kept in his satchel.

Hastening to her chamber, still hoping to see her safe with Margeret, his heart dropped when he entered the empty room. He searched her wardrobe for some practical shoes, grabbed a chemise and working gown before heading back downstairs.

Surely Fife would have his horse readied by now. James skidded to a stop in the kitchen, wrapped a few dried meats, pieces of fruit and a loaf of bread into a cloth and shoved the bundle into his bags. He snatched a bladder of water on the way out the door.

"Fife!" He sprinted across the courtyard.

"Aye, lad!" Fife handed James the reins once he secured the saddlebags.

"Give me those two bottles of lamp oil there!"

Fife tossed the glass bottles to James, who wedged them into the side of his saddlebags. Mounting his gelding, he kicked its side and galloped through the front gate.

James yanked on the reins when he bounded into the camp. Nicabar approached, clutching a scrap of parchment in his hands. "This had a dagger stuck through it on a caravan." He handed it to James as Davina ran forward.

"Still no sign of Margeret, James." Tears stained her pleading face. "They may have snatched her thinking she was me."

James had also mistaken Maggie for Davina at a glance. He read the note aloud. "Glen Morin."

"'Tis nothing else?" Davina grabbed the note. "Glen Morin?"

"Does it mean anything to you?"

She shook her head, her brow furrowing even more and tears welling anew in her eyes. "Oh, saints help us, this message is for Broderick alone. Somehow they knew he was gone."

Guilt crept into James's soul. He had told his father as much before he knew Alistair was bent on revenge. He was somehow behind this. James clenched his jaw so hard it ached.

"James!" Rosselyn waved frantically from down the road to the north. "Here!"

With a quick kick to his mount, he approached Davina's sister, a crowd of people drawing up behind him.

"Look! This must be Cailin's!" She ran forward and handed him a green, glass-beaded slipper.

"Aye, 'tis hers! Where did you get it?"

Grabbing her skirts, she ran forward. "Here," she panted, pointing to the ground. "I found it here."

James eyed the muddy road and trotted along, studying the various tracks. With the multitude of marks from foot and hoof, it was difficult to discern which—if any—belonged to Cailin's captors. He increased his gait and continued several yards until the tracks thinned down to what appeared to be four sets of hooves. These went for a long stretch, cup-like tracks imprinted into the mud, and he darted his eyes from the hoof prints to the road ahead and his heart lurched.

"*Hah!*" he barked to his gelding and kicked his horse forward. Pulling up short, he jumped from the saddle and picked the soiled green shoe from a peak of mud. He mounted, galloped back to the pursuing crowd and tossed the shoes to Nicabar.

"This is the path they took!" He turned his gaze to the sobbing but hopeful face of Davina. "I shall get her back, my lady."

"Be watchful, James!" she warned. "He is obviously not working alone and may have other surprises along the way."

He nodded and wheeled his mount around, hastening down the path after his betrothed.

Cailin's head pounded. Her body bopped up and down in an uncomfortable rhythm and something pushed against her midsection in the same aggravating tempo. Nausea roiled in her stomach and she ached. Blinking her eyes didn't help. She was still surrounded by darkness. An acrid, musty odor accompanied the gritty dust in her mouth. The thumpity-thump of horse hooves seemed somewhat in synch with her bobbing and her memory rushed to the forefront of her mind.

The shouts. Maggie trying to get her to safety. The thwack against her skull.

Based on her position, she was slung over the back of a horse and her hands were bound in front of her and tucked under her stomach.

"Should we not pick up the pace?" Cailin recognized Alistair's voice and remained still, as uncomfortable as this was.

"They won't know where we be takin' them." That was definitely Jasper. "That note only had a name and I'm guessin' Davina and Cailin are the only ones who know about Angus's childhood home. Since they be with us, no one should be following."

Dread gripped Cailin's heart. *Nay, they could not have taken M'ma! Only me! It was only supposed to be me!*

A moan sounded and Cailin guessed that to be her mother.

"Hold up," Jasper said and the horses slowed to a stop.

Some rustling, some footsteps, and a pair of rough hands gripped her calves, yanking her from the saddle. Thankfully, she fell into a pair of arms and the sack was jerked from her head.

She inhaled cool, clean breaths of fresh air…at least until Jasper's yellow-stained grin and sour breath assaulted her. "Ay there, ducks!"

She coughed and turned her head to recover from the stench. "M'ma?" Cailin turned in Jasper's arms only to be dragged to the side of the road and thrown to the muddy ground. Lying on her arms while on the back of the horse had rendered them useless, for now they ached and refused to respond to her wishes. Margeret was also pushed to the ground at Cailin's side.

"'Tis not Davina!" Alistair shouted, pointing a finger at her companion. "'Tis Cailin's handmaid, Margeret!"

"I thought ye said that was Davina!" Jasper accused.

Alistair paled and shook his head. "It looked like her. I swear, I thought it was her."

Yanking a dagger from his belt, Jasper stepped forward and grabbed Margeret's hair.

"Nay!" Cailin scrambled on her bound hands and knees to reach Jasper, but Alistair beat her to him.

"What are you doing?" James's father grabbed Jasper's wrist, staying the dagger.

"'Tis a dead weight she is." Jasper's eyebrows scrunched in disbelief. "Angus willna let her live and she'll only slow us down."

"What do you mean Angus won't let her live?" Alistair retained Jasper's wrist in his grip, Jasper's other fist still in Margeret's hair as she whimpered.

"Slitting her throat will be an act of mercy, my friend. Angus will torture her just for amusement."

Alistair's mouth twisted with rage. "You never told me any of this! What kind of man is Angus that he would do this?"

Cailin groaned inwardly. Alistair obviously didn't know what he was getting into, joining the likes of Angus and his henchmen. What lies had Jasper told Alistair?

Jasper released Margeret and lowered his knife to his side. "What did ye think this venture would be about, lad?" A cold smile crept over his mouth. "Ye didna think this through? Ye must have known people were going to die." He placed a comforting hand upon a bewildered Alistair's shoulder. "Come now, Alistair. Remember why yer doin' this. Think of poor Fiona's throat slashed open. This is what ye wanted and it may be difficult, but ye have to see this through. Revenge is a nasty business."

Alistair stared at the ground. But when Jasper stepped to grab Margeret's hair again, Alistair grabbed his shirt. "Wait! Why do we have to kill her? Let her go. Let her fend for herself out here."

Cailin scanned the horizon, illuminated by the setting sun, and a chill skittered through her body. They were indeed in the middle of the wilds with no civilization for miles.

"The night is coming and she'll be alone." Alistair glared at Margeret. "She'll not survive, but I'll not have her blood on our hands."

Jasper shook his head, assessed the whimpering Margeret, and then nodded. "Very well, Alistair." With the hilt of the dagger in his fist, he clobbered Maggie on her head and she slumped into Cailin's lap. Blood oozed down her temple, staining her cheek.

"Maggie!" Cailin struggled to hold onto her handmaid as Jasper yanked Cailin to her feet, her bare toes dragging through the mud.

"Now get yer sweet little arse up in that saddle." He grabbed Cailin's shoulders, forcing her to face him. "An' if ye dinna listen to what ol' Jasper tells ye to do." He grabbed a handful of her breast and she struggled to free herself from his hold. "Then ol' Jasper is finally gonna have his way wit' ye." Laughing, he whirled her around and urged her to mount the horse. "Up wit' ye now or I toss yer skirts where we stand!"

Repulsion catapulted Cailin into the saddle and she kicked her leg when Jasper's rough hand smoothed over her calf. He chuckled and handed the reins of Margeret's horse to Alistair.

Taking Cailin's reins, he snickered then tied her horse to his saddle and mounted. "Come, lad. We need to keep movin'. I dinna wanna take any chances someone may still be on our trail."

Hands still bound before her, Cailin squeezed her knees to stay firmly astride and looked over her shoulder at Margeret's body retreating in the distance. Tears slipped down her cheeks and she choked back her sobs. *Please, Lord. Watch over her. Give her enough daylight to find a safe haven.*

The wind whipping past his cheeks and tugging at his hair, Broderick continued on his trek through the English countryside toward the destination of *Stanenges.*

"You are sure to see it on the horizon," the English farmer had told him, pointing down the road. "Though they are not much to look at—just large stone pillars in the middle of a field—they are a curious site. Must have taken a hundred men to move just one stone."

Now, two hours after sunset, the said stones loomed ahead, tall silhouettes on the horizon. Slowing to a cautious stroll several yards from the site, he studied the area. No sign of anyone. Stepping into the circle of monoliths, he rotated, gazing at each towering figure. "Curious to be sure," he mumbled.

"Well met, Vamsyrian."

He spun to face a robed figure holding a lantern. *Where did she come from?* He nodded and eyed her suspiciously.

"I am Malloren Rune," she said with a husky British accent. She pushed her hood back to reveal a head of long, coal-black hair with silver streaks at the temples. Judging by the slight creasing at the corners of her eyes, the subtle lines in her forehead, this handsome woman had to be in her late forties. "I am whom you seek."

Cocking an eyebrow, he stepped forward, his eyes darting around as he approached. "Greetings, Mistress Rune."

"Please, Malloren will do." Her dark-brown gaze assessed the stone giants. "This place will one day be known as Stonehenge." Locking her eyes with his, she stepped forward and a small grin crooked the corner of her pouting lips—pouting lips that held a trace of familiarity. "But that is another time. Come with me, Broderick."

After pivoting on her heels, she marched out of the stone circle, not looking back. Obviously, she expected him to follow without question. Taking another glance around the area for signs of anyone else, he pursued her across the field for a goodly distance. She knelt down, pulled a large iron ring and opened a grass-covered door. The hatch was suspended by two chains attached to the edges of the door, the other ends spiked into the ground. Still not acknowledging Broderick's approaching, she descended into the earth on an iron ladder. The light of her lantern retreated into the hole.

Broderick harrumphed. "Even more curious." With a sigh of resignation, he followed the mysterious woman into the darkness and closed the hatch behind him.

"Please latch the door." Her voice echoed up to him as he perched on the ladder.

Though dark, through his immortal eyesight, the latch she spoke of remained visible and he slid the well-oiled mechanism into place. Rung by rung, Broderick descended into the earth a near fifty feet before he reached the bottom. He stood at the end of a stone corridor lit by wall-mounted oil lamps, the orange glow guiding his way as he proceeded with cautious steps. He reached out with his immortal senses, not detecting any other Vamsyrian presence. The corridor curved and opened to a high-ceilinged chamber.

Row upon row of bookcases held an endless array of scrolls and leather-bound tomes. The unmistakable aroma of parchment, leather and age wafted through the chilled air. The library rose three levels, various finely finished ladders scattered about the platforms, giving the keeper of this collection access to a wealth of information. More oil lamps—multitudes of them mounted between each bookcase—lit the massive room enough to satisfy any need for study no matter where one stood. Small tables sat against iron railings on each platform and were arranged evenly about each level to provide plenty of opportunities for perusal of the written materials. In the center of the massive room, and a level lower than where Broderick stood, were larger tables piled with more volumes and scrolls in what appeared to be active stages of research and reading. Malloren Rune stood behind one of the tables, the lantern sitting on the corner, serenely waiting with her hands clasped before her.

"Impressive," Broderick said, his deep voice echoing in the vast space.

She dipped her head in acknowledgment. "I am a Keeper of Secrets." She spread her arms wide, presenting her collection. "A prophetess who sees visions and records various bits of knowledge about supernatural and magical beings through the ages." She strolled around the bottom level, touching books as she passed. "This underground chamber dug from the earth, and these rooms lined with stone, were crafted over a one-hundred year period. I am the twelfth generation of prophets, my mother before me, her mother and so forth."

By taking the stairs down to the lower level, he met her beside the table and performed a quick calculation of years gone by. "So you are a tradition stretching back approximately two-hundred and fifty years?"

A knowing grin spread across her lips, and again there was something familiar about her pouty smile. "No, Broderick MacDougal. The first prophetess was born over one-thousand years ago."

"One-thou—" He redid the math, originally estimating a generation to be rounded to near twenty years. Twelve twenty-year generations would be two-hundred forty years, so he had been generous on the estimation. Confusion mixed with wonderment. Malloren Rune may not be as young as he supposed.

"I am one-hundred, two-and-sixty years, Broderick," she replied to his unanswered question.

"But you are mortal," he protested.

Malloren removed her cloak, pulled down the neckline of her robes and bared her right shoulder. Markings, in what appeared to be made from black ink, branded her skin with the same design on the amulet he'd left with Cailin. "I am a member of the *Tzava Ha'or*, and as a prophetess of the Army of Light, I have a longer life span than most mortals."

"*Most* mortals?" Broderick was astonished at this world opening before him. "What other mortals have such long lives?"

Her soft chuckle swarmed around the illimitable chamber as she righted her gown. "Your kind is not the only miraculous species on this planet. There is much to know about this strange world in which we live, Vamsyrian."

Species. He had never heard the term, but in context of her phrasing, perhaps the general meaning of the word implied a race of peoples. "So, with these visions and vast knowledge you have, this explains why you know how the amulet Amice gave me was created."

"That is correct. But I have brought you here for more than just magical charms of protection, Broderick MacDougal. You are a piece of a grand puzzle I can help you assemble."

Broderick narrowed his eyes as he considered her words. "And what puzzle is this you speak of?"

"A prophecy." Malloren twirled and snatched her lantern and cloak from the table. "Come, Vamsyrian." Grabbing a handful of her skirts, she ascended the stone staircase on the opposite side of the room and faced him when she stood behind the iron railing on second level. "Let us retire to a more comfortable atmosphere. We have hours of information ahead of us to review."

Turning her back to him, she disappeared through a door between the bookcases and he quickened his pace to catch up with the prophetess. She led him down another long corridor glowing with oil lamps. The path turned and twisted, many doors dotting the walls along the way, stimulating images of more corridors and rooms filled with tomes. Walking behind Malloren afforded him a study of her figure. She wore simple tan robes beneath a long, dark-brown apron tunic, but even this non-descript garment couldn't hide her voluptuous figure. Her hips flared generously, and as she turned the corners through the halls, her narrow waist and heavy bust peeked through. Broderick frowned. Even her figure seemed familiar. Yet he had never seen nor even heard of Malloren Rune before, so he shook off the nagging notion.

The corridor finally ended at a wide set of oaken double-doors. With a flip of the latch, Malloren pushed the doors open and they stepped into a warm, lived-in chamber. A fire burned in the hearth where a cast-iron bean pot hung from a hook fastened to the stone by a hinge. He imagined Malloren sitting in the cushioned chair by the fire, swinging a meal over the flames to simmer in the pot.

She bustled about the chamber, hung her cloak on a hook in the wood-paneled wall by the door and placed the lantern on the mantel. "Please make yourself comfortable."

"How did you know I would—"

"Leave your family on such an unknown quest?" She poured a beverage in the small kitchen area occupying the far-side of the chamber next to the hearth. Holding up the mug, she said, "Mead?"

Broderick shook his head.

"I thought not, but it would be impolite not to offer." A gentle grin played upon her lips and she sat on the cushioned chair by the hearth. Broderick sat on a tapestry couch across the space from her. Malloren set her mug upon the simple, crafted table that stood between them. "I knew you would be here because I saw you in my visions. I knew exactly when to expect your arrival. I saw Amice, the Gypsies traveling with her in their caravans. I knew Amice would die before she delivered the amulet, and I knew Rosselyn would complete the journey for her."

"I left the amulet with my family." He settled back into the couch and crossed his ankle over his knee. "Did you see that in your visions as well?"

She nodded. "It was a wise decision to give the amulet to Cailin."

An uneasiness settled over Broderick at all the information she had about him—his name, how the amulet came into his possession, what he did with it and when he would arrive—in comparison to how little he knew of her.

"The power of the amulet does not lie within the piece itself," she continued, "but rather the incantation attached to the medallion. This is what I will teach to you and what you truly seek to protect those you love."

"Why are you, a member of the *Tzava Ha'or*, teaching me a method that will protect my family? Why would you help one of my kind? Are we not enemies?"

"The *Tzava Ha'or* is not at war with the Vamsyrians. We were put in place by Jehovah to be the balancing force of their creation. But we will delve into the origin and history of the Vamsyrians while you are here. For now, let us stay on the subject of the incantation." She sat at the edge of her seat, sipped from her mug and replaced it on the table. "There are three parts to the incantation which invokes the power of the Christian God, Jehovah. The first erects the protection, the next is the request for the protection to be removed, and the final is the response to the request, which removes the protection."

Broderick nodded and waited for her to proceed.

She held up her palms toward him. "*Veh atah adonai mahgen bah-adee, k'vodee u-merim roshee.*" She recited the words with ease and they tickled his memory. The oppressive weight that fluttered across the space, however, brought back his full recollection.

"Evangeline," he whispered. "That was what Evangeline chanted when I tried to attack her the night I—"

"Yes. The night you became a Vamsyrian. It is a Hebrew chant, and what a person envisions when they say the chant will determine its use and boundaries. When I recited the incantation, I envisioned a barrier around my person with a radius that reached only to where my palms were placed. Try to take my hand." Malloren laid her hand open, palm up.

Broderick stretched his hand toward her and his fingers slammed into a wall…only there was no wall to see. A small wave of exhaustion rippled from his fingertips through his body as well.

"*Pitkhu li sha-ahray tsedek, avoh bahm ve odeh yah.* That is the request to remove the protection. *Zeh ha-sha-ar adonai. Tsadikim yavou bo.*" The oppressive atmosphere disappeared. "That is the response to remove the protection."

"Why the three parts?" Broderick sat back, relieved the protection—and the discomfort it caused—was removed. "Why not just the placement and removal?"

Malloren also settled back into her chair, mug in hand. Shaking her head, she said, "I do not know. As Jehovah has proved over and over again, nothing is without purpose. The truth of that has yet to be revealed to *me*, at least."

"So you are not all knowing?"

She chortled. "Far from it." After downing the last of her drink, she rose then placed the mug upon a table in her kitchen. "Come with me." She strolled to the double-doors, where they had originally entered. "We'll move to a more spacious chamber where we'll have more working room for you to learn the incantation."

He rose to follow her. "Working room? How much space do we need to recite words?"

That knowing smiled crossed her pouty lips. "Be prepared to be shown the force of Jehovah, Vamsyrian." She pivoted on her heels and glided down the corridor.

Broderick groaned. *I have a distinct feeling I am not going to enjoy this.*

James cursed at his lack of progress. During the summer weeks the sun did set well into the evening hours, giving him much-needed daylight, but following tracks in the mud demanded a slower pace. Thankfully, Cailin's captors were among the first to travel after the rains, leaving only one set of tracks to follow versus trying to discern their hoof prints among many others on the road. However, though the moonlight was enough to guide him, it did not lend the illumination needed. With the lamp oil Fife gave him, a narrow branch and one of the drying cloths, James fashioned a torch to light the way. Darkness now blanketed the terrain and his arm ached from holding the torch aloft. A scream startled both him and his gelding, causing James to drop his torch and gain control of his rearing mount. Reining in the animal, he searched the ground to find a figure cowering in the amber glow of the still-burning torch.

"Have mercy!" she pleaded.

"Margeret?" James jumped from the saddle and grabbed the torch before crouching beside her.

"Master James?" She turned her face toward him and he winced at the dried blood crusted on her cheek and matting her hair in a dark, tangled mess.

"Sweet Lord, what have they done to you?" He comforted the sobbing woman clinging to his vest. Stabbing the end of the torch into the mud to keep it upright, he left her side for a moment to grab the salve, the water bladder and a drying cloth from his saddlebags.

"Oh, Master James," she whimpered as he cleaned the blood from her face and what he could from her hair. "The saints be praised you found me. I knew you and Davina would not give up so easily as to wait for Lord Broderick's return."

"Who grabbed you and Cailin, Maggie? Do you know where they're taking her?"

"I heard them say something about Angus's childhood home being scrawled on a note they left behind."

"Glen Morin."

"I've never heard of Glen Morin. All I know is they may be taking her toward the Highlands, Master James. 'Tis an awfully large target to search, though."

"Why do you think the Highlands?"

"When Broderick learned my husband was from the Highlands, he told me his childhood home was just off the shores of Loch Etive. In other conversations, he mentioned Angus's home lay somewhere between Loch Etive and Loch Awe." She frowned as he continued tending to her head wound. "'Tis sorry I am I don't know the exact location, but surely 'tis better than having no direction at all."

"Right you are, Maggie." He struggled to keep despair from his voice. As he heard it, those two lochs stretched for miles with just as much land spanning between them. He applied some salve to the gash in her scalp. "'Tis a nasty knot you have there. Can you stand?"

She nodded and rose on unsteady legs.

He couldn't leave Margeret here. Nor could he take her back to Edinburgh, having ridden several hours already. Certainly, he was lagging behind Cailin by at least two or three hours as it was. He couldn't afford any more lost time. "Come, Maggie. Climb into the saddle and we shall see what we can do about getting some help."

Once Margeret was mounted, he grabbed the torch and sat astride behind her. He kicked his heels and they started down the road again after his betrothed.

"I noticed they're sticking to the roads," James commented.

"Aye, the saints be praised. 'Tis grateful I am of their overconfidence."

"Meaning?"

"They're cocksure no one knows where they be headed and only Broderick will be the one to pursue them."

"Well, that certainly works in our favor. I may not be behind them as far as I thought." He could tell Margeret did what she could to keep a distance between their bodies, but she surely needed to rest. "You may lean against me, Maggie. I promise to keep my hands to myself."

She chuckled and leaned back. "'Tis old enough to be yer mother, I am." She continued laughing and smacked his knee before she relaxed. His soft chortles joined hers.

They were silent for a few paces while he eyed the tracks they followed in the mud. "Master James…"

"Aye, Maggie?"

"'Tis something of import I need to tell you." She paused so long, he almost said something to coax her to finish. "Your father…"

James tightened his grip on the torch. "He was one of the captors, wasn't he?"

"Aye." Her voice a whisper.

Tears threatened to come forth and he fought against them. Though he had his suspicions, he hadn't really believed his father would go as far as to put others in danger. He sought revenge against Broderick, not his family. And yet his father took the cowardly path as Campbell did. *Why should I be surprised? My father has always been a coward.*

"Are ye well, lad?"

He appreciated her motherly tone. "Aye, Maggie.

As they topped a rise in the road, the glow of a fire peeked between shuttered windows.

"'Tis a cottage ahead," Margeret exclaimed.

"Aye, I see it." He urged his gelding forward at a trot and Margeret put her hand to her wound, groaning. He slowed their pace again, praying the residents would be able to give Maggie refuge while he went after Cailin.

Pulling on the reins, he stopped the horse and reconsidered his approach.

"If we're lucky," he whispered and dismounted, snuffing out the torch in the dirt, "this might be them. Stay here." Handing her the reins and the smoking stick, he encouraged her to go into the trees and wait for him. Once she was tucked away, he crouched and padded across the field. He dodged a plow stuck in soft soil, his boots sucking through the mud as he continued to advance. The baying of distant sheep echoed across the farm. The small, thatched building loomed before him and he crouched below a nearby window, noises and conversation coming from within.

"Mum, what a lovely jumper you be knittin' there!" a woman's voice exclaimed.

"I had to mend Richard's today for the last time," an older woman answered. "Yer husband certainly keeps me busy mendin', he does."

Male laughter was the response. "Mary, I'm forever beholdin' to yer skillful hands."

Only three people in the small cottage appeared through the shutter gaps. A fire burned brightly in the hearth and the aroma of some kind of mutton dish greeted his nose. Seemed safe enough to approach.

He ran back to Margeret, taking the more direct route of the well-worn path from the road to the cottage, and led the horse back along that same pathway. After helping her down from the horse, he assisted her to the door and rapped on the worn wood.

The casual conversation reduced to whispers before the door swung open and the man named Richard stood with an axe in his hand. "State yer business."

"Well met, fine folks," James greeted. "'Tis sorry I am to bother you, but we're in need of assistance."

The silhouette of the younger woman peeked around his shoulder. He pushed her back, not taking his eyes off the strange visitors. "What kind of assistance?"

Would they help if they determined how much trouble just arrived on their doorstep? *Sometimes it pays to be honest.* "My betrothed has been taken hostage by a clan enemy. This is her handmaid, who has only just escaped with her life." He encouraged Margeret into the light to show the gash on her head and Richard's wife gasped. "She needs shelter while I pursue the men who took my promised bride." James waited with hope. Some people would shut the door on trouble like this because they didn't want to put themselves in danger, and he could hardly blame them if these folks made that choice.

Richard's wife tugged at his arm. He glanced over his shoulder and nodded. "Aye, bring her in." Though his reply was gruff and guarded, a touch of compassion softened the man's eyes as James and Maggie stepped through the door and into the light. The couple appeared to be in their fifties, worn by hard labor and years.

"Thank you." James helped Margeret to a chair at the table. He offered his hand in greeting to Richard. "James Knightly. This here is Margeret."

"Richard Drummond. My wife Bess and my mother-in-law, Mary."

Everyone nodded their salutations.

"Mum," the woman said with a beckoning hand. "Bring the kettle."

"Aye, Bess." Mary hunched to the fire and did as her daughter asked before she joined Maggie at the table. Patting Maggie's hand, she said, "Are ye hungry, child? We have some hot mutton stew in the pot."

Margeret smiled and raised the old woman's hand to her lips for a grateful kiss on her wrinkled knuckles. Mary cackled softly and patted Maggie's hand again.

Bess doused a folded cloth with hot water and pressed it to Maggie's head then grabbed a bowl and headed toward the hearth. Richard stood in the corner, axe still in hand, his eyes following every nuance. Again, James could hardly blame him.

Stepping outside, James trotted to the horse and dug in his saddlebags for some coin. When he returned, he placed a small pile of the currency on the table. "For your troubles. I hope it will cover your needs."

Richard's jaw dropped and he gawked at James in disbelief. "That be a lot o' coin, lad."

"We're greatly imposing on you and your family. Are you heading into Edinburgh anytime soon?"

"With that much money, I can certainly make a trip for ye."

James sagged with relief. "Maggie here needs to get back there to let my bride's family know what's happened. Can you leave on the morrow?"

Richard nodded.

"I can guarantee the MacDougal's will be generous with more coin once you see me safely home," Margeret interjected.

"MacDougal?" Richard's gaze darted back to James. "Knightly. Is that the same MacDougal & Knightly Shipping Company?"

"Aye, sir, that it is." James allowed a smile.

"Ye help me keep food on the table, James. I take my wool to MacDougal & Knightly for export." Richard put the axe down and leaned it against the wall next to him. He slapped James on the back. "It would be my honor to take Maggie home."

"Saints be praised!" Margeret exclaimed and the room filled with laughter and voices.

"I cannot thank you enough for helping us," James said. "Maggie, I have to make haste."

"Aye lad." She grabbed his hand before he stepped away. "Be careful, laddie."

"Where are ye headed?" Richard asked.

"Maggie tells me they took Cailin toward Lochs Etive and Awe. I look for a place called Glen Morin."

The room fell silent and Richard's family all exchanged horrified glances. "Glen Morin?" Bess gasped.

James shivered and fear crept into his gut. "What—"

"Hush now, Bess." Richard rubbed his wife's back. Diverting his attention back to James, he said, "Glen Morin is a castle owned by Clan Campbell for generations. Though far from here—

ye have a trek ahead of ye, lad—the tales of the place are far reaching."

"Why?"

"It be haunted," Mary said.

"About fifty years ago, the elder son of Fraser Campbell went mad," Richard explained. "Killed his father, his younger brother and the entire household."

"I lived in the Highlands as of ten years ago," Margeret said. "I never once heard about no tales of a haunted castle called Glen Morin. How is it you know about it this far east?"

"Near around five years ago," Richard answered, "stories drifted through the merchant routes about torches lighting the old ruins."

"Some people says they seen someone walking on the grounds," Bess whispered.

"On the merchant routes?" James turned the Margeret. "Have you heard the MacDougals speak of such stories?"

She shrugged.

"Sounds like the place has been taken up again," James offered.

Richard shook his head. "They said it be Angus Campbell wandering the grounds. The son of Fraser Campbell. Being the murders happened over fifty years ago and the place abandoned...well, it either be Angus's ghost or a mad man."

James and Margeret exchanged glances and the warning in her eyes reflected what he wanted to voice: *Say nothing!* These folks might kick them both out on their arses if they knew who had a hand in capturing Cailin.

"I dinna understand why they would take yer Cailin to Glen Morin," Richard said. "But you may be in for more than a few surprises."

"That may be," James stated firmly, "but I need to get on that path. Do you know the way?"

"That road there will take ye, lad." Richard advanced to the door, pointed to the road they'd been on and waved north.

James nodded as Richard explained a detailed route that would take him past major milestones and lakes, burning the directions into his memory and repeating the information back to the older man when he was done.

"Just stick to them old roads, lad," Richard encouraged. "Anyone along the merchant route should keep you on the path."

"'Tis all well," Margeret said, waving off Bess' attentions. She shuffled to the door and urged James outside. James expressed his gratitude to the Drummonds and stepped with Maggie to stand beside his gelding. "Doncha be worrying about a thing, Master James. I don't intend on breathing a word about Angus."

"'Tis a wise idea, Maggie."

"What I do not understand is why them that took Cailin do not seem to know—"

"About how well-known their location is?" he finished and nodded. "Perhaps they were counting on it. Maybe they *are* expecting someone other than Broderick to pursue." Urgency was nagging at James's heart. He had to go. "Listen—"

"Get after her, James," Margeret encouraged. "Guessin' the whys will not save her."

"Aye." After planting a kiss on her cheek, he swung into the saddle, nodded to her and waved to the Drummonds before he kicked his mount forward and set on down the road toward Glen Morin and his sweet Mouse.

"Here." Jasper shoved a piece of dried meat at Cailin and she raised her bound hands to accept the food. Not entirely filling, but she took what they offered to keep up her strength. Her bottom was sore from riding and her wrists were tender and chaffed by the rope. She could only hope she'd be able to face Angus when the time came. Shifting her seat on the round stone by the fire, she made a futile attempt to get comfortable then leveled her gaze at her future father-in-law.

Alistair sat brooding on the other side the fire, the yellow glow casting severe shadows on his face and creating harsh angles. Cailin shivered. His hands turned over a small, smooth stick in a repetitive, nervous movement. He glared at her, his frown deepening. "Stop lookin' at me."

She kept her eyes trained on him. "I do not understand your motives, Alistair."

"Shut yer mouth."

"You've joined forces with the man who killed your wife," she persisted.

"Shut. Yer. Mouth." The stick snapped in two.

Jasper rasped a hearty laugh. "Easy now, Alistair." He patted James's father on the back like an old mate. "Yer lettin' her get to ye."

Cailin wasn't certain why, but she wanted to press Alistair more. "Mayhap, I'm hitting too close to the mark." She kept her voice as level as her gaze. "Do you think dear Fiona would approve of you escorting me to my death?"

The harshness of Alistair's eyes softened just enough for Cailin to understand that James's father had indeed not thought his plans through to the end. A certain measure of panic rose in her throat. He was going to get himself killed, and didn't have the slightest idea the position he'd put himself in *or* the monster Angus truly was.

"'Tis enough out of you, ducks." Jasper rose and yanked Cailin to her feet. "Time to give that mouth o' yours something more productive to do." His calloused hands gripping her elbows wrenched a cry from her and she growled, struggling to keep him from dragging her into the woods. Her bare feet slid uselessly through the mud, scraping on rocks and pebbles, adding to her misery.

"Enough!" Alistair grabbed Jasper by the shoulder and spun him around. "This was not in the arrangements!"

"What do ye think Angus is going to do to her when he has her?" Jasper protested, his steel grip still on Cailin's elbow. "No better way to defile a woman and incite the wrath of her father than—"

"Nay!" Alistair pushed Jasper aside and started untying Cailin's bonds. "I cannot go through with this. This was wrong! This was not—"

Warm liquid spurted across Cailin's face. Echoes of the past. She squeezed her eyes shut and pursed her lips closed as the warmth dripped down her cheeks and over her lips. Her breath stayed trapped in her lungs. *I've killed him!* When Alistair yanked on her hands, pulling her to her knees, her eyes popped open. He collapsed to the ground. *But he tore my dress, he'd tried to…* Thick red blood oozed onto the dirt. A strange noise assaulted her ears—a raspy, rapid panting that grew faster. She marveled over the realization that it was *her* breathing. She fell back onto her rump and stared at Jasper, standing over her, shaking his head.

"Damn fool," he growled, pity in his eyes for Alistair. Pity for the man he had just killed as if he had put an animal out of its misery. "Ah, 'tis better to have ended his life now. He surely would have tried to kill me once he discovered I killed his wife." He diverted his gaze to Cailin and his eyes drooped in a failed attempt at compassion. "Aw, now lassie. Doncha be mournin' the life of a man who handed ye over to yer enemy." Seizing her hands, he yanked her to her feet and snaked his arms around her. With a hefty handful of her bottom, he said, "And now ol' Jasper has ye all to himself." He winked and escorted her back to the horses. "Not a very romantic settin', a dead body an' all." Cailin allowed him to hoist her back into the saddle. He patted her thigh. "Aye, yer not quite here, are ye, lassie?" He chuckled.

Cailin stared at Jasper as he dragged Alistair's body into the bordering forest. She heard what he'd said. Yet why did she not respond over learning the truth of Fiona's death and how far back Angus has inserted his henchman? She saw what he did to her future father-in-law. Her heart was numb. She knew she had the chance to run away, on horseback, while he was busy with his task. She just couldn't get her body to respond to her mind. If she could keep this immunity to emotion while she faced Angus, she may be able to accomplish her goal. But the fragility of mortal life loomed before her. Alistair never knew what happened. With a flick of his wrist, Jasper had slit Alistair's throat and his life was over.

Another realization trembled inside her belly. Jasper only threatened to assault her to solicit a response from Alistair. He somehow needed the excuse to kill him. Her life could be over just as easily, especially at the hands of Angus. Jasper was a mortal man who had no regard for life, except mayhap his own. Angus would be worse.

Jasper approached her side and she met his eyes. Handing her a wet kerchief, he cocked his head at an angle and smirked. "Not so tough without yer knives, are ye lassie?"

Her face was a mask of neutrality. Her cheeks, still dripping with Alistair's blood, would not respond though she wanted to grin. "You, Jasper, will be the first life I snuff out like a candle flame." Only then did her face gain mobility and the corner of her mouth turned up.

Jasper's lips parted and he hitched a breath, his eyes growing just a fraction wider. Then he frowned and shuffled away.

Cailin glared at his back as he urged their horses forward, leaving Alistair's body behind. She placed her hands over the silver-plated dagger still strapped to her thigh and imagined the blade sinking into Jasper's back. Hands returned to her lap, she nudged the blade at her forearm. She wiped the blood from her face and tossed the kerchief to the ground. After several yards, the indifference melted from her body. She sobbed.

CHAPTER SEVEN

Thud-thud-thud-thud-thud-thud. The monotony of the horse's hooves hitting the dirt as they trotted along at a steady pace grated at James's patience. He wanted nothing more than to jab his heels into the side of his mount, lean forward in the saddle and ride the horse into exhaustion. However, doing so was a death sentence for Cailin. At a steady trot, a horse could continue for hours. A hard gallop may get him farther in a short period of time, but the resting would be a fatal set-back. The only thing maintaining his sanity was his endless study of tracks in the torchlight. He tossed another prayer of thanks toward the heavens for the rain they'd had and how far-reaching the weather had stretched. The road was still soft and Cailin's journey was imprinted in the mud. He was also grateful his father and whoever he worked with were such fools. They made no attempt at all to cover their tracks, but this also made James wonder if their lack of effort was intentional. It mattered not. He would rather get to Cailin and deal with a fight than lose the trail and be helpless in coming to her aid.

The tracks disappeared. He pulled the reins and doubled back more slowly. When had they vanished? He'd been so caught up in his thoughts, he hadn't noticed until now. *There!* Picking up where he regained sight of the tracks, he followed them as they veered off the trail and to a small clearing just off the side of the road. Remnants of a camp littered the area. Grass matted down in the amber glow of the torch. He hovered his hand over the dead campfire and, in finding no warmth, eased his hand into the ashes. He smiled when a subtle warmth greeted his fingertips as he touched the earth.

Sweeping the torch around the area, he noted long marks in the dirt and held his breath. He pushed forward, reticent to follow, his feet dragging from an unseen weight. No more than a dozen steps inside the dense trees, he clenched his jaw. A pair of man's boots. Upon closer examination, he groaned at the wide-eyed expression of his father. Alistair's mouth hung open, the front of his shirt and coat dark with blood from his gashed throat.

James whirled away from the sight to catch his breath. "Stupid fool!"

Giving himself enough time to gain his composure, he inhaled deep and faced the body of his father once more. James knelt and fought the tears threatening to come forth. He stabbed the torch into the soft earth and leaves to keep it upright, and touched his father's hand. The warmth still present in Alistair's skin gave James *some* hope, as this indicated he hadn't been dead for very long. His own experience with death at the *Fechtschulen* and over the years provided him at least that much information.

James shook his head and quelled the rising anger and sorrow, cursing his father again. Another bout of steadying breaths, he stood and paced the forest.

Cailin, it appeared, was much closer than he had hoped, but staying behind to give his father a proper burial would put that much more distance between him and her.

He growled at Alistair's prone form. "Damn you, Father. I must tend to you later." No longer able to stay the tears, James let them fall as he pulled fallen branches, brush and leaves over Alistair's body. He grabbed the torch when he finished and started for his horse, but stopped. James twirled, reached through the debris into Alistair's coat pocket and found what he sought.

The laudanum. *If Cailin is wounded during this ordeal, this may actually help her.*

He stomped out of the forest and shoved the half-filled bottle into his saddlebags before swinging into the saddle. Several yards down the road a white speck amongst the dirt gleamed under the moonlight. He dismounted and picked up a dirty kerchief stained with blood. Clenching his jaw, he mounted and continued once more at a steady trot, hoping the stains on the cloth were not Cailin's blood.

"*Veh ata...adonai...mah— mahgen—*" Broderick growled.

"You are almost there, Vamsyrian," Malloren encouraged. "I know you are weary from the incantations draining you. Just this one last time."

Broderick nodded and took a deep breath to gather his strength. He had already been at these exercises for several hours with the prophetess, bringing up the shield, lowering it, casting the incantations over various objects and areas. However, the casting was limited to what he was. He could not cast such a protective boundary around himself without causing great pain. The incantation was designed to cleanse an area of evil, moving from the center point of the target outward to the designated boundary. Broderick disliked the idea that he was evil more and more with each demonstration of Jehovah's power. He was anxious to learn the history of the Vamsyrians, to learn why he was considered evil other than in his choice to turn against God. Though Malloren Rune shared that the incantations would protect against any spawn of Satan, she insisted he would learn such things once he performed the incantations to her satisfaction.

Speaking slowly, Broderick extended his hand at the candlestick again and recited while envisioning a small bubble around the object. *"Veh atah adonai…mahgen bah-adee, k'vodee…u-merim roshee."*

The subtle oppression resonated from the candlestick. He tried to touch the protected item and ran into the expected barrier…and the anticipated weakness rippled from his fingertips up his arm.

"Very good, Broderick," she whispered.

He nodded again. *"Pitkhu li…sha-ahray tsedek,…avoh…bahm ve odeh yah."* The request to remove the protection. *"Zeh ha-sha-ar…adonai. Tsadikim…yavou bo."* Broderick sighed as the oppressive atmosphere vanished.

"Excellent." Malloren smiled at Broderick, stepped forward and recited the incantation to erect the boundary.

With a blow to his chest by an unseen but familiar force, Broderick flew across the small room and hit the stone wall with grunt. He bellowed in agony as an intense pressure crushed his chest. Malloren recited the last two parts of the incantation and his body fell to ground in a heap. After several minutes of panting, the pain finally subsided enough for him to breathe easy. He shook his head to clear the dizziness and glared at her. "What in blazes was that about?"

The corner of her mouth turned up in a half-smile. "The last lesson for this evening. Davina or Cailin can use the incantation, setting a desired boundary, to cast away any evil in their midst. As you can see, it is quite effective." She held her palm up and again recited the first chant.

Broderick staggered to his feet and groaned from the oppressive force. "Was it really necessary, though?" He kept his distance.

"Recite the request," she commanded.

He did as instructed and Malloren recited the final part of the incantation. The shield disappeared.

"Remember, the request alone is not enough to lower the protection. The person who originated the defensive guard must be the one to respond and remove it."

"Or someone of the same bloodline," he amended, based on what had she told him earlier.

"That is correct. Otherwise the protection is permanent, such as what has happened with the amulet you left with Cailin. Because the person who created the cleansing amulet has passed on or is unknown, it cannot be removed from the amulet."

"And that particular protection was the cleansing," he said more to himself, reviewing their lessons for the evening.

"Yes. You envision the item as cleansed instead of with a barrier. Cleansing burns. The shield repels. That is why—"

"Aye, why the amulet burned me instead of repelled me," he grumbled. Again, the idea that he was *evil* did not sit well with him. He also pushed away the nagging thoughts that he may have not left much protection for his family after all, with the amulet only being cleansed. He was here now. He knew the incantations. He would be home shortly.

"I realize it has been a trying evening, but you must understand the weapon I have given you and its limitations."

"Aye." He sighed.

"This is how the incantation is used. Davina and Cailin should invoke the protection. Either you or they request for its removal. They should respond."

"Understood."

"Come, Vamsyrian." Malloren turned and opened the door, exiting into the corridor. "I will show you to your accommodations."

Another trek through the turning and twisting lamp-lit hallways, he became increasingly agitated. "And just how am I to find my way through this labyrinth on my own?"

She stopped and faced him, tilting her head as if pondering the idea. "Who says I will allow you to wander my halls alone, Vamsyrian?" Without waiting for his answer, she spun and continued through the maze.

Broderick grumbled after her.

They finally arrived at a door, which Malloren opened and stepped through. Broderick followed. The room was lit by more oil lamps. "Surely, you must have a monumental supply of oil at your disposal." He smirked.

The prophetess pursed lips as if to suppress a smile. "I only light what I need when I need it. Since I knew of your coming, I made the appropriate accommodations for our duties this evening. I usually carry my lantern to light my way."

She twirled around the room, showing Broderick his lodgings. A good-sized, box-frame bed was positioned along the far wall. A small table sat near the head of the bed with the oil lamp. The walls were bare. A crudely woven rug lay at the bedside. "Nothing as fancy as your grand fortress in Scotland, to be sure, but suitable for your needs I hope."

He cocked an eyebrow and crossed his arms. "You already know it will suit."

"Yes, I do." She sauntered to the doorway and stepped into the corridor, pointing down the hall. "Walk in this direction, Vamsyrian, and you will come to another ladder. Ascend that ladder to the surface and you may exit to do some much-needed feeding." Her eyes traveled down and up his body. "Be sure to make note where you emerged from these chambers so you may return."

"Thank you, Malloren. For everything."

"Do not thank me now, Vamsyrian." She regarded him with cold eyes. "You may not be so grateful on the morrow."

Broderick narrowed his gaze as she strutted away from the entrance of his chamber. Stepping forward, he poked his head through the doorway...only to find she had already disappeared through some hall or door...or into thin air. He harrumphed and frowned. She was right, though. He needed to feed.

Securing his satchel by slipping it under the simple box-frame bed, Broderick then headed down the hall in the direction she'd indicated, found the iron ladder and climbed the rungs until he reached the hatch. He scanned the night sky then lowered the door into the grass and surveyed the area. He had emerged on the eastern side of the circle of stones. He studied the arrangement of the monoliths, noted the alignment and started toward the circle, counting his paces until he reached the formation. After turning about-face, he counted as he paced forward and found the door again. That should suffice as a "map" of the door's location. Broderick set off toward the establishment in the distance, his fangs already extending in anticipation of the hunt.

"This is completely unnecessary, Jasper." Cailin inwardly cursed at the fear in her voice.

Her captor grinned as he continued to re-tie her hands in front of her. They had stopped to make camp for the evening. Jasper had led her off the path, several yards from the road over a shallow rise, and settled them behind the mound so as to be hidden from any passersby. With his bedroll laid out and the horses secured, Jasper pulled her to the ground with him.

"Please, I promise I won't try to escape."

A raspy chuckle brushed her cheek as he finished tying the rope around his body, securing Cailin to his person. "Ye must think I be daft if ye expect me to trust ye'll stay the night. Ye shall be tied right by my side so I can get some rest without worryin' about ye troddin' off on yer own."

Unbeknownst to him, he was leading her straight toward her goal. So if she protested too much— and if by some remote chance she was able to talk him into letting her sleep alone, he would be suspicious by the morning when she didn't try to escape. But having to sleep in such close proximity of his stinking and vile presence was something she didn't think she could abide.

To her disgust, he scooted close behind her, nestling his groin against her bottom.

"Hmmm." He nuzzled her ear.

Cailin veered away, struggling to stave off his attentions, but Jasper grabbed her throat and squeezed until she stilled. His other hand clutched her skirts and she panicked...and not just because he trod upon territory she despised him exploring. Fighting against him in spite of the gagging hold he had on her, Cailin failed to keep his hand from creeping up her leg and finding her prized possession.

"Oy!" he exclaimed when he came in contact with the knife she had strapped to her thigh. She cried out when he ripped it off her. "Thought you could sneak that in, did ye?" He laughed maniacally. "Ol' Jasper did good by havin' his way!"

Cailin's spirits sank.

Jasper chuckled and bile rose to her throat as he ground his erection against her backside. "Relax, lassie." He growled and grunted as he continued to rub himself against her. "As much as I want to—" He grunted again. "Bury my cock in yer sweet body." Another grunt. "Angus has made it very clear he's to be yer first." Jasper chuckled and hissed in her ear, "But he also promised to let me have ye when he be done."

Cailin squeezed her eyes shut against the pain of him gripping her throat and his lewd actions behind her. His bucking increased and his hand eased from her neck, but his clumsy hands found her breasts while he continued grunting and finally shuddered his release. Lying spent behind her for several moments, Jasper eventually maneuvered his body within the bindings so they lay back-to-back. "Just a sampling of what is yet to come, lassie." He laughed again.

Cailin lay very still, waiting, her eyes staring off into the darkness. Eventually, she heard the slow, even breathing of her captor in sleep. Only then did she release her tears. Trembling and loathing her situation, she silently encouraged herself to sleep. *You need the rest. How can you face Angus if you are exhausted?*

Staring up at the waxing moon, she locked her gaze onto the partial silver disc in the sky as a focal point for her thoughts. Had her family been able to track her? Was James searching for her? She was sure her father had not yet come home, so would James even know where to find her? Did Maggie make it to safety?

Exhaustion finally claimed Cailin and she descended into blessed darkness.

Broderick dropped the stinking thief next to his partner, his head thumping the forest floor. These two had followed him through the streets of Amesbury, the small town just east of the circle of stones. Broderick led them to the small patch of forest bordering the modest establishment where he performed the mock task of making a camp. That's when they jumped him, thievery on their minds. One of them had murder in his heart.

He shook his head and wiped his mouth as he tried to force the images of their lurid lives out of his mind. Everyone had a past. Everyone traveled a certain path which lead them to the point in time when he encountered their nefarious intentions to rob or murder him. Every one of them had a sorrowful story.

Evil doers are not born, they are grown. All children begin their lives with open hearts and a desire to love and be loved. The world teaches them to distrust, to withdraw, or to lash out. Life strips them of their innocence and leaves a legacy of hatred and selfishness in order to survive. Some become prey. Others become hunters. Worse, some become parasites, like these two.

The surprising lesson Broderick had learned from the memories he harvested through the blood of his victims was this: Not one person who attacked him ever thought they were acting improperly. Wrongdoers did not see themselves as evil. With all their hearts, they believed their actions were justified. Life owed them. Or they felt what they did was necessary for survival. Or any number of other reasons, each as unique as the individual. Guilt may pepper their intentions, but that is usually explained away or conveniently forgotten.

He stared down at their pathetic forms with a measure of his own guilt. "Do I not also justify my actions as you do?" he whispered. "Surely Angus does as well."

He breathed deep and eyed the coming dawn on the horizon. Kneeling down, he placed his palm on each of their foreheads in turn, wiping the encounter with him from their minds. They would wake in a few hours, bewildered, weak, and after seeing the efforts at making a camp, they would think they had slept a drunken night in the woods.

He turned to leave the two on the ground, unconscious heaps of flesh, but stepped back and placed his hands on his hips, chuckling. For his own amusement, Broderick arranged the two men, one behind the other in a cuddling, sleeping repose. Wrapping the arm of the man behind over his partner in front of him, he said through his chortles, "Sleep well, gents." He continued to laugh at his imagining of their reactions to waking in each other's arms.

Broderick dashed across the field and arrived back at the circle of stones, then counted his paces to where he found the hatch to the underground dwelling of the prophetess. He locked the hatch behind him and descended the iron rungs. It was a short stroll back to his temporary chamber.

He started with surprise. Malloren sat on his bed and he frowned, not yet stepping into the room. "Shall I find another place to rest for the day?"

"That is not necessary, Vamsyrian." She rose from the bed and loitered around the room before meandering to the door. He stepped back to allow her space to exit. Instead, she stood before him…a little too close for his comfort. She gazed up at him, pouty lips curling into a seductive grin, hooded eyes staring at his mouth. When she tried to touch his face, he seized her wrist.

"Do I frighten you, Broderick?"

"Not at all," he drawled and raised a warning brow. "Your attentions, however, are unwanted. Surely, with that all-knowing power you possess, you must know how devoted I am to Davina."

Amusement softened the seduction in her expression, but she still near-purred as she leaned back against the door frame, her eyes now smoldering. "I can see why she was so attracted to you."

"Last recollection," he said, crossing his arms, "she is *still* attracted to me."

Malloren nodded with a smile as if she pondered some private joke. She sauntered down the corridor before stopping to face him again, her serious prophetess mask upon her face once more. "Tomorrow night I will teach you the history of your race, reveal your purpose in this prophecy and why you are here." Her eyes raked over his form and the seductive smile returned. "Rest well, Vamsyrian." Though husky and alluring, her voice sent a chill of apprehension skipping up his spine.

He narrowed his eyes at her retreating figure and a wave of lethargy rippled through his body. Dawn. He closed the door and secured the bolt. Though she may very well have a key to the room, the action lent him a subtle security. He could at least make some small attempt at keeping her out while he slept.

Another wave dragged through his form, buckling his knees. He doused the oil lamp, plunging the room into blackness. The box-frame bed creaked in protest when he lay upon the mattress. His last thoughts were of Davina's sweet lips, her sapphire eyes, and the dread of spending another day without her loving presence in his dreams.

Jasper gave her good shove and Cailin stumbled into the dust-coated and dingy chamber. She struggled to keep herself from falling on her face and whirled to glare at him.

"Ye better get some rest before Angus rises," he growled.

She held her wrists up to him.

"Nay, lassie." He grinned. "Ye shall keep yer bonds until Angus decides to cut them." He closed and latched the door, his grating laughter fading as he continued down the corridor.

She gritted her frustration and shoved an arm chair against the wall, sending clouds of dust into the air. Wrinkling her nose, she ambled to the partially parted curtains and pulled them back, sending more showers of dust about her. Cailin coughed and waved her bound hands in an attempt to clear the air. A useless gesture. However, with the curtains now parted, the thin window high in the wall allowed the fading sun of the day to stream fingers of clouded light across the chamber. The room was sparsely furnished with an empty canopy bed void of any bedcovers, mattress or curtains, the chair she'd pushed, a broken settee at the foot of the bed and a small trestle table under the narrow window. On the table sat a bowl and urn. Hope bloomed in her chest when she saw no dust on the chipped pottery. She sighed with relief when she peered into the urn. Water. Using the bottom of her skirt, she attempted to clear the dust from the chair, then fetched the bowl and urn and sat. Though difficult to maneuver with bound hands, she managed to wash her cut and bruised feet, wincing as her wounds stung from her ministrations.

She returned the bowl and urn filled with muddy water to the table. Only then did she notice the looking glass, propped against the stone wall, and dusted its surface to reveal her haggard appearance. Even though Maggie had done a right tight job at plaiting her hair, wisps about her head created a disheveled halo. Dark circles shadowed her eyes. Spots of Alistair's blood still dotted her face. After dipping a fairly clean part of the hem of her skirt into the edge of the muddy water, she did her best to wipe the remains of crusted blood from her skin. She loosed her hair from the braids, scrubbed her scalp, then tied her mass of hair at the nape of her neck with the one remaining ribbon worth salvaging.

Exhaustion weighted her body and she abandoned her attempts at grooming. Though the wooden chair with its worn padding wasn't as comfortable as she'd hoped, it was surely more comfortable than the hard-hewn, wooden planks of the floor.

Jasper had awakened her no more than a couple of hours after sunrise, based on the sun's height at the time they vacated the camp. Sleep had been fitful and their journey languorously long, so it was no wonder she was spent. Judging by the colors of the sky through the narrow window, it was very late in the day and at least a few hours before sunset…before Angus would rise for the evening. Jasper was right. She needed what rest she could get.

With her stomach rumbling from hunger, Cailin settled in as much as the oaken chair and her bonds would allow, and closed her eyes.

James had followed the instructions from the merchants of the various stops he'd made along the way, the murmurs and whispers over why anyone would want to go chasing ghosts rippling behind him as he sped on toward his destination.

He'd kept his purpose to himself and asked only of Glen Morin. He'd stated, "I have my reasons," too many times to remember, and the monotony of the inquiries stretched on as endlessly as the road before him. Had he made a wrong turn and put more distance between him and Cailin? Were the tracks he followed only leading him to some merchant's home in the Highlands? Fear and uncertainty pressed upon his chest with every passing moment.

Rounding a bend in the path and over a rise in the road, the tracks of the horses imprinted just a bit deeper and farther apart. The sun had set and having purchased more fuel, he had enough oil to still light his torch. However, it was getting harder to see the hoof prints in the drying soil. But there was no mistaking this increase in speed. Why had they picked up their pace?

Settled into the glen just yards before him, a castle in partial ruins sat glowing against the silvery landscape. Sconces burned along the broken, outer wall. He gasped. He may have actually arrived at his destination, and only too late did he toss his torch to the road to douse it from view of anyone who might be near.

At that belated thought, a sharp pain slammed into his shoulder and knocked him from his mount. His gelding trotted to the nearby trees.

Disoriented from the fall and the agony that shot through his body, he shook his head and clutched his shoulder. The point of an arrow protruded through his upper arm. Cursing for letting his guard down and from the injury, he finished putting the flames out and crawled through the brush toward the safety his mount had sought.

Another arrow whizzed by his head. "Damn!"

After reaching the refuge of the trees and a large, fallen log, he examined the damage. As previously observed, the bolt went cleanly through from the back of his arm. Though still in pain, he sighed from relief at sheer luck or the bad aim of his attacker. The bolt had pierced the fleshy, outside part of his shoulder, missing the bone. *Small favors!*

Peeking over the rotting trunk, his eyes trained over the dim landscape and he ducked when two hovering shadows bobbed across the moonlit field. James drew his sword and remained crouching as he waited for them to come closer. With concerted effort, he kept his breathing as quiet as possible. God the burning in his arm was blinding! After several tense moments, footsteps thrashed through the soggy leaves and twigs. He held his breath. *Snap!*

James stood. One man raised a bow. James leapt over the log and swung his sword, severing the man's head from his shoulders. His body collapsed to the ground. The other man stepped from behind a tree and fired an arrow, missing James by mere inches.

He charged. The man turned and ran. James pounced, sinking his sword between the man's shoulder blades. He yanked his sword from the body and wiped the blood on the body's tunic.

His eyes scanned the landscape again. All was quiet, save for his panting. Falling to his knees, he groaned. The ache in his shoulder spread across his chest and back and he hugged his arm to his side.

He rose on unsteady legs. Sheathed his sword. Shuffled back toward the log. The open and glassy eyes of the severed head regarded him. Though not a stranger to taking a life—journeying back from *Fechtschulen* had its trials and, unfortunately, had forced him into opportunities which put his newfound skills to the test—doing so never sat well with him. In each situation, it was him or them. Self-defense didn't make the toll of death easier on his conscience, though.

He kicked some leaves over the gawking face and perused the terrain once more. Still no sign of others. If he was lucky, no one saw the skirmish and no alarm would be raised. He had the advantage of dusk's dim light.

He staggered to his horse, speaking soothing words to the agitated animal. Reached into his saddlebags. He pulled out a drying cloth and the laudanum. With a groan, he sat behind the fallen log. No sense in keeping himself exposed just in case others did come around.

He took a few sips from the spiced-brandy mixture. Though unsure of exactly how much to take, he had an idea, and based his estimation on the small amount his fencing mates drank whenever they used it. He knew there was a point of "too much" and saw the listlessness the elixir could induce. *Let us see how effective this draught can be.*

And he waited, allowing his body to recuperate and for the laudanum to take effect. A certain peace settled into his limbs after several minutes.

Not wishing to waste too much time, he turned his attentions to his wound. He stuffed a cloth into his mouth and bit down. Grabbing the fletching, he inhaled a few deep breaths to prepare for the pain and snapped off the end, his grunts of discomfort muffled by the gag. *That was not as painful as I anticipated. Perhaps the laudanum has indeed helped.* With a hiss, he pulled the rest of the projectile from his flesh and threw the offending bolt aside. After ripping the drying cloth into strips, he wrapped his arm to stay the small flow of blood.

Several more minutes passed and the burn of the wound lessened. However, a disconcerting haziness swept over him…similar to the effects brought on by drinking wine or ale but with its own characteristics of rhapsody and reaction to the world around him, to the injury. Though his shoulder still throbbed, it was bearable. In fact, he didn't particularly care about the wound.

"Well," he said rising with a grunt. "Such an indifference to pain may prove helpful." He absently scratched at the tingling itches across his abdomen.

Tying his horse securely to a low-hanging branch, he checked the stilettos at his hips, positioned them the way Broderick had shown him, and adjusted his baldric to settle the sword at his side.

He breathed deep. As Cailin had instructed him before their sparring session, he closed his eyes and imagined the construction of a brick wall around his mind. The mason workers stacked the bricks, but then began to argue over the inconsistency of the job being done. James imagined himself coming on the scene and scolding them, being the task master to bring about accord. Reluctantly, the workers resumed, casting disapproving, sideways glances at each other while he supervised.

James opened his eyes and chuckled. "Very interesting indeed," he mumbled and crouched low, heading toward the castle structure.

He stopped and let his eyes roam the landscape. When had the sun set? He shrugged and slinked through the darkness.

Broderick stepped down from the last rung on the iron ladder, turned and almost collided with Malloren Rune.

"Very wise of you to feed before our sessions."

At first taken aback that he hadn't heard her, Broderick eventually nodded. "I was unsure of how many exercises we would do this evening. I thought it would be best if I had my full strength."

She continued to stare at him. Crossing his arms, he waited for her to make the next move. The corner of her mouth turned up in amusement and she twirled to proceed down the corridor. Broderick cocked a suspicious eyebrow before following her.

Malloren led him through the various corridors and doorways, navigating their way through the labyrinth until they emerged into the library where he'd first entered the underground chambers.

"Please proceed to the center on the lower level. We have tomes to consult."

Broderick did as she instructed, and she mumbled the initial incantation as she slid the bolt. A tingle of apprehension thrummed in his gut. She padded down the stone stairs to the lower level, seated herself at the center table and, with an open palm, motioned for Broderick to join her.

"What do you know of the origin of the Vamsyrians?" She settled back comfortably in her armed chair.

"Evangeline told me only briefly that…" He was about to say "they", but the nagging thought of the choice he'd made forced him to include himself in this race. "She told me briefly that *we* are creations of Satan…and that making the choice to become a Vamsyrian is turning our backs on God. However, that is all I know."

She nodded. "Vamsyrians are Satan's revenge against God. They are a mockery of Christ's redemption." She rose from her seat and strolled slowly about the room. "Jesus shed His blood so that humanity might have eternal life. Satan created Vamsyrians to shed the blood of the innocent so they might have immortality. The ultimate goal for Satan is to trap the human soul within the body, forcing the Vamsyrian to kill and build an increasing mountain of sins against the soul, thereby preventing it from obtaining any redemption."

"So that is why we have turned our back on God, by choosing to become…an offspring of Satan."

She leveled her eyes at him. "Yes, Vamsyrian."

Broderick clenched his jaw. As much as he did not want to admit his part in this choice, he was fully conscious of his decision. His wife Evangeline had betrayed him and he believed, at the time, she was responsible for the slaughter of his family. When she had been the one to stand before him as one of "God's chosen", he wanted nothing to do with God and his ways. He consciously rejected God.

"There is hope for redemption, though, Broderick."

He squinched with skepticism. "But Evangeline said once we made this decision, there was no turning back."

"Jehovah rarely creates such inescapable situations." She raised an eyebrow, hinting at the many secrets she held.

Broderick grumbled. *God's blood, this woman enjoys this position of power knowledge affords her!*

"I spoke of a prophecy."

He nodded.

"This prophecy foretells of a warrior created who will be the Deliverer of God's wrath on the Vamsyrian race. Through their destruction, there is redemption."

Broderick rolled his eyes and shook his head. "So, the redemption of which you speak is through death."

Malloren's unemotional silence was his confirmation.

He stood and paced. "How appropriate." The ramblings of the Church in his youth—of sacrifice and suffering in the name of the Lord—needled his shoulders with its endless lessons fraught by guilt and judgment. "It seems God's salvation is always through suffering and death."

"As you recall," she went on, ignoring his rants, "making the choice to become a Vamsyrian had to be an educated decision. You had to face a member of the *Tzava Ha'or* and—"

"Hear both sides of this coin," he grumbled. "Aye, I remember."

"It is important, Broderick MacDougal," she stressed. "If someone is changed unwillingly into a Vamsyrian, Jehovah will release His wrath on the Vamsyrian race, cleansing the earth of their presence."

Broderick ceased his pacing and faced Malloren with his jaw dropped in disbelief. "The choice had to be a willing one, Elder Ammon said. But I did not know the full extent of the choice I made." The realization hit him like a stone to the chest. "You are telling me God is releasing his wrath on our race because of me?"

She smiled a knowing grin. "In a manner of speaking, yes."

"Come now, lassie." Jasper's gruff voice invaded her fitful dreams, his meaty hands inconsiderate of her body or sleepiness as he yanked her out of the chair and dragged her through the dusty chamber. "Lord Angus wants to see ye in the Grand Hall."

Cailin struggled with the blurriness of heavy eyes and limbs and tripped several times, yelping at her already sore feet. Jasper grunted and pulled her along, shoving her into a cushioned armchair. Surprisingly, the chair felt good and she arranged herself more comfortably as she surveyed her new surroundings. Blinking to accustom her eyes to the light, she focused on a massive hearth which came into view, a blaze dancing in a fireplace large enough for one to stand in. Torches burned along the walls of the Grand Hall. In the center, a gargantuan chandelier hung with myriad candles flickering and dripping their wax onto the floor below. This room seemed well-used. There were no signs of cobwebs or dust in the high-ceiling rafters or on the tables in a rectangular U-shape formation around the room and behind her. The chair in which she sat was positioned at the mouth of the "U", Jasper standing just behind her and to her right, while she faced a raised platform that housed a long, head table.

She glared over her shoulder at Jasper, who winked at her, and she delivered an equally scathing glower to the rest of the men stationed around the room. An observation platform edged the entire hall—starting at the back-right, skirting along the right wall, the front wall and the left wall, ending at a door to the back-left. At the entrances to this second level, two more men stood on post. She directed her attention back to the head table and grumbled. *Six men plus Jasper and only one small blade.*

"Sweet, sweet Cailin," a deep voice drawled, echoing in the vast room, and gooseflesh rose on her skin at the eerie familiarity.

CHAPTER EIGHT

Cailin snapped her head to the right and caught her breath as Angus swaggered toward her. The corner of his mouth curved sensuously, his hooded gaze seductive and alluring. Frowning and standing before her, he tipped her head up with a curled index finger under her chin and hitched his breath.

"'Tis beautiful enough to steal my breath from me...in spite of your disheveled appearance." Angus stepped back and surveyed her, the crease between his brows deepening.

In a blur, he back-handed Jasper, who fell to the floor, gasping. Cailin squeaked her surprise.

"I did as you asked, m'lord." Jasper wiped the blood from his split lip. "She is here for your pleasure."

"Dotard! And what pleasure am I to find in this poor lass, half-starved and spent from your mishandling?" Angus closed his eyes and inhaled deeply, clenching his fists. Training his gaze on her once more, his eyes softened. "Please forgive this dolt, Cailin." He bent forward, brushing his cheek against hers, and scraped her skin with his whiskers. Inhaling deep, he caressed her brow with his mouth as he feathered his way to her other cheek. "I shall tend to your needs," he whispered.

Cailin shivered at the heat of his words against her ear and shrank from him.

Angus chuckled, but did not stand upright. He placed his palms on the arms of the chair, his face still hovering above hers as his deep-green eyes roamed her features. The last time she had encountered Angus, she was ten years of age. He had made similar arrangements to have her and her mother captured and brought to some holdings closer to Edinburgh than this location. Though he looked the same and he still used the same taunting voice, his effect on her was entirely different. His mannerisms toward her were purely…sexual. *Aye, that is the difference.* He oozed with sexuality and lustful intentions.

Cailin gasped when his knee settled between her thighs. His gaze dropped to her mouth and his tongue swept his lips as if he prepared for a scrumptious feast. With his hand at the nape of her neck, he held her in place as he kissed her. Sensuously at first, then growing more urgent. Cailin refused to open her mouth to him, though his tongue and lips made insistent demands. *So much for this amulet preventing him from touching me!*

Angus pulled back. He panted and his brows drew up in what appeared to be confusion. After several moments of his searching gaze and his breathing seemed to return to normal, he grinned and stood.

"Welcome to Glen Morin, sweet Cailin." Grabbing the throne on the opposite side of the head table, he lifted the wood chair and swung it over to his side. Cailin blanched as the solid thump of the dense furniture confirmed its weight and size...and he had tossed it about as if it were hollow.

Angus sat upon the velvet cushions and threw a leg over one of the arms, propped his elbow on the other and rested his chin in his palm. With a frown, he regarded Jasper. "Cut her bonds. She is a guest in my home."

Jasper scrambled to his feet, procured her silver-plated dagger from his belt with a smile and sliced through the ropes binding her wrists in a single swipe. He nodded appreciatively at the weapon, winked at her and replaced the coveted knife in his belt.

"I am impressed...about many things," Angus complimented. "You have grown into quite a vision from the gangly little waif I saw so many years ago. Knowing my friend Jasper here, and judging by the rawness on your wrists…" He glowered momentarily at Jasper before diverting his gaze back to her, the lust returning in his eyes. "'Tis obvious you did not have a pleasant journey here, yet you remain steadfast in your scathing glares against me. I see every indication that if you had the opportunity, you would drive a silver stake through my heart…and perhaps relish in the experience." His soft laugh caressed the air around her. "Am I right, sweet Cailin?"

She nodded.

He laughed outright this time and sat forward, resting his elbows on his knees and amusement sparkling in his lustful gaze. Cocking an eyebrow and squinting, he rubbed his chin as he considered her. "I am curious, though, over how well you have managed to block your thoughts from me." He sat back and crossed an ankle over his knee. "My dear brother must be getting better at teaching you such skills. Even with Davina, I caught a glimpse here and there of her precious little musings."

Cailin inwardly sighed with relief. *At least the amulet is working in that regard.*

Angus averted his eyes to one side, apparently looking to the back of the room, and he nodded. Directing his attention back to Cailin, he said, "Hungry?"

A thin, elderly man shuffled forward to the raised platform, carrying a tray overloaded with fruits, breads, cheeses, roast chicken, a pitcher and two goblets. He grunted as he precariously set the tray upon the head table.

"Thank you, Malcolm." Angus nodded at the servant, who nodded in response and shuffled out of the room. "Please, my dear." Angus sauntered forward and gingerly took her hand in his. Not wishing to be confrontational at this point, she allowed him to escort her, limping in the process. He stopped and looked at her feet, then glared at Jasper. Cailin gasped as Angus swept her into his arms and carried her the rest of the way around the table. He seated her in the matching throne armchair in the second place of honor. "Help yourself," he encouraged. Turning his chair to face her from across the table, he again sat in his casual display, leg hung over the arm.

Cailin's mouth watered as the buttery aroma of the bread teased her senses. She near-drooled at the roasted chicken, skin glazed golden-brown and crisp to the eye. The grapes, round and plump, would surely burst in her mouth. She very much wanted to partake of the bounty before her, but this was Angus Campbell and he was not to be trusted.

Her host chuckled. "Come now." He rose and poured her a cup-full of deep-burgundy wine. "Do you think I would have you brought all this way just to poison you?" He poured himself a cup and drank deep. "You must know I would derive no satisfaction in such a heinous act."

Moving too fast for her mortal eyes to witness, he appeared at her side. His nose nuzzled the dangling strands of her hair away from her ear. "Nay, my luscious little morsel."

Cailin's breath quickened.

His tongue darted out to taste her lobe and she gasped as his fang pricked her skin. She tried to pull away only to find his steel grip on her neck immobilizing her. He moaned and suckled her blood. "I cannot kill you…at least not yet." Yanking her chair to face him, he knelt breathless before her, his lips red with her blood. "You are the bait, sweet Cailin." His hands cupped her breasts and she slapped him away. Angus chuckled and gazed at her with hooded eyes. "Torturing you in front of Broderick will be a thrilling task, indeed." Inhaling as if savoring her aroma, he sighed, his eyes roaming over her body leaving icy trails of repulsion. "But I am of a mind to help myself to your charms before he arrives." He regarded her under his brow. "I am a demanding lover, Cailin." He rose to his feet, leaned over her and, nose-to-nose, whispered his threat. "Eat to gain your strength. You will most certainly need it."

"In a manner of speaking?" Broderick frowned at Malloren. "Enough of the riddles. I am either the cause of this redemption or I am not."

"It is your role in the prophecy that will bring about the end result."

He crossed his arms. "Explain."

For once, Malloren appeared uncertain. "I cannot say exactly at this point in time."

He pointed an accusing finger. "Malloren, if you do not—"

"Calm yourself, Vamsyrian," she protested as she held up her palm. "I'm not the one speaking in riddles. I'm just the messenger and I'm not always given all the information." She marched to the table and her hands pushed around and lifted the various scrolls and tomes. Settling on one particular scroll, she unrolled it, her eyes moving over the parchment, and then lowered the paper to consider him. "The full prophecy has been lost for centuries. For several decades, I have been given visions to help me piece together, find and uncover the missing parts." She sat in her chair once more and leaned forward, encouraging Broderick to join her again by waving her hand toward his chair.

He grumbled and sat.

"Satan created the first Vamsyrian shortly after the crucifixion of the Christ. As it has been told through the teachings of the *Tzava Ha'or*, Satan wanted revenge for giving humanity a definitive path to the salvation Jehovah offered His followers. Satan seduced a woman with the promise of being the mother of a new nation, a new race of invincible warriors."

"The first Vamsyrian is a woman?"

She hesitated before speaking. "No one actually knows for certain, but that is how the history is taught. The creation of the Vamsyrian race is very similar to man's fall from grace, so the chronicles have been handed down in the same fashion."

"Mmm-hmmm." Broderick raised a skeptical eyebrow.

Malloren challenged him with a lift of her chin. "You do not think a woman is worthy of being the leader of a nation?"

He waved a dismissive hand, not wishing to get into this debate. "The first Vamsyrian was created, the mother of a nation of warriors. Go on."

She pursed her lips. "It is told that the Angel Gabriel approached Satan and his new creation, stating conditions."

"God did not challenge this creation? He allowed it to occur?"

"Gabriel told Satan and the First Vamsyrian that God would never interfere with the free will of mankind. That is a gift given by God and something He will never take away." She leaned forward again for emphasis. "It is the reason Satan rebelled against his creator, Vamsyrian. He was not allowed to choose or not choose God, and thereby was cast out of heaven for taking liberties not given to him. It is the core reason why Satan hates mankind." Malloren perused the many scrolls and tomes again while she spoke. "Gabriel said since God does not interfere with the free will of man, and man has always had the option of turning away from Him, so must the choice be for those becoming Vamsyrians. No one must change another unwillingly. If this happens, God will destroy the Vamsyrians."

"By *unwillingly*, you mean the transformation cannot be forced upon someone?"

She nodded.

"Then I am not the Deliverer you speak of."

She shook her head.

"Everyone becoming Vamsyrians must do so willingly," he mumbled, repeating what Elder Ammon told him. "'Tis fair, I suppose." His voice held a touch of sarcasm. "Satan creates a race of killers and God permits it as long as his people go along willingly with the creation." He shrugged. "Go on."

Malloren tapped her fingers in irritation. "A balancing force needed to be set in place to ensure the choice made was a willing one. Satan is a liar and God did not trust that those facing the choice would be provided the entire truth. That is why the *Tzava Ha'or* was created. We are the balancing force and provide the last chance for such victims to choose God."

Broderick scrunched his brow and *he* leaned forward in emphasis. "I do not understand why God would set up provisions to *preserve* this race Satan created. Why not just let them to their own devices and allow them to kill themselves by fouling up the rules?"

"Then those who made such a choice could never be offered redemption. I do not think it is wise to question Jehovah," Malloren warned.

"Bah!" Broderick sat back and shook his head. "It is my free will to question him, is it not? I have often pondered the usefulness of God's creations over the decades, Satan being one of them. If God is all-powerful and all-knowing, did he not know Satan would rebel? That he would tempt Adam and Eve in paradise? That man would fall from grace by choosing to bow to Satan by disobeying God?" He harrumphed.

"The pain and the suffering in this world are caused primarily by Satan, Broderick."

"Nay, caused by God, Malloren! And to what purpose?" He stood and planted his fists on the table, glaring down at the prophetess. "God created Satan, who is the cause of evil. Thereby, God created the pain and suffering in this world. I see the lives of the victims I feed from, their innocent beginnings falling prey to the evils of God's creation." He pushed away and turned his back on her. "Do not tell me God did not have a hand in any of this."

Malloren placed a comforting hand upon Broderick's shoulder, but he did not turn to face her. In a voice full of compassion, she said, "I did not say God did not have a hand in any of this, Vamsyrian. But I am saying I do not question His motives. Who are we to question God's ultimate design? I believe He does have a plan and you are indeed a special part of the redemption for your race."

Broderick opened his mouth to protest, not wanting to be a part of this manipulation to an unknown end.

But Malloren reached up and placed tender fingers upon his lips. "Do not turn your back on those who may have realized they made a mistake by choosing immortality." Tears welled in the eyes of the prophetess as she pleaded her case. "If you do not care about God or the salvation He offers, please do not throw away the second chance He has given those of your kind to make a different choice."

Guilt washed over Broderick as he weighed her words, as he considered the glassy pools of her dark-brown eyes under her pleading, raven brows. He sighed. "What part do I play in this plan?"

Malloren bowed her head and kissed his knuckles before returning to her seat. "It is unclear as to how many years, decades or even centuries passed before the prophecy was revealed to the *Tzava Ha'or*. As it has been passed down—and with some of the information I have gleaned from the many visions I have received over the years—the Angel Gabriel appeared to a leader of our Order with this message." She picked up the scroll she once held and read.

God's mercy is infinite and He wishes all of His children to receive salvation…even those who have chosen to turn their backs on Him. The Vamsyrian creator is choosing to keep God's path to redemption a secret. I am here to expose that truth to the light and declare how this truth will be revealed.

"So Satan has known about this prophecy since the beginning?"

"As we have come to understand it, yes." She continued.

God has foreseen that by the conflict of two Vamsyrian brothers will the path toward redemption be known. Their family wars will propel them to make the choice of immortality, bonding them by blood not only through their lineage, but also their transformation.

Broderick leaned forward in awe, his palms on the table. "Did Angus know of this prophecy?"

Malloren's brow creased. "Angus? No, not that I am aware. Why do you ask?"

"Bonded by blood," Broderick whispered.

"I beg your pardon?"

"Angus spoke those words the night he transformed me. 'Brothers for all eternity now, forever bonded by blood.' At the time, I thought he was only referring to how the transformation had bonded us in blood, thereby making us brothers as Vamsyrians." Broderick sat, his eyes staring into the past and seeing the final confirmation of his connection to Angus. Until this moment, he'd still harbored doubts about Angus being his brother.

"I had not seen Angus since the night of my turning. Seventeen years ago, we clashed, both of us seeking to settle decades of vengeance. It was in that confrontation I learned we were brothers, both sons of Hamish MacDougal." He brought himself back to the present and regarded Malloren. "Both of us sought immortality for our own reasons of revenge. I learned that Angus was immortal when he murdered my...*our* brothers...and their families." *Will that heartache ever fade?* "Angus left me for dead and Cordelia saved me before..."

Choosing over the years not to dwell on the events that led to his transformation, Broderick had ignored the part Cordelia played in this drama...until now. "*Cordelia* knew we were brothers. But how? *I* did not know." He rose and resumed pacing. He turned to Malloren. "She knew

Angus. Mayhap she had been the one to transform him."

"I revoke my claim on Broderick MacDougal." Cordelia's proclamation and her taunting expressions thrown at Angus echoed through the decades.

"She must have known about the prophecy! Cordelia manipulated Angus and I to be the brothers to fulfill the prophecy. That is why she backed away from doing the transformation herself. She wanted…nay *needed* Angus to perform the transformation."

Malloren sat with her hands folded neatly in her lap.

Is that a hint of pride in her smirk?

"You are correct, Vamsyrian." She stood and cautiously stepped toward him. "Cordelia does indeed know about the prophecy."

Broderick tilted his head and narrowed his eyes at the prophetess. "Why do I feel you know more about this than you are leading me to believe?"

"Please sit." She turned her chair to face him. "You will not like what I have to say."

"So you have continued to make abundantly clear." Broderick scowled.

Cailin grabbed a second leg from the roasted chicken and set it on the trencher before her. Gathering a few more grapes and blackberries along with another chunk of bread, she continued to enjoy the meal before her. True to Angus's word, the food was appetizing and—more to the point—excellent for regaining her strength. With what little rest she was able to snatch in the dusty room and the nourishment of this fine meal, new confidence about confronting her enemy surged through her. Certainly Angus would bide his time, waiting for Broderick to come after her, so she took advantage of the opportunity.

Angus chuckled. "Have you been rendered mute, my little morsel? I do not believe you've uttered a single word since your arrival."

She swallowed her mouthful and washed it down with the rich vintage in her cup. "Apologies to my host." Her voice sounded husky, a sure sign she was fatigued. She cleared her throat. "The food is delicious, but I hesitate to thank you, for I feel as if I am the calf being fattened for the feast."

Angus threw his head back and laughed. "Well said, my dear." He leveled sparkling eyes upon her. "Well said, indeed." He strolled to the far-right doorway at the back of the hall and mumbled something to the man standing post, who nodded and reached into his pocket. Angus took the small jar he handed over and glared at Jasper as he passed by on his path back to the head table. Tossing the jar before Cailin, he smiled and she caught it before it skittered over the edge. "Salve for your wrists and feet."

"Thank you," she whispered.

Angus sat and waved off the courtesy. "Of course." A roguish grin tilted his lips. "As you say, another measure to fatten up my little calf." His eyes dropped to her neckline, lingering until a flushing heat crept over her skin and she had difficulty swallowing.

"I am surprised Broderick has not yet arrived," he deliberated. "Do you think he has abandoned you? Perhaps you are not as important as his beloved Davina? I am very sad to see *she* is not here." He seethed momentarily.

Unmoved by his taunts, she took another sip of wine to wash down the last of her meal. "My father has other business, as I am sure Jasper informed you, but he will be along." The sudden thought that her father might not arrive for at least another day—perhaps even longer—sent a shiver of uncertainty through her. Though she had not originally counted on his assistance, even wanted to handle this herself, the reality she was indeed on her own to finish this confrontation loomed before her. Because she would rather die than let Angus touch her in the ways he threatened, she feared she would not live long enough for her father's rescue.

Angus peered around his shoulder toward his head henchman and the color drained from Jasper's face. "First you do not bring me the complete package," Angus growled. "And now I learn Broderick was away from his family?"

"I had no time to inform you, m'lord! I had only learned—"

"You and I will discuss this later, much to my enjoyment." Turning his attention back to Cailin, Angus dropped his mask of anger and his face melted into pleasantry once more. "You address him as 'father', I see." He feigned a wounded expression. "Pray tell, do not say I am the one to break your heart by informing you he is truly not your father."

She chuckled. "Fear not, Angus. You need not weather the burden of such a task. I am well aware of my parentage. But Broderick MacDougal has been more of a father to me than that monster Ian Russell could have ever hoped to accomplish." She would have to get closer to Angus, but at this moment still wasn't ready to do so and aimed to keep the conversation going to buy the time needed to build her courage.

"I am relieved, then," Angus continued with his taunting. "Being so well-informed about your situation, sweet Cailin, I am assuming you must also know that my dear brother is only using you and your mother to make up for past sins?" He leaned forward and poured himself another cup of wine, then settled back into his chair with a devilish glint in his eyes. "A truly well-adjusted and astounding woman you are if this be so."

Broderick had warned Cailin several times that Angus Campbell was a liar and lived a life entrenched in his own delusions about the truth of their heritage. Yet she struggled with the trepidation rising within her over his words. "If you speak of the past sins regarding the lives he has taken, I know of them and that is not the purpose of our family."

"Nay, Cailin." Angus placed both feet on the floor and propped his elbows on his knees, cradling the goblet of wine in his hands. He stared into the cup almost as if he wished to divine the past from it. "I speak of the guilt Broderick harbors in his black heart over abandoning his own flesh and blood." The lower registers of his voice and his piercing eyes regarding her from under his fiery brows gave Cailin great pause over such deadly intent. He sighed and sat back again, boredom washing the anger from his face like rain washes away a layer of dust.

She fought the urge to shake her head from his dizzying mood swings. Angus's unpredictability in his ever-changing countenance was unnerving. He sipped his wine. Eyes roaming about the Grand Hall, he relayed his history as if he reflected on the latest conditions of the weather. "Our father, Hamish MacDougal, seduced my mother, Alyssa Campbell. Hamish knew my mother was with child, and yet he did not claim me as his son." And like the weather, shifted into a black demeanor as suddenly as an unexpected storm. "The man married to my mother—Fraser Campbell—was far from being a loving father, but at least *he* took on the responsibility of raising me." Angus brooded over his cup. "Fraser never let me forget how the MacDougals abandoned me and deprived me of my rightful place as Hamish's son."

Cailin frowned at Angus's perspective of her family history. How much blood had been spilled over a possible misunderstanding? "Angus," she dared to offer. "Are you certain Broderick knew? What if Hamish—?"

For a moment, sadness clouded Angus's eyes. Then mayhap even a measure of hope glimmered. A mirthless laugh rumbled from his chest and he threw his cup against the wall behind her.

The clanging of a bowl or cup startled James and he winced from the stabbing pain in his shoulder. He stole a sip from the bottle in his pocket. He had snuck over the field unnoticed and dispatched the three men standing guard at the castle entrance. A sharp blade and the indifference he gained from the laudanum made the task an easy one. Mortals must surely be ineffective at defending and fighting immortals, so he spent little time pondering the lack of protection posted around the grounds.

The activity centered around what, he assumed, was the main hall of the castle and stairs led to a second level. He crept up the stairs and peered around the wall, sizing up the distance between him and the man standing at the door on the landing. Checking behind him once more, James advanced slowly…quietly…stiletto poised.

"I was the bastard son of Hamish MacDougal!" the voice below yelled. "The man who waged war after war against *my* home and what little family I had, trying to kill me to erase his mistake!"

James eased the body to the floor, having slit his throat, while the man in the main hall screamed over his history.

"But that was *Hamish*!"

James snapped his head up. *Cailin!* He crawled across the floor and peeked through the doorway, the stretch of landing before him. He chanced peering over the half-wall thankfully hiding him.

In one stride, a man—who strongly resembled Broderick MacDougal—slammed his fists onto a table and towered over Cailin. "Broderick MacDougal stood right by Hamish's side in battle! Rick stood by our father, boasting his position as eldest son and heir to their small fortune, not wanting to share his legacy with the *tainted* blood of a Campbell…even though MacDougal blood ran through *my* veins. Rick carried on the legacy of our father after his death, never stopping the wars. So do not tell me Rick did not know." The man James now assumed was Angus Campbell turned away from Cailin and raked his fingers through his shoulder-length auburn hair…aye, so much like Broderick's. From this distance, he appeared a younger version of James's future father-in-law. How had Broderick never seen the resemblance?

Stealing one more glance at Cailin, he was grateful that at least she was not in Campbell's grasp. He peeked out just a tad farther and groaned inwardly when another man stood at his post on the opposite landing across the room.

James sat on the floor and sighed. He would need to sneak around to the other side and repeat a death blow to the other guard.

Cailin gulped her wine for courage and did her best not to cower before Angus. He reveled in the fear of his victims.

Angus returned his murderous glare to her. "Now that you know the truth, you must realize his motivations for taking in a family, for caring for you as his own daughter, do you not?" He strode forward and rested his fists upon the table once more as he loomed over her. "He thinks he can salve his guilty conscience with a good deed." A sneer curled his lips and he rose to his full height, crossing his arms. "Truly, you are nothing to him but his failed attempt at redemption."

Broderick loved her as if his own blood ran through her veins, as if he had been the one to plant the seed in her mother's womb. The years in his fatherly embrace, the endless memories of his comfort, advice and their laughter were Cailin's testimony against Angus's lies. Yet why did her throat tighten with grief? The nagging pins of doubt pricked her resolve.

Why else would Broderick take such a chance with our lives, his very presence putting us in danger from his enemy, if not for another reason? Surely if he loved us, he would have sacrificed living with us as a family if it meant our survival. These were the arguments she'd had with herself whenever danger reared its destructive head.

"Broderick stays with us *for* our protection," her mother assured her when Cailin had voiced her questions after Angus's first successful abduction.

Angus's whisper at her ear startled her into the present. "I see the doubt in your eyes, sweet Cailin." His chuckle brushed warm against her cheek. "The sooner you realize the truth…" His tongue flicked out to taste the tender flesh behind her ear. She shivered. "The sooner you will be free from the prison of Broderick's fantasies."

Cailin pushed away from Angus and rose from her chair, escaping on unsteady legs around the table, to stand at the center of the Grand Hall. She eyed the doorway, longing to run...but she couldn't. If she did, Angus would easily overpower her. The moment had come. She did not relish the thought of Angus touching her, but she would not have the opportunity to strike unless he had her in his grasp. Swallowing the lump in her throat, she stood her ground.

She hissed with fright as Angus appeared at her side. Cailin clutched her forearm, using the hardness of the blade in its sheath for comfort. Pivoting to stand behind her, Angus wrapped his arm around her waist like a steel band and nuzzled his mouth against her ear. "Why do you leave me so breathless, Cailin?" he panted. His hand reached up to cup her breast while his other hand grabbed a fistful of her skirts.

Where is the protection of this cursed amulet?

Drawing her trembling lip between her teeth, she blinked and a tear slip down her cheek. Her eyes darted about the room. As she feared, Angus's men closed in to watch the show. How would she attempt to slip her blade from the sheath up her sleeve before they were upon her? Like dark clouds moving in, dread settled in Cailin's heart. *Have I failed?*

Where is the so-called protection of this amulet?

James clutched the rail of the second level while Campbell wrapped his foul arms around Cailin. With the other dead guard at his feet, James clenched his jaw as his frightened betrothed search her surroundings for an escape. His own eyes darted about the room for anything that would give him the advantage. She was in the arms of the enemy and this man would use her life as leverage. James needed to get her out of his filthy grasp...but how?

Biting back his anger, he inwardly cursed as Campbell's men closed in. One of them shoved his hand into his breeches, fisting himself as he eyed Campbell's hands roaming over Cailin's body. *You will be among the first to die, my friend.*

James's lips curled into a snarl.

Malloren's warning echoed around the library as Broderick waited for her to continue her games. He cast wary eyes as she inched across the room.

"You must listen to and heed my words." She took a deep breath and exhaled as if to gain strength. "There are certain events that must take place in order for the prophecy to be fulfilled."

"I tire of this prophecy, Malloren," he growled. "And I tire of your delays. Make your point be known."

"I receive visions constantly." She continued her path around. "They guide me each step toward a fulfillment and discovery of the prophecy and its milestones." She stopped before the doorway where Broderick had first stepped into this den of mystery. "I saw a vision of your family in danger."

The blood drained from his face.

"This event was inevitable and no matter what your actions, Angus was still going to strike."

Panic seized Broderick's chest and he panted his anxiety.

"You will understand when this is over, but the key to fulfilling the prophecy..." Her eyes flooded with compassion. "Was to stop you from interfering with their capture."

He sprang toward the door, but slammed into an invisible wall with a force that knocked the breath from him and dashed him to the stone floor with a grunt. He quickly gained his senses and air filled his lungs again, but the impact had drained him. He forgot she had recited the incantation when they entered the room.

"You are saying he has them now!" he accused. "You lured me down here! Why?"

Malloren gazed down her nose at Broderick, tears spilling over her lashes. "I told you...so the prophecy would be fulfilled."

CHAPTER NINE

James struggled with the helplessness threatening to consume him and disciplined his mind to conjure a solution. Campbell groped his filthy hands over Cailin's body, his henchmen gathering ever closer and becoming more lewd with their gestures and comments.

Careful to keep his grumblings to himself, James diverted his eyes away from the source of his rage, hoping to quell his fury and find *something* to spark an idea.

A large, wooden chandelier hung over the center of the hall. It was suspended from the ceiling by a thick chain, rope and pulley which were probably used to lower the fixture to light the many candles. The thick rope was tied securely at a pair of iron hooks on the second level…just a few feet away from where he seethed. The weight of the chandelier was obviously greater than his own. He eyed the rope. He glanced at his knife, surely strong and sharp enough to make it through the taught fibers…and shook his head. A vivid and disturbing image of him cutting the cord and using the weight of the chandelier to propel him into the scene only ended in him slamming against the ceiling and falling to his death.

However, his mouth dropped open as an idea emerged from that fiasco.

He stayed crouched and inched his way toward the iron hooks securing the chandelier. He peered over the wall to be sure Cailin and that bastard were clear of the chandelier where they stood. They were, to his relief…just barely.

His Wootz blade at the ready, he pursed his lips and sucked air into the corner of his mouth, making a familiar chirping sound.

Cailin anguished over how she was going to get the blade from her sleeve. She had one chance and her only advantage was that Angus could not hear her thoughts. The *only* thing she gained from this amulet.

"The rapid beating of your heart betrays you," he grunted. He licked a wet trail from her shoulder to her ear where he, again, pierced her lobe and groaned. Cailin hissed and jerked her head to the side, away from his mouth. He chuckled.

A wonderful, familiar twittering echo against the walls of the Grand Hall.

James!

The pace of her heart quickened—if that were even possible—and she frantically searched the room.

Angus moaned. "Oh, Cailin, you must know the fearful beating of your heart only arouses me more." He ground his erection against her backside. "'Tis time I buried myself in your sweetness."

She gasped as James's precious face peered over the wall from the landing above. *He is going to get himself killed!*

"Broderick MacDougal!" Malloren shouted over his cries of outrage as he repeatedly slammed against the impenetrable barrier she had erected. "You cannot break through!"

Broderick repeated the incantations to remove the barrier, even knowing they wouldn't work, his voice growing hoarse. "If my family dies, I will personally enjoy tearing you apart!" Yet the more he threw his body against the unseen wall blocking him from her and his exit, the weaker he became and the more hope drained from his soul.

I knew this was a trap. God's blood, I knew it!

James pointed at Cailin and then at to the wall to her right. *What in…Oh! He wants me to get away from Angus. Easier said than done.* In spite of her reservations, she nodded and clung to the small hope that Angus was preoccupied enough with his "seduction" to allow her the few moments James needed to do whatever he planned to do. Then his head ducked behind the wall and her mouth dropped open. *But when do I—?*

James's hands reached up and sawed at the rope tied to the hooks on the wall. Her eyes followed the path of the rope to the ceiling…and the large wooden chandelier.

With a screech, Cailin vaulted herself from Angus's unsuspecting arms and dove for the shelter of the head table as the chandelier crashed down on a few of the men who stood groping themselves. The sickening cracks of their bones and odd twists of their necks had Cailin teetering between revulsion and elation.

James jumped from the landing, using a henchman to break his fall, and dispatched the man so swiftly, Cailin blinked in disbelief.

She had just enough time to slide the blade from her sleeve before a steel grip on her ankle snatched her from under the table. Angus yanked her to her feet and she swiped her small dagger at him when she spun around.

The edge sliced across his chest and he gasped, knocked the blade from her hands and stumbled backward. Her knife skidded across the stone floor. James appeared, shoved his stilettos into her hands and drew his sword, putting himself between her and Angus.

She brandished the daggers, ready for anything…except for the dumbfounded state in which Angus flailed around.

Blood coursed down his chest, staining his shirt now lying open from the slash she'd made. Confusion marred his brow as he studied himself. His cut did not heal. She had seen Broderick cut himself with a silver-gilded blade before, so even silver would not prevent the incision from healing, though a scar would remain. Something was different. Angus's breath labored and his steps and stance were lethargic. *Perhaps the amulet has worked after all!*

Anger replaced confusion and Angus drew his sword, lunging at James with a growl. The once-confused and gawking henchmen resumed their own advances and Cailin faced her foes with daggers twirling.

Still somewhat dazed and hazy from the laudanum, James was dismayed he could not remember the maneuvers Broderick or Cailin had taught him. And since he no longer had the element of a surprise attack on Campbell, James resolved to fight the immortal with the skills embedded into his spirit through *Fechtschulen*, routines he could execute in his sleep. Knowing Cailin's skill with her daggers, he wasn't particularly concerned for her wellbeing, but still kept her in his peripheral vision as he continued to spar with Campbell. However, the body count piling up at his feet at the hands of his betrothed had him paying less attention to her and focusing more of his efforts on the enemy before him.

Campbell lunged. James parried and swept his blade around for a swipe, cutting Campbell's shoulder. The Vamsyrian hissed and spun away, putting distance between them.

Advancing again, Campbell slashed at James's thrust, batting the blade away with his own. James dodged and twirled, arcing his sword and slicing Campbell's back. He growled and faced James, panting. This immortal was supposed to be a formidable opponent. Save for the skills he obviously possessed over the men he'd hired, Campbell did not seem any more challenging than a mortal. Though Campbell was a bit faster, he never came near the speed at James the way Broderick had. And more importantly...Campbell did not seem to anticipate any of his moves. The immortal's face reflected James's surprise and confusion.

Executing a specific routine designed to snatch a winning blow, James thrilled when his blade sank deep into the shoulder of Campbell's sword arm. Both staggered backward in a moment of stunned silence. Anger twisted Campbell's lips and he thrust forward, returning the blow…his sword sinking into James's sword shoulder in retaliation.

Gritting his teeth, James grunted from each blow Campbell dealt, driving him backward across the room. Weakened state or not, Campbell forced James to question his stability.

Sufficiently drained from his attempts, Broderick laid on the floor, panting.

"I am sorry, Broderick, but this was necessary." She stepped next to his prone figure and she was either a fool for trusting him to come so close and risk getting into his grasp, or she knew exactly how incapable he was of taking any action. He feared it was the latter.

"What is the difference…between the two methods?" He struggled to gain enough strength to speak or sit up.

"What two methods?"

He lay on his back, weak like a newborn, drawing deep breaths. "Other than…the burning versus shielding? To what purpose…would someone use…the cleansing?"

"The cleansing allows a subtle form of protection, something the blood of the cursed would not recognize because it slowly drains away the power of the immortal. The burning prevents the item of protection from being removed. Though a Vamsyrian may be able to feed from such a protected person, wearing the cleansed item would *taint* their blood, as it were, further weakening the immortal."

Broderick shuddered at the thought of how little that might protect Cailin after all and felt even worse about having left his family behind.

"However, now that you are silent enough to finally listen to me, I can tell you I have also foreseen that your family will not die."

In spite of the helplessness of his position and the lack of trust he had in her at this moment, relief still soothed his exhausted spirit.

"They will survive and your efforts to come here will not be in vain." Malloren strolled to the table littered with scrolls and seated herself. "If you ever hope to have the prophecy fulfilled, you must never kill Angus Campbell."

The laughter started low in his belly. He rolled onto his side and let it run its course, his guffaws echoing off the many books and shelves and reaching high above him. "I believe, woman," he said after his amusement subsided, "that I must be losing my wit. I thought you just told me I must never kill Angus Campbell."

"You're not in a frenzy, Vamsyrian."

He struggled to prop himself upon his elbow and glared at the prophetess. "I don't give a damn about some fucking prophecy!"

"You had *better* give a damn." She raised a critical eyebrow. "If either you or Angus Campbell dies, Davina's soul will be destroyed."

Six bodies littered the ground around them and Cailin near stumbled over one of them. Four men—including that damned Jasper—crawled away wounded or moaned in a corner of the room. Only Angus stood—sword poised before him—facing Cailin and James, who held his own sword aloft in spite of the wound in his shoulder.

His brow furrowed in confusion and his mouth twisted in frustration, Angus faltered on unsteady legs, blood streaming down his torso from the gaping wound at his shoulder and the slash Cailin had inflicted across his chest. The amulet must have made him weak, and gave them an advantage over the immortal.

Angus stepped out and jabbed his blade toward James, but Cailin successfully blocked him with her dagger in one hand and she thrust the amulet forward with the other, breaking the thin leather cord. Angus howled as Cailin pressed the relic to his chest and he stumbled back, recoiling. His gaze dropped to his new wound and then to the amulet she held toward him like a shield.

He squinted, studying the medallion. Recognition dawned on his face, and he stood bewildered for a moment—his eyes searching Cailin's for answers—before he dashed through the door, escaping the Great Hall with Jasper limping behind him.

"I am none too pleased at that strange departure," James murmured.

"Agreed." Turning to face him, Cailin pulled the collar of his shirt back from his wound.

"Later, Cailin," he scolded and waved her hands away. "We cannot bide while he may be fetching reinforcements. Come."

She nodded, embarrassed she didn't think of that danger herself. Following close, she kept a watchful eye behind them as they navigated their path through the ruins and out onto the glen leading to the bordering trees.

"There, laddie," James cooed to his horse as he approached and untied the reins from a low-hanging branch. Cailin hopped up into the saddle at his encouragement and James mounted behind her, kicking the gelding into a fast trot. "Not sure how far we can get with him carrying two riders, but I hope 'tis far enough for us to find a place to rest. This poor animal needs it."

"As do you," she reminded him. "Are you still bleeding?" She tried to turn and peer at his wound over her shoulder only to have James set her to rights before him.

"'Tis fine I am," he growled. "I shall tend to it later."

Cailin huffed and bit back the tears needling her eyes.

It seemed an hour or more of riding passed before James slowed enough for them to circle about and face the direction from which they retreated. "I see no signs of anyone pursuing us," he said after a long pause, his voice gravelly.

He reined the horse back down the path they headed. Exhaustion had caught up with Cailin and her body ached from the last two days of her ordeal. She couldn't image what James must be suffering after being stabbed. Shifting in the saddle behind her, he hissed and leaned back. His arms coming around her, he uncorked a small bottle, took a swig and replaced the cork.

"What is that?"

"'Tis an elixir called laudanum. For pain." After a moment or two of silence, he said in a whisper, "I grabbed it from my father's body."

Cailin pulled James's arm tighter around her waist. "Oh, James, I'm so very sorry."

He grunted, but said no more on the matter.

The orange glow of torches dotted the horizon, giving evidence to some establishment in the distance. Eventually, they rode into a small village. "Thank our Lord, they have an inn." Cailin breathed a sigh of relief.

"Aye." James sagged against her back and his arms briefly squeezed her midsection. "Let us make haste." He steered the gelding toward the shadows, lowered Cailin to the ground then dismounted himself. Grabbing a cloak from the back of his saddle, he donned the garment with a grimace and made an effort to hide the blood on his shirt. "I want to avoid any chance they may turn us away, thinking we bring trouble."

She nodded.

After unloading his saddlebags from the horse, James handed over his gelding to the groomsman at the stable and ushered Cailin into the inn. At this late hour, she hadn't expected so many people to be seated at the tables and standing around the lamp-lit room of the public area.

Taking her by the hand, James led her to the side serving counter. "Do you have a room available?"

A tall lanky man with a shining bald head and bulbous red nose eyed them both and pursed his lips in disapproval. "Who be askin'?"

"My wife and I have been on a long journey and we need a place to rest for the night."

Cailin clamped her lips closed at his lie and the flutter of excitement tickling her belly…or was that her stomach growling over the tantalizing aromas wafting out from the kitchen behind the innkeeper?

"Aye, I have a room for ye." The innkeeper's apprehensions seemed to fade only by a margin at hearing they were "married", but he still eyed them with subtle suspicion. "Come with me." He nodded to the stout woman behind the counter and she dipped her chin in return.

The gangly innkeeper wiped his hands on his smock as he led them to the back of the noisy room, up the stairs and down the narrow hallway to the last room on the right. "'Tis grand enough for the king," he snickered as he threw open the door and gestured with an open palm to enter.

The accommodations were sparse and small, but comfortable enough for the two of them.

"Would you bring up a tub and a few buckets of hot water?" James asked and handed him a note.

The man's protests died upon his lips as he studied the currency. "Aye! I shall have them brought up straight away, sir. And for this price, ye shall have a nice hot meal for ye and yer lovely wife. Fresh baked bread, too."

"Thank you." James closed the door behind the innkeeper and faced the window. "Am I right in thinking we are fairly safe from Angus once the day is upon us?"

She glanced toward the darkness outside. "Aye. If his men are following us, though, I am not sure—"

"Oh, I have no doubt we can handle them." He shuffled to the box bed and sat upon the mattress, the leather supports groaning from his weight. He sighed.

A knock sounded at the door. Cailin scampered to answer it and the stout woman, whom the innkeeper had nodded to earlier, stood in the hall with a tray of two generously filled bowls of stew, a half-loaf of bread and a wide grin upon her face. "My husband tells me you two are famished!"

"You have married a very attentive man, mistress," Cailin confirmed, returning the grin. "Please, come in."

The innkeeper's wife chuckled a merry sound and set the tray upon the small, square table before the hearth. A wee lass resembling the woman followed behind with an earthen pitcher and two mugs in her arms. She smiled her greeting through dirty cheeks framed with blonde braids that matched her mother's.

"Thank you, Tenny," the woman said, taking the load from the girl. "Now run along."

"Aye, mum." She nodded and ran from the room.

"Och! Dinna run like that, Tenny! Ye nearly knocked me down the stairs!" The innkeeper carried the promised tub and some drying cloths. Two young men followed behind, each carrying a pair of buckets.

Cailin stepped back in the suddenly crowded room and stood beside James, who observed their duties with a smirk on his handsome face.

"Careful now, lads," the innkeeper instructed as the boys poured the steaming water into the tub. One by one, they all left the room with a smile and a nod.

Cailin closed the door behind them. "Finally, some peace."

At last James took off his cloak, grunting as he did so. Cailin rushed to his side and tried to help him remove the garment.

"I can do this myself," he growled.

"'Tis obvious you are in pain. If you will only—"

"I said I can take care of myself," he snapped.

She struggled to keep her tears at bay. He was furious with her. She knew it. Even though necessity had forced him to hand the daggers to her himself, he must be angry she was—again—the exact opposite of what he wanted. Turning away because she could not stand to watch him grimace through his self-administrations, she searched the room for something to do. What *could* she do?

The drying cloths were neatly stacked on the stool by the tub. The food sat waiting for them to eat. She could pour the beverage! And she did, filling the mugs. Now what?

"Oh, if you must have something with which to occupy yourself," James groaned, "you can get the cloths I brought for wounds. They're in my saddlebags."

Embarrassed her restless nature was so obvious, she cast her eyes down and pulled the saddlebags to the bed. Kneeling, she grabbed the said bandages. "Is this a salve?" She held up the jar she found.

He nodded.

She suppressed a grin when she saw he had also packed a spare change of clothes for her, including a sensible pair of slippers and a chemise. His groan drew her attention once more and she frowned. When she attempted to pull his bloodied shirt back to assess the wound, he shrugged off her attention.

Cailin stood and punched her fists onto her hips. "And just why did you tell them we were married if you did not want my help?"

"What?" He stared at her as if she'd sprouted a tail.

"I assume you told them I was your wife so we could be roomed together. Surely you were seeking some assistance."

"I just trekked halfway across Scotland to rescue you from that monster. If you think I'm going to let you out of my sight for the sake of reputation, 'tis daft you are."

"'Tis daft *you* are if you think I'm going to stand by and watch you tend to your own wounds." Cailin ignored his scowl and scuffled about the room, using the hot water to clean the crusted blood from his skin. Half-covered, he created a tempting vision that forced her to divert her attention away many times so he would not catch her ogling him.

His gentle hand circled her wrist and their eyes met. "If you're going to tend to my wounds, it would be wise to watch what you're doing." His roguish smile made her heart flutter.

She nodded and continued, but gasped when she uncovered his left shoulder, which was also bandaged. "James!" She jumped to her feet. "You have *two* wounds? But why didn't you tell me you–"

"Cailin." He glared a warning.

With a huff, she grumbled and snatched fresh bandages. After changing the soiled dressings from his shoulder and cleaning the last of his wounds, she fetched a clean shirt from his saddlebags. James mumbled his thanks, donned the garment and shuffled to the door.

"Where are you going?"

"To hire a courier." He stepped into the hall. "I have to send a message to your family to let them know you're safe." His sea-green eyes, worn and half-lidded, searched her face. A tired grin turned up one corner of his mouth before he closed the door.

Broderick's head whirled with exhaustion, fury and the jumble of words Malloren had thrown at him. "Woman, none of this makes any sense to me so you had better start over and leave out the useless details."

Malloren breathed a heavy sigh and seated herself at the scroll table again. "The purpose of Davina's soul is to complete the final milestone of the prophecy."

"Now stop right there. What in Hades does that mean?"

She closed her eyes as if to brace herself for a blow. "The complete answer is unclear."

"Sorceress, I vow—"

"Forgive me, but I am not given all the facts!" she shouted over his words. "All I know is Davina's soul is the key to the end of this conflict between you and Angus Campbell, and thereby the key to the prophecy. If either of you dies before the final milestone can be completed, her soul will cease to exist because your conflict will no longer be giving her soul purpose."

"What does God want with us?" He gathered enough strength to at last rise from the floor and lean on the table, glaring at her. "He plays with all our lives with no regard for our hearts. Is he not supposed to be a god of love?" He snorted in disgust.

"I know none of this is pleasant to hear—"

"An understatement, witch."

She scowled in disapproval. "If you had been home when Angus abducted Cailin, you would have dueled with Angus and won...thereby destroying Davina's soul."

"Cailin? I thought you said he seized my *family*. Did he not also take Davina?"

She shook her head. "I received a vision while we were conversing. James was a good choice as her husband. She is now safe with him."

Broderick flopped into the chair across from Malloren. "Thank G—" He stopped himself. *God has nothing to do with her safety.* He glared at the ceiling, imagining the clouds through the layers of stone and earth. *I am not finished with you yet.* "Both Davina and Cailin are safe, say you?"

Malloren nodded.

He rested a moment, his head in his hands, grateful his loved ones were out of danger. Raising his head, he asked, "What happens if Davina dies before the final milestone is complete?" Broderick waited, his breath stuck in his chest.

"I honestly don't know. There is nothing I have read or visions I have seen that indicate disaster."

"How is that possible if she is the final milestone?"

She sighed and slouched in defeat. "I told you, I don't know."

They both brewed in silence before he rose. "I must leave to feed and regain my strength."

She nodded and recited the incantation to bring down the wall. The oppressive atmosphere lifted. "I believe you know the way out." She rose from the chair and padded up the stairs to the door opposite the one Broderick would exit. "You should stay here one more day. Sunrise is almost upon us. You will have difficulty finding shelter elsewhere." She pivoted on her heel and disappeared through the doorway.

Broderick shook his head and clenched his jaw as he glared heavenward. "I swear to you, we are not yet finished."

CHAPTER TEN

Using the water, salve and cloths, Cailin tended to her own minor cuts and abrasions, most of them on her arms…grumbling throughout her task over her insufferable betrothed. She cleaned up after herself, set the tiny room to rights as much as possible and waited by the hearth for James to return. The bowl of stew for James grew cold, so she dumped the contents into the cast-iron pot hanging by the fire and swung it near enough to the flames to keep it warm without risking it burning. She rested her chin in her palm, her fingers tapping her cheek.

Eyeing the warm water and cloths, she considered taking a bath. She glanced at the door, then at the tub and back to the door. Throwing her chin forward in defiance, she disrobed with shaking fingers. *If he discovers me nude while I cleanse…well, it would serve him right for being gone so long.* Her sex clenched at the thought. She raised her foot to step into the hot water and stopped, glancing over her shoulder at the entrance again. Exasperated with her cowardice, she stomped to the door and slammed the bolt in place. With a huff of defiance, she returned and stepped into the basin, wincing at the heat against her tender feet. The soothing water eased some of the tension from her body and she sighed.

A soap cake lay on the drying cloths. Taking advantage of this opportunity, she washed the grime and uneasiness from her weary form. She would reapply the salve when finished. Before leaving the tub, she removed the ribbon from her hair and submerged her head and long auburn locks into the water. Rising to her feet, she wrung her tresses, the patter of water droplets mixing with the crackling of the fire.

The door burst open and James stood with his fists clenched at his sides, his legs in a wide, low stance, ready to do battle. The snarl on his face melted into astonishment when his eyes settled on Cailin...and traveled down her naked, wet body. She snatched the cloths on the stool, attempting to cover herself.

James gawked a long moment before he spoke. "God's blood, Mouse! What are you doing?"

He dashed inside the room and closed the door, turning his back to her. A furious knocking accompanied by protests sounded from the hall. James reached into the sporran at his waist, cracked the door and shoved his hand through the entry. "My apologies, master innkeeper. This should cover the damages. All is well."

He slammed the door and shoved a chair in front of it, apparently using that in place of the bolt he'd just dislodged with his dramatic entrance.

"What are *you* doing?" Cailin demanded, scampering to the saddlebags to get to her fresh chemise.

Still facing away from her, he paced in front of the hearth. "I knocked but you didn't answer. I thought...well, I thought someone had..." He growled. "Why did you lock the door?"

"Obviously, so I could bathe in privacy!" She fumbled with her undergarment and managed to pull it over her damp skin, grumbling and cursing at the uncooperative material. Shoving her feet into her slippers, she began plaiting her wet hair and stomped to the door, her gown tucked under her arm.

James grabbed her shoulders and faced her. "Where are you going?"

"I need a few moments to myself. I shall speak with the innkeeper's wife and make amends." She tried to shove him away from her, but he held tight.

"Oh, no you don't! How do you expect us to resolve our differences if you keep running each time we quarrel?"

Cailin gasped and struggled to break free. "I'm not running! I-I'm trying to contain my temper, which I cannot seem to do around you!" She still could not wrest herself from his grip.

"Control your—" He exhaled in exasperation. "Why are you trying to control it? I want it! 'Tis better than what you *have* been doing. What are you afraid of?"

She ceased struggling and barked in his face. "You and your mockery of who I am! Just let us go back and end this farce of a betrothal so you can be free to find the woman you want!"

"And just what kind of woman is that?"

"You stated it plainly when I told you how much I had changed!"

There was that expression again, as if she'd grown an additional appendage. "Stated *what* plainly?"

"You said I wasn't what you were expecting."

"That is an understatement, my lady!"

Cailin opened her mouth to gloat, but James jumped on her words.

"I also said you're not what you pretend to be. You're atrocious at embroidery, which you claim to do often, and you try to hide the fact that you fight better than most men I know!"

"Precisely! What kind of man desires such a woman as that?"

James tipped his head back, hearty laughter pouring from his mouth.

The rush of shame and humiliation to her face blurred her vision and she struggled to see through the onslaught of tears. *How could he be so openly cruel?* Sobs choked her and she whirled to struggle with the chair blocking her escape.

James seized her by the arms, dragged her across the room and threw her to the bed. Before she could rise and make a dash for the door, his body covered hers. Her arms flailed and struck his shoulder, causing him to snatch her hands above her head as he buried his face in the mattress to stifle a roar of pain.

Through labored breaths, he managed to still her legs with his own, imprison her wrists with one hand and grab her face with the other, forcing her to face him. "Why are you pushing me away?"

"Release me, James! I cannot bear this empty promise of a union with you. We will go back to Leith and finally settle the matter and you can be done with me."

"What have I done to make you think this, Mouse?" Accusations gone from his voice, James's eyes implored Cailin to near tears. "Was there something I said to hurt you in one of my letters?

Whatever it is, tell me. I will move the earth to prove my lo—"

"Nay, James!" Cailin squeezed her eyes shut. "'Tis nothing you did. I...just...please let me go." Sobbing, she fought the memories clanging against her resolve.

The tender, seeking lips of her betrothed invaded her nightmarish thoughts. Though she held firm against him, he teased and caressed, his tongue traced her mouth and lapped away her tears...and his voice entranced and sapped the fight from her bones.

"Shhh, Mouse." He suckled her bottom lip with warmth. "Relax, m'dove." He nibbled her chin. "Look at me, Mouse."

She kept her eyes shut against his sweet words and could bare his kindness no more. Trying to dislodge his hold on her, she wriggled beneath him, sorrow almost choking her with sobs.

"Cailin." James held tight but she still fought him. *"Cailin!"*

"Let me go," she ground out through clenched teeth.

"Not until you tell me what's warring inside your heart."

He wouldn't release her. She was a fool to think she could bury the truth in the darkness from him, from herself. She blinked through her tears and gazed at the compassion in his sparkling jade eyes.

The kindness would turn to cold stone once he knew, but where could she hide? The words rushed out in a whisper. "I killed a man, James."

He gasped. Just a small intake of breath, but enough to suck the life from her soul. *I've lost him.*

She renewed her struggles but continued to gain no purchase against him.

James pressed his palms firmly to her cheeks. "You listen to me, Cailin MacDougal."

She calmed and braced herself for his chastisement. But he did not hold judgment or conviction in his eyes. *How can this be?* They radiated warmth, understanding and, sweet lord in heaven, unconditional love. His finger traced her mouth, open with awe. "The fact that you are burdened with such guilt and remorse proves to me you are not the vicious woman you must think yourself to be."

"Nay, you don't understand. I took this man's life without even blinking."

"How is that possible?" Was that doubt in his eyes? Did he think she was lying?

She trembled at the memories of her dagger sinking into the man's chest. Echoes from the past. She struggled to banish the sensation of his warm blood flowing over her hand and spurting against her face, the coppery taste of his life in her mouth even now.

She swallowed over the lump in her throat. "It happened so quickly." She bit her lip and diverted her attention to James's shoulder, focusing on the blood-stained bandages, anything but his face. "Only after he lay slumped on the ground before me, did I realize how quickly everything transpired. He grabbed me from behind. Like the wind, I slipped my daggers from their sheaths as I spun around. One blade…sliced his throat. The other buried in his chest." She fought the sobs so she could finish. "His hand clutched my breast, ripping my gown as he fell to the ground." A half-laugh, half-moan warbled from her mouth and she whispered, "Da wrapped me in his arms and ran." She gathered the courage to endure his judgment. *Deep breath.*

He searched her face with pinched brows and a glassy gaze.

"Why do you look at me so?"

"Because I know your pain, Mouse." He inhaled slowly and pressed his lips to her temple. "This is a cruel world and I…also had my hand forced in self-defense."

"See, you *don't* understand. I am a mindless killer. All the man had to do was reach for me and—"

"How did you learn to fight with blades?"

"My father, but you can't blame him. I insisted he teach me."

"But why?"

He asked for answers he already knew, so Cailin pondered his questions. "Be…because of Angus. Because I felt so helpless when he had kidnapped my mother and I."

James frowned. "Can you not grasp the truth in this? The threat on your family forced your hand. I know what it's like to feel defenseless. But I also know the courage a blade seated in your palm can give, and I don't blame you one bit for wanting that."

She opened her mouth to protest, but he placed a finger on her lips.

"When one is instructed the way I know your father has trained you, thinking is not an option. Life is decided in a matter of seconds and I, for one, am glad it was you who prevailed." He brushed a tear from her cheek with his thumb. "Do you really want to know what kind of man desires a woman such as you?" The corner of his mouth turned up in the wolfish grin that always set her insides to quivering. "I am. I am exactly the kind of man who *needs* a woman such as you."

"But—"

"You cannot embroider to save your life. I can tell you're still learning your way around managing a household. You have a temper as fiery as the hair upon that beautiful head and a tongue as sharp as your daggers…and I would not have you any…other…way."

"But—"

His mouth descended and claimed hers with sensual delights once again until she trembled in his arms. "Silence, woman, and make love to me."

He nibbled a path to her chin then regarded her with hooded eyes as his hand hiked the hem of her chemise. The calloused pads of his fingers contrasted against her tender skin and she shivered when he caressed her inner thigh. "Let me touch you, Cailin." His words feathered against her ear. "Let me inside you." His finger flicked the sensitive bud hidden in the curls between her thighs and she gasped. "Let me show you how you are the only woman I will ever love."

She surrendered with a whimper and claimed his mouth with her own, her tongue sweeping in to taste him. James groaned, fueling their urgency to remove the barrier of their clothes. Within dizzying moments, Cailin lay naked on the bed before him, his gaze hungry and raking her body as he stood before her.

"My God, you are so beautiful."

She dropped her eyes to his shaft, jutting proud and challenging. There it was. All her curiosity over what the male member actually looked like, what James would look like, were satisfied in a single glance. Yet her curiosity over this mysterious organ fueled new questions.

Sitting forward, she diverted her gaze to his face as she licked lips suddenly gone dry. James gasped and his hand grasped his cock. The heat rushing to her sex elicited a moan from her throat and she marveled as a clear drop wept from the crown of his shaft. ·

She reached out and caught the warm fluid with her fingertip, then touched it to her tongue.

"Cailin!" She hardly had time to explore the salty taste as he descended swiftly upon her and buried his head in her neck, grunting. He nestled his cock along the slick folds between her thighs…not penetrating, but sliding the length of him against her. He pumped his hips, sending delicious shivers of pleasure through her legs, her breath rapid pants. The tip of his cock stroked farther back…back to caress and tease her anus with each thrust. She shuddered with delight and surprise.

His pace slowed and she mewed in protest as he pulled away and placed a fingertip to her lips. "This will hurt at first, but—"

"Silence, you rogue, and make love to me!" She thrust her hips forward, aching to feel those scrumptious sensations again.

A deep rumble of laughter undulated through James, vibrating against Cailin's breasts and she arched against him. His laughter transformed into a moan and he bent his head to draw her nipple into his mouth, teasing the peak with his teeth. "James! Please!"

"Anxious for me to fill you, my little Mouse?" His deep voice hummed across her tingling skin.

"Aye!"

Cailin caught her breath as the tip of his cock hovered against her maidenhead. She locked her gaze with his and he nodded. This would consummate their betrothal. They would be as good as married.

She nodded in response.

He thrust forward and she grunted, the pain swift and fading as he pumped against her. James moaned and shackled her wrists above her head, rocking in and out. "Uhhh, Cailin!" His breath dampened her cheek. "God, I could stay buried inside you forever." His hands smoothed down her body to cup her bottom and angle her entrance upward to meet each thrust.

She had heard, though never imagined…how could anyone describe…her mind swirled with the pleasure coursing through her body, the slickness of his wonderful shaft stroking the center of her universe, and she gasped at the pressure building inside, climbing, rising… "Oh…God…James…I…" Cailin tossed her head to the side and clutched his back, crying out as he continued to drive her over a crescendo of bliss.

James threw his head back and thundered his release, his thrusts slowing as his thighs trembled. Cailin wrapped her legs around his waist and held tight. Their labored breaths mingled with their sated kisses and moans of endearment. Collapsing to the bed, James rolled onto his back, panting.

"I can now see why you have been so anxious to wed me," she cooed, snuggling up against his side and twirling her fingertip around his puckered nipple.

"Och, woman!" He stayed her hand. "Continue your toying and I will take you again."

Cailin giggled and leaned forward, lapping her tongue against the pink pebble she just fondled. James pulled her atop his body to straddle his hips, his knees bending to cradle her back comfortably against his thighs. Her mouth opened in surprise. "You cannot take me thus…can you?"

That wicked laughter rumbled in his chest and his wolfish grin set her heart to fluttering. "Oh, my sweet Mouse…there are *many* ways I may take you."

Her brows shot up at the possibilities. "Truly? What other ways?"

His hand snaked between her legs, his fingers caressed her sex. "Oohhh, sweet heavens!" Cailin bucked her hips against the glorious sensations as she held tight to her thighs.

He groaned. His fingers rubbed against that life-centering bud, teasing, stroking, smoothing through her wet cleft, touching farther back against that wicked little hole the crown of his cock had brushed against earlier when his shaft slid between her legs. James slowed his fingers and she opened her eyes and frowned. "Why did you stop?"

His eyebrows waggled and a devilish smile graced his full lips. He reached to the bedside table and grabbed the oil lamp. Puffing out the flame, he lifted the top and wick and sniffed. "Ahhh…olive oil." He coated his fingertips with oil and seemed to test the texture by rubbing it around his finger pads. Nodding, he replaced the lamp then reached around Cailin. His oiled fingers fondled the tight hole of her anus and she gasped.

"How naught—" But her protests died in her moans of approval when his other hand continued to tickled her pleasure bud. Both hands, slick and glorious, stroked between her legs, exploring her sex and a place she had never dreamed to go.

"Lean forward for me," his husky voice coaxed.

Hands on his rock-hard chest, she did as he bade and the motion pushed her bud between his fingers. Cailin jerked against his hand, grunting as both sides of her nub received attention. She near-squealed when the tip of his finger behind her penetrated her anus and she ceased rocking. "James!"

"Easy, dove," he soothed, a mischievous grin playing upon his mouth. "I'll go no farther." He pulled his finger out…then slid back in.

"Ooohh…oh, James…"

Out…then in. His other fingers continued to stroke her quim in the same, lethargic rhythm.

"Just tell me if you wish me to stop," he whispered.

"If you stop now," she panted, "I shall never speak to you again."

James's delicious rumble of laughter sent more heat to her sex. The slow movement was no longer enough. Cailin rocked faster and James matched her pace. He removed his hand from her bud and, before she could complain, he replaced it with the side of his shaft. His hand still gripped her from behind, his one finger still penetrating her as she slid against his thick rod laying along his belly. With a swift wave of sweet ecstasy, Cailin shuddered and cried out her release, her eyes wide with amazement as the most incredulous pleasure rushed through her limbs.

"Sweet heavens!" She gulped for air. "That was wondrous." She collapsed to his chest.

"Oh, 'tis far from finished with you I am, woman." James lifted her from his lap just enough to grab his cock and position it upright before he thrust his hips and buried himself to the hilt inside her. With the encouragement of his hands on her arse, Cailin bounced atop James, bracing her hands on his chest. How could it be possible that this position was even more divine than the other?

Cailin diverted her eyes from the ceiling back to James's face and she bit her bottom lip to stay the laughter that threatened to bubble forth. Through the marvelous grinding, she managed to say, "Why James, 'tis though you have stolen the king's jewels. What is that mischief in your eyes?"

Her betrothed—nay, now he would be husband—eased his cadence and reached up to caress the bottom swell of her breasts. Eyes feasting upon her flesh, he said, "I have stolen away with a jewel more prized than any king's ransom. Cailin Mac—Cailin *Knightly*, a woman whose passion meets that of my own, whose skill with a blade makes me want to impale her." He thrust upward and she moaned. With a gentle hand to the nape of her neck, he pulled her down for a tender kiss. He cupped her face with his palms. "And a woman whom I can count as my dearest friend. You have not changed much these years, Mouse…except to become more beautiful and entrancing. You have always been the adventuresome, practical and passionate person who is my perfect mate."

Cailin's smile melted into a frown. "But how freely can we enjoy our life together if it is haunted by the threat of Angus Campbell?"

"We will overcome that threat," he promised. "For now, let us not spoil this time together." James moved his hips under her, successfully wrangling her thoughts back to their lovemaking, and they rode to another climax in each other arms before they lay entangled and satiated and drifted off to sleep.

Angus scowled in the darkness. His body trembled with weakness. His mind swirled with confusion and anger. What had transpired while in possession of that wretched girl?

This sickness upon him was much like the weakness that lorded over his body for three years after Broderick had driven Davina's silver-decorated blade into his heart. The silver had poisoned him and his recovery was more extensive than he had ever imagined possible. Three years...before he returned to being somewhat normal again. Three years of living like an animal, feeding off the weak and frail like an outcast wolf waiting for scraps, before he was strong enough to pursue any real kind of hunt. Three years to seethe over the lies Broderick MacDougal either believed himself or was foolish enough to think Angus would believe.

Fingering the welted burn on his chest where Cailin had touched the medallion to his skin, he snarled. The crude symbols from the piece, he was sure, would mark his skin permanently. "The *Tzava Ha'or*," he growled. Why was the Army of Light protecting them? How did Broderick obtain this, being a Vamsyrian?

"Lord Campbell?" Jasper's raspy voice intruded upon Angus's thoughts. But the smell of blood drifted through the cracks of the dark, chamber door and gave Angus strength.

He grinned. Jasper and three of his henchmen were all Cailin and James had left behind. All four of them were wounded. Even in his weakness, Angus had overpowered and shoved them into the adjoining chamber, locking them inside before the lethargy of his daytime slumber rendered him unconscious.

He rose on shaky knees, inhaled deeply to savor the aroma of their fear and stalked to the door. Swinging it open, Angus surveyed the four men lying about the room, propped against the walls, their eyes searching the blackness through which only Angus could see. The thick scent of their blood swept over him like a determined lover, arousing his urgency. By their gasps, Angus knew the silver glow in his eyes had flared to life, a sign of the *Hunger*.

"Good morrow, Jasper." The grave tone of his voice pleased him.

Jasper squeaked some unintelligible word, cleared his throat and tried again. "Ye said ye wanted to wait until the next day to ask yer questions. We be ready to aid ye, m'lord."

"And that you will, Jasper." Angus filled the doorway…their only escape. Narrowing his eyes at them, he struggled to discern their thoughts. He sensed their fear, but the words of their minds drifted incoherently in and out of reach, like a shout lost on the wind, a figure fading intermittently through fog. "Tell me, Jasper, what has transpired as of late that you have kept from me?"

"T-transpired, m'lord?" His voice trembled.

"Aye." Angus crossed his arms. "The thought patterns I hear from you and your men…" A spike in Jasper's fear stabbed at the *Hunger* and Angus smiled. "They are very much like the thought patterns I heard from the young James Knightly." He knelt before Jasper and grabbed his shirt when the wretch tried to slink away. "I can smell your fear, Jasper. Conspiring with the enemy?"

Jasper's jaw bobbed up and down and he stammered, "N-nay, m-m'lord! I-I—"

Dragging him to the corner by his shirt, Angus tossed Jasper aside and pounced on the next man within reach. Fingers buried in his greasy hair, he yanked the man's head to the side and sank his fangs into this throat.

Blessed euphoria flooded his body and Angus surrendered to the sweet song of the man's dying soul. Though he gained knowledge of this man's life through his blood, as with any other feeding, this exchange was a silent one. No rambling thoughts. No cacophony of words. Just the absorption of knowledge from his miserable life of thieving and opportunistic choices. *Ohhh*…and as this creature's body sagged in his arms, the life fading away, the euphoria *continued.*

Angus gasped as the man dropped to the floor like a sack of grain, forgotten and inconsequential compared to the rapture coursing through his veins. *What is this heaven?*

The pleasure of feeding normally ended—and rather abruptly—when he released his victims. This bliss continued to glide through his limbs, building, and merrily settled into his groin. Panting, Angus stepped forward and slapped his palms to the stone wall to steady himself as an unaided and ravishing climax surged through his shaft. His ballocks jerked into his body and he roared his release. Gasping for air, he shook his head to clear the haze of the lingering thrill.

"Huz-*zah*!" Snapping his head toward Jasper, he said, "What *is* this laudanum?"

Jasper swallowed. "B-beg yer pardon, m'lord?"

The other two men had made for the exit while Angus fed. One had succeeded in slinking into the hall, the other halfway over the threshold. "Oh nay, my little delicacies!"

With strength renewed by the fresh blood and this miracle drug, Angus snatched both men back from their retreat and tossed them into the corners of the room, slamming the door and bolting it.

He turned to Jasper once more and pointed to the body. "The experiences of that man, as you know, told me you gave these men something called laudanum to ease their pain." He stalked forward and his henchman scrambled away on the floor. Angus backed him against the wall. Nose to nose, Angus chuckled at Jasper. "He did not know what it was made of, but true enough…the elixir eased his pain and gave him quite a sensation in the process."

Jasper nodded in the dark. "Aye, m-m'lord. 'Tis something Alistair brought back from his journey to Germania when he sought after his son." He panted for a moment before saying with a calmer voice, "Did ye gain some pleasure from the tonic in his blood, m'lord?"

Angus threw his head back and laughed. "Pleasure, my dear wretch, is *exactly* what I gained." He turned to the man groaning across the room and, before the pitiful sod could scuffle away, Angus plucked him from the floor and fed.

Another rippling and gratifying climax surged through his body. *'Tis well and good Vamsyrians no longer spill seed. My breeches would be filled!*

The third man lay curled into a ball, crying and pleading for his life…petitions which fell upon deaf ears. Angus gloried in the third climax, his roar of approval filling the chamber. "Jasper, you must tell me about this wonderful elixir!"

The fear ebbed from Jasper, his breathing and voice more stable. "Well, yer lordship, I-I know not how it is made. Alistair had a source in Germania and—"

"Come now, Jasper." Angus crossed his arms and stood before his now-shrinking servant. "Have you not yet learned I know when you are lying?"

"Nay, please, m'lord," Jasper whimpered. "I—"

Angus pulled Jasper to his feet and sank his fangs into his throat, drinking deep, and a fourth climax rolled through his body. Angus stood trembling as the sensations ebbed. He absorbed and examined the full truth—the recipe for the elixir and how Jasper had learned one side-effect of the tonic. It clouded musings so Vamsyrians were unable to clearly hear the thoughts of mortals.

"So, Alistair learned of this through his brief exchanges with Broderick," Angus said to Jasper's crumpled form, dying at his feet. "And you, my friend, decided to try it out on me to gain an advantage." He smiled as a death rattle thrummed from Jaspers mouth. "Thank you for the thrilling experience and the knowledge of such a treat."

Angus stalked from the room, through the ruins and out the front gate. The wind teased his cheeks as he dashed through the trees and toward his destination. Though strengthened by the blood and exhilaration of the feedings, he had not yet recovered his full strength. This meant he would not reach Edinburgh before dawn...but he may have a chance to catch up to James and Cailin before *they* reached the city.

James obviously obtained the laudanum from Alistair in spite of being on ill-terms with his father. This must have been how James was able to keep his thoughts clouded and why I could not anticipate his battle moves.

"Hrmmm...very clever, young Knightly." He smiled as he glanced at the rising moon and increased his pace. "Let us see how clever you feel when I drain the life from *your* body and revel in another climax over your death."

The moon, almost finishing its arc for the night, beckoned Broderick to make haste. Edinburgh— and home—were too close for him to stop now. He pressed on as fast as his limbs allowed.

Though the night before Malloren Rune had encouraged him to stay another day, Broderick rushed to cover as much ground as possible in the few short hours remaining in the evening. The words of the prophetess had attested her gift in most everything she had predicted, and yet he still did not trust her completely. He would not waste another moment away from his family in spite of her warning. He had also thought with his heart instead of his head and near regretted his decision, as finding a suitable shelter before dawn had almost been his undoing…just as she had said. Fortunately, he discovered an abandoned farmhouse with a root cellar that needed little preparation. He grudgingly offered thanks toward heaven as he lost consciousness. Due to his furious pace, the need to be home driving him ever onward and his familiarity with the route, the return trip proved shorter than his initial journey toward Stonehenge.

Yet, however short the journey home, he still had many hours to ponder these last few days. And a single point of contention nagged at his conscience. Distracted with the safety of his family and rushing home, he had never followed up on Cordelia's part in this puppet show controlled by God. What was her connection with Malloren Rune? And what was Malloren's role other than assembling the prophecy? He grumbled at how she had manipulated the amulet into his possession. Malloren knew he would not take such a piece from a stranger. Passed between too many hands, the relic's source would be unknown to him. Amice was the perfect messenger, for he did not even question the necklace's origin since it came from her. "What other machinations have you sorceress?" he murmured under his breath. "Where do they end?"

MacDougal Castle loomed in the distance on the edge of the horizon and remained the single focus of his spirit as he crossed the rocky terrain. As he neared, the Gypsy camp came into view. It seemed serene with little activity, nestled beside the road at the base of the hill on which perched his home…though the smell of campfires seemed unusually strong. Pounding down the darkened path, past the surrounding forest and up the road to the fortress, Broderick finally slowed his pace as he crossed the bridge and approached the gate. He slammed his fist into the thick oak monstrosity. "I bid entrance into my home!" he bellowed.

"Lord MacDougal has returned!" a voice shouted from atop the high curtain wall. "Open the gate!"

Panting, Broderick waited for the long bolt to slide back and the gates to ease open on their massive hinges. With just enough breadth between the two doors, he dashed through and darted for the entrance. He'd barely pushed open the door and stepped into the front hall when Davina padded down the stairs. Her hair unbound and hanging to her waist, her thin night shift whispering around her like a spirit, Broderick almost couldn't believe the vision before him. She picked up her hem and sprinted into his embrace, throwing her eager arms around him. Her body trembled as she sobbed against his neck. A mixture of fear, sadness and relief swarmed around them like a whirlwind.

"I know, Blossom," he comforted. "I know Cailin was taken. I also know she is safe with James."

She pulled back and her teary eyes, filled with confusion, searched his face. "But how? How did you—"

He covered her mouth with a hungry kiss and lifted her from the ground as he crushed her to his body. *I am cursed, for I can never get enough of this woman and I know I shall surely perish without her.* Only after the fever of their lips died to languorous caresses did he force himself to set her down. "We've much to discuss. Pray tell me exactly what's transpired since I left. I only know what I just told you and that Angus was behind it. I know not the details."

Davina pulled Broderick by his hand and up the stairs to their chamber, telling him of the fire at the betrothal celebration and how Cailin and Margeret were both captured. "Broderick..." She encouraged him to sit on the settee at the foot of their bed. "Alistair worked with a man named

Jasper in the scheme. I was meant to go with Cailin. They had mistaken Maggie for me."

He clenched his fists and stood. "Jasper! That was the man who accosted Cailin several days ago."

"Cailin was...oh, the day she followed that urchin into the alley?"

"Aye." Broderick paced the room. "Angus planned this at least a fortnight ago, mayhap even before that."

Davina nodded. "Aye, Jasper answered to Angus."

He continued circling, too agitated to stay seated. Even though Cailin was safe, the anxiety of the events needled his patience.

"Maggie returned home the following afternoon," Davina continued. "James had found her on the road where Alistair and this Jasper left her to fend for herself. The Drummonds were kind enough to take her in and see her home, Rick."

"Richard Drummond? Near Fawkirk?"

She nodded and handed him a slip of paper. "This is the note her captors left behind."

Broderick's heart sank at the name of his enemy's childhood home. "Glen Morin."

"Thankfully the Drummonds knew of it." When Broderick frowned at such news, she explained about the ghost stories. "If it wasn't for the Drummonds, James wouldn't have known where to find Cailin." Davina strolled to the writing desk at the other end of the room.

He cast a glare heavenward and cursed under his breath. These happenchance blessings only aggravated him more. "I am not finished with you yet," he grumbled to God.

"Say again?" his wife said, approaching him with a parchment in hand.

"Nothing. I shall explain shortly." He jerked his chin toward the paper. "What is that?"

"A message from James." She handed him the note.

My Dearest Family to Be,

I send this message before me and as soon as I was able, to inform you that Cailin is safe and with me. She is as unharmed as can be under the circumstances, only minor abrasions. Nothing she cannot handle. As I write this, I wonder if there is anything your wondrous daughter cannot handle. I am humbled and so very proud I will soon call her my wife and I can call myself kin to you and yours.

As the journey was arduous for us both, the ordeal of her rescue taxing, I am confident you understand the need for us to rest. Cailin and I are housed at an inn regaining our strength.

Broderick scanned the rest of the contents, gripping the paper when he did not find what he sought. "He does not say where they are *housed?* Are they in separate rooms? Who is—?"

Davina cleared her throat. "My overprotective husband."

He looked up from the parchment to the amused expression of his wife as she sat on the settee.

"I would venture to say we will not need a betrothal ceremony upon their return. Since they are promised, and it is quite obvious they have most likely—"

"Hush, woman!" Broderick tossed the message to his wife's lap and paced anew.

"Where did you stop reading?" Her eyes searched the scrawlings while he glared at her.

"Does this not concern you at all?" he snapped as he waved his arms in frustration.

Dropping the paper back to her lap, she pursed her lips in disapproval. "Whether or not you are willing to grasp the notion that our daughter is no longer a child—"

Broderick pointed a rigid finger at her and ceased pacing, silencing her for only a moment.

She sighed. "The fact still remains that Cailin is now a woman."

All the protests died on his lips. His breath left him in a defeated gust. *Cailin is now a woman. When did that happen?*

Davina rose and pulled him down for a tender press of her lips upon his own. "My sweet, sweet, loving husband and the true father of my flesh and blood." She led him to the settee and eased him to sit upon the cushion once more. "I am rather surprised to discover I am prepared for this moment and you are not." She caressed his cheeks with her warm palms. "She is James's responsibility now. He successfully pursued and rescued her. We cannot look after her forever." She paused and shrugged. "Well, *you* may be able to, but probably should not. We will just have to trust that we have chosen the right man to watch over her…and it seems we have." She raised James's message as her evidence.

Broderick nodded, yet still bewildered. "Does it not bother you that she, well…"

A sympathetic smile curled her mouth and creased her brow. "Cailin is alive and safe with James. Whether or not her maidenhead is intact when she returns is the least of my concerns. It matters not as she surrendered her virtue to the man she is to marry."

Broderick agreed. "Well, since you term it in such a way." He took up the letter and scanned the rest of the contents. "I will make arrangements on the morrow to recover Alistair's body." The rest of the missive informed them James and Cailin should return home later in the afternoon the following day. Rising, he set the parchment aside and kissed Davina's knuckles. "My journey was successful. We have an added tool that will allow us to protect this family, at last, from Angus Campbell and any other evil entity who might do us harm. It is time I shared with you what I have learned. We have a few more hours before dawn and I wish to impart this information to you now, to be sure you are able to use this tool as soon as possible. Are you able to endure the rest of the night?"

She stepped into his embrace and seared his lips with a kiss, causing Broderick's shaft to harden. "As long as we have enough time for you to make love to me before you slumber for the day, then aye. I will endure."

Broderick glanced at the window and judged the hours ahead. Sweeping Davina into his arms, he strode to the bed, wisped her night shift from her curvy figure and hastily stripped off his clothes. "Lessons will wait. I cannot bide another moment to be with you."

He bent to capture her mouth with his, cupped her bottom in his hands and lifted her onto his rigid cock to bury himself in her warmth.

Cailin snuggled into the arms of her *husband* while they sat astride their mount, traveling back to Edinburgh.

James groaned. "Keep that up, woman, and I shall have to stop and take you in the bushes."

She chuckled and wiggled her backside in response. James grabbed her hips and ground his erection against her bottom, nibbling at her shoulder. Laughter poured from her mouth and she hugged his arms about her waist. "Aye, I will behave!"

"Nay, never behave. I like you just the way you are." He kissed the crown of her head and patted her thigh. "We are very close now."

Cailin's eyes scanned the darkened landscape. They had traveled the day away from the inn and, an hour or so into sunset, they were approaching Edinburgh. Just the path from the city to their castle and they would home. "Though I would have enjoyed a more leisurely ride with you for such a great distance, I am grateful for this time to learn about your adventures at feck...feckt..."

"*Fechtschulen*...'fencing school' in the German language."

"Aye, that." She stroked the back of his hand with her palm. "I wouldn't have imagined all the things you experienced." Her heart tightened over her own experience at killing a man. "All the death. You have a strong spirit to withstand the ordeal of taking another's life."

"Mouse." He shifted in the saddle until his eyes became level with hers. "Warring and battle are the ways of men. You shouldn't have had to endure what you did, being a woman. And yet you are stronger than any woman I know. Allow me the honor of defending you, even though I know you are capable of taking care of yourself."

The lump in Cailin's throat prevented her from speaking, so she kissed James with the love and appreciation she could not say. "I'm proud to call you my defender, but know I will always have your back, should the need arise."

He chuckled and hugged her close. "I pity the dolt who would dare cross blades with you!"

Pride swelled in her breast. James truly did love her for everything she was, blades and all. They were, at first, friends and the years they spent together in childhood provided her heart a stable foundation. He kissed her shoulder and teased her skin with his tongue, setting her belly fluttering. *May that feeling never disappear*, she prayed.

They sauntered around the bend and, through a break in the trees, MacDougal Castle hovered on the horizon—torches blazing on the curtain wall, the moonlight casting silvery highlights against the slate roofs. James kicked their mount into a run and galloped up the road to the front gate, which opened upon their arrival. Broderick rushed out to the stables to meet them and swept Cailin into a crushing embrace, burying his face in her hair.

"God's blood, child!" His muffled voice reverberated against her neck. "'Tis good to have you home." He knelt, Cailin sitting on his knee as he continued to hold and rock her in his arms.

Cailin had thought she released the tension of the journey. She thought she'd expelled enough of the grief and sorrow over the last few days already in the crying and talking she did with James on the journey home. Now, in her father's arms and his love creating a cocoon of safety in his embrace, new tears poured from her and she clung to his neck. After long, racking sobs left her sniffling and breathing deep, a hand stroked her hair. She turned to find her mother waiting with tear-filled eyes and open arms. She rushed to be enveloped in Davina's embrace and more tears fell down her already wet cheeks.

"I owe you more than I will ever be able to repay you," Broderick said.

Cailin turned as James and her father grasped each other by the forearms and yanked into a manly hug, slapping backs.

"I would have battled the mightiest dragon for her, my lord." James cast adoring eyes her way and a rush of heat flared up her neck and through her cheeks.

"Come, let us get inside beside a warm fire and put some food in your bellies." Broderick wrapped his arms around both James and Cailin, ushering them up to the front entrance. The small procession of well-wishers and members of the household herded them down the halls, peeling off and going their separate ways as Cailin, her parents, Maggie and James continued toward the kitchen. Davina and Maggie bustled about to gather the supper already prepared. Cailin's stomach rumbled. She hadn't realized how hungry she was until the luscious aroma of the beef roast and baked bread surrounded her. Broderick poured wine for the five of them, and James and Cailin sat at the trestle table to dig into the food on the trenchers placed before them.

"Broderick," James began between bites. "I will need some assistance in reclaiming my father."

"Aye, son. I am sorry to hear of your loss as well as know how your father was involved."

James nodded in response. "As am I. I cannot help but feel a measure of responsibility for his—"

"Nay!" Broderick slammed his fist onto the table, silencing everyone. "I apologize, but never take the burden that is mine onto your shoulders. None of this would have happened if not for Angus, and *I* have brought him into the lives of all you good people."

Her mother laid a comforting hand upon Broderick's arm. "'Tis well you know how I feel about that position you take. I, for one, am grateful for your presence in my life and regret nothing."

Everyone at the table agreed and Cailin also reached her hand out to touch her father. "'Tis

Angus that chooses to draw us into his feud with you... not you, Da. We have never blamed you."

"What happened?" Broderick turned his eyes on James. "Were you able to apprehend her before she reached Angus?"

James shook his head. "Nay, sir. I was not." Regret laced his words.

"Da." James had done his best to rescue her from Angus and she did not want her father doubting his heart in the matter. She rose and padded to Broderick's side of the table, removed the repaired leather cord with the amulet from around her neck and handed it to Davina. "The quickest way to know all that happened would be to feed from me." Cailin offered her wrist.

Broderick cradled her wrist in his fingers, darted his eyes around the table, then back to Cailin. She nodded. Broderick opened his mouth and pressed his lips to her tender skin.

"Are you sure you want to do that?" James asked with a tremble of apprehension in his voice.

Cailin's eyes locked to her now-husband and widened, realizing what he implied. "Nay, wait!"

Too late to respond, Broderick's fangs pierced Cailin's flesh. Her knees weakened and she slumped to sit on the bench beside her father. Only a moment later, he pulled back from the bite, licking her blood from his lips. When Cailin gained her composure, she gazed upon her father's saucer-like eyes and burning red face. The heat rushed to Cailin's cheeks and mortification consumed her.

"Well." Broderick cleared his throat. "'Tis right you are, Davina. They are consummated." He glared at James and Cailin in turn.

Davina covered her mouth, yet stifled laughter spilled through her fingers. Through her chortles she said, "I must say, Broderick, I do believe this is the first time I have ever seen you blush!"

The table erupted into laughter…save for Broderick.

"Oh, Da!" Cailin's hands covered her heated cheeks. "I'm truly sorry—"

"Hush, child!" After doing a double-take, he slumped. "I suppose I can no longer refer to you as *child*, can I?" He glowered at James.

Cailin kissed her father's cheek and returned to her seat. "I'm so sorry, James. I forgot about that other part of our trip."

"Forgot? Surely 'twas more memorable than that!"

More laughter and James silenced Cailin's protests with a kiss.

However, Broderick continued to scowl at James. "Those are images I will forever need to cleanse from my mind! Impatient buck! If you had but waited, you—"

"Da!" Cailin stood and punched her fists into her hips. "You act as if I was a reluctant participant!"

Her father frowned and the laughter flared once more before gradually dying around the table.

Recovering from the shock of James and Cailin's coupling—the images still swirling around in his head, much to his dismay—Broderick eventually sifted through the information he gleaned from Cailin's blood. A heaviness pulled upon his heart. "Cailin, I am sorry for the turmoil your spirit endured while you listened to Angus's lies."

The table fell silent and he rose to pace about the room, uncomfortable with the doubts Cailin had harbored for so many years. He could not blame her and was relieved they did not take any real root in her mind, but he needed to offer an explanation. "You should not have heard as much from Angus. I should have been more forthcoming about my history with him."

"'Tis not necessary to explain, Da. I have—"

"Nay, Cailin. I need to say this. If anything, James will gain from my words."

She nodded and put the amulet back around her neck.

"In spite of what Angus said, I did not know we were brothers until that night seventeen years ago. He had used your mother to get to me. 'Tis his way of revenge…he uses those closest to his enemy. I never understood why until now." Angus ranting at Cailin while he fattened her for the feast chafed Broderick's spirit. "My father Hamish never told us why we were feuding with the Campbells. We had grown up fighting them and I only continued because of everything we had already lost at the hands of Fraser and Angus. And because Angus never stopped attacking. As far as I knew, the Campbells had been the catalyst of these battles. Angus initiating an attack may have been his retaliation from the last battle, just as our retaliations may have seemed an initiation on our part to him. And so the vicious cycle must have repeated through the years."

He shook his head and absorbed this new information, putting more pieces to the puzzle in place. "In truth, Angus was bent on revenge over what he felt was an injustice to him and his mother." Broderick squeezed his eyes shut at the memory of his brothers, Maxwell and Donnell, and their families slain by Angus. "I still cannot forgive him for slaughtering his own family, though!" He fought the tears pressing against his eyes and mayhap pleaded with his family now. "Angus *knew* we were kin and yet he still killed them—children and all—leaving me crucified to a table to gaze at their bloodied bodies with the intention of returning to slit my throat once he felt I had suffered enough!" He raked his fingers through his hair. "I will never forgive him for taking their innocent lives. If Angus had a feud with me, he should have settled it with me, not them!"

Davina rose and wrapped her arms about his waist. He hesitated in accepting her warmth. He wanted to cling to his anger to justify his own reasons for revenge, his own decision to become immortal. He did not want to explore the idea that Angus may have been justified in his actions or at least in his position at being the bastard son of Hamish MacDougal. If so, were Broderick's reasons to become immortal for naught? *But he killed his own brothers!*

He surrendered to the arms of his wife. He accepted her embrace and comforted her as she wept.

The hairs at the back of his neck tingled and rose. A faintly familiar chill rippled through his limbs. *Angus!*

He gripped Davina's shoulders and held her at arm's length. "Get everyone into my underground chambers. Now!"

CHAPTER ELEVEN

"I will do no such thing!" Cailin protested.

"You will do exactly as I tell you, child!" Broderick boomed and turned to James. "Take her in hand and go with Davina!"

Cailin fumed and drew her blades, running after Broderick's departing figure.

"Cailin!" James's voice faded behind her as she ran out the front door and into the courtyard to stand beside her father.

Broderick snatched Cailin's blades from her hands and sheathed them back at her hips in the span of a moment.

"I—" Her world twirled upside down and sideways as he tossed her over his shoulder and stomped across the courtyard, throwing her into James's arms.

"Get her inside!" her father ordered.

James set Cailin down, grabbed her by the hand and marched—surprisingly—*toward* her father. "Why did you bother training her to use her blades if not for this moment?"

"Aye!" Cailin agreed with a surge of enthusiasm fueled by pride in her perfect mate and, at last, someone who understood who she was to her core.

Broderick opened his mouth to protest, his index finger poised for an argument, but nothing came from his lips. His eyes darted from Cailin to James and his mouth fused into a straight line of disapproval. He shook his head. "You are both too stubborn for your own good." His eyes diverted to Davina. "Blossom, get inside!"

"Broderick, the gates!" Davina shouted, pointing.

He whirled around and dashed for the massive doors, still standing open from when Cailin and James had arrived not one hour ago. Her father reached the oaken doors and closed them, but before they could be secured, a reverberating *boom* pounded Cailin's ears and she staggered back when the doors slammed open, throwing Broderick across the courtyard. Hanging off their hinges for a few lingering seconds, the doors teetered and careened to the ground as guards scattered to avoid being crushed. The ground shook as the oaken beasts hit the cobblestones. Angus Campbell, sword drawn and face contorted with rage, stood at the entrance of the gate, his eyes searching.

Broderick growled, drew his sword and Angus's attention, and advanced, their blades clashing. The dizzying effects of the two Vamsyrians engaging in battle was enough to make Cailin tremble and seek refuge in the protective arms of James. Davina, James and Cailin stood with their mouths agape as the two immortals fought in flashes of fury, their arms and swinging steel blurry streaks through the air.

Reality tumbled down upon Cailin like a rain of stones.

No mortal would *ever* be a match for a Vamsyrian. No amount of training or thought-blocking or sneaky maneuvers would ever give her the advantage over such a force. Broderick only trained her to help her overcome her fears. He knew she would never be able to defend herself against any immortal. No wonder her father risked the journey south.

"Come to me!" Davina hissed.

Cailin and James whirled, and her mother's opening arms beckoned, a pleading expression on her face. Cailin stepped toward her mother and stopped short when Angus suddenly appeared behind Davina, his blade at her belly. Angus panted, fierce eyes daring anyone to make a move.

Broderick stood before Cailin and James, guarding them as he faced Angus with Davina held captive in his arms. "Your war is with *me*, Angus!"

"I shall cut her heart out as you and Hamish have cut out mine!"

Cailin's mother shook her head, her eyes beseeching. "*Veh atah adonai mahgen bah-adee, k'vodee u-merim roshee.*" On the last syllable Davina uttered, Broderick and Angus each let out a cry of agony, both thrown back through the air. Cailin ducked and gawked as Angus sailed over the side curtain wall, his heel catching on the top stone and sending him spinning head over heels out of sight. Whirling toward the direction her father flew, she winced when Broderick slammed into the front curtain wall. Just a foot higher and he would have vaulted over the towering structure as Angus had!

Her father twisted and writhed, bellowing as he remained pinned to the wall.

Through his cries and grunts, he rambled some incoherent words. "*Pitkhu li sha-ahray tsedek, avoh bahm ve odeh yah.* Davina! Say the response!"

Her mother knelt, hugging her belly as she whimpered, "*Zeh...ha...ha-sha-ar adonai. Tsadikim yavou bo.*"

Broderick fell the height of the wall to the ground with a resounding *oomph!* Panting and scrambling to his feet, he rushed to Davina's side. As he pulled her into his arms, Cailin gasped and crouched before her mother. Blood stained her gown from the gash in her abdomen to her hem. "M'ma!"

"He...cut me...as he flew," Davina managed through her moans and gasps.

Broderick snatched one of Cailin's daggers, hissed as the silver blade cut open his wrist, and let his immortal blood flow into and over Davina's wound. "Stay with me, Davina!"

She grunted, her eyes gazing up at her husband. Cailin bit her knuckle to stifle her sobs.

"Do you hear me, woman!" Broderick demanded as he slit his flesh again and administered more of his healing blood. "You stay with me!"

"Stop...yelling at me...you brute," she stammered. Davina breathed easier, her painful gasps calming to more even breaths. Though still in obvious pain, the smile crooking the corner of her mouth spoke to the miracle of her healing.

Cailin collapsed with relief.

Broderick grinned. "Aye, Blossom." He bent forward and gave her a tender kiss. Davina's breath quavered and Broderick checked her wound. His shoulders rose with his heavy sigh. He nodded to Cailin.

She will live! Cailin let the tears flow as James held her in his arms.

With a palm extended toward Cailin and James, Broderick murmured, "*Veh atah adonai mahgen bahadee, k'vodee u-merim roshee.*"

Nothing happened. Cailin darted her eyes around for any noticeable changes in her surroundings, but found none. She gazed back at her father.

"You will not feel it, but I do," he said. "That incantation has put a shield of protection around you and James. I invoked it just as a precaution for the moment. It's similar to the protection that is around the amulet you wear. I shall teach you the differences and you will learn it just as your mother did last night." Cradling Davina in his arms, he kissed her brow and caressed her cheek. "You learned it well, Blossom."

She smiled.

"I don't understand, Da. What happened? What threw you and Angus across the courtyard?"

"The incantation invokes the power of Jehovah, starting from the focused center and outward to the imagined boundary." He grinned at his wife. "You were the center and you imagined the boundary to encompass the curtain wall, aye?"

"Aye."

"That was stronger than any barrier the prophetess erected. Well done, my dove."

Cailin shook her head swarming with confusion. "But I still don't understand why you were thrown. I—"

Broderick's sad expression turned to Cailin. "Come. Let us get your mother inside. I will explain everything once we have her settled."

"Will Angus not return?" Cailin glanced around the courtyard as if expecting him to do just that.

Broderick rose on shaky legs with Davina in his arms. "As weakened as I feel from the blow, I would imagine he feels just as drained. I hardly think he's strong enough to do battle. And when he is, it will not matter. This protection will prevent him from ever harming any of you again."

Hope surged through Cailin. "Then we can, at last, kill him and end this?"

The sadness in Broderick's eyes deepened. "Nay, little one. As I said, all will be explained. Come."

Turning toward the front entrance, Broderick carried Davina, murmuring against her cheek and nuzzling her. James hugged Cailin close to his side as they followed. They stopped at the threshold and she turned to face the blackened sky.

"What, Mouse?" James kissed her temple.

"I have a strange feeling this journey my father took has opened a door to…" She couldn't quite put words to the foreboding in her heart.

"To what?"

"Considering what he just said and this lingering...I know not, James. I just know this is not finished. There's more than just a safety we now have with this protection."

"Then let us go inside and hear what Broderick has to say."

She nodded and reluctantly tore her gaze from the partial moon rising in the sky.

Cordelia paced the center of the stone circle, glancing at the full moon above. "Where are you?" she chanted, her frustration mounting. "Where are you?"

"I am as impatient as you are, my dear."

Cordelia jumped at Malloren Rune's voice and cursed under her breath.

"Again, you weren't paying attention." That mischievous light in her eyes, she winked at Cordelia and waved a hand, motioning her to follow.

"Is it finished?" Cordelia scampered after the prophetess, holding the satchel secure at her waist. "Did everything go as you said it would?"

"As we have been hoping, my child." Malloren stopped several yards from the stone circle and raised the hatch door. They both descended the iron ladder and into the vast chambers below.

Her immortal eyes allowed a clear view of the narrow passages as she followed Malloren's path into the center library chamber, the golden lamplight casting a halo around the Keeper of Secrets. Malloren padded down the steps to the center table and set the lantern beside the scattered scrolls. Cordelia sniffed the stale air and grinned. "I can still smell him."

Malloren pursed her lips and crossed her arms. "You should not still fancy him. You know where his heart is and his role in the prophecy."

Cordelia rolled her eyes heavenward and placed her satchel on the table before pulling a throne-like chair back to sit. "Of course. I like the way he smells, though."

The corner of Malloren's mouth twitched. "Well, I can hardly blame you there."

Leaning forward and clasping her hands before her to contain her excitement, Cordelia pressed the prophetess for information. "I did exactly as you instructed. I delivered the package. Pray tell me what transpired."

"You know exactly what transpired." Malloren sat in the chair opposite Cordelia and tossed her long, black braid over her shoulder. "You saw Alistair deliver the box containing the relic of protection to Amice…even though I told you not to stay around."

Cordelia clenched her hands together painfully, a monumental effort to control her embarrassment at being caught.

Malloren turned her palm up and flapped her fingers in a come-hither gesture. "Give me the shackles."

Cordelia cursed and tossed the lamb-skin satchel to the prophetess. "How I ever thought I could keep anything from a seer is beyond me."

Malloren pursed her lips. "Did you think you went on that little errand to retrieve this relic on your own?" The prophetess pulled the iron shackles from the bag and examined them.

Cordelia cursed again and sat back, pouting. "I should have known you were behind it."

The corner of Malloren's mouth turned up in amusement. "Cordelia, I know you too well and you know I have the gift of sight. Your curiosity gets the better of you sometimes. How else was I supposed to keep you from following that amulet all the way to Scotland? Besides, this errand was too important to have dabbled the way you did."

"Which errand? The one to bring the amulet to Alistair? The one to get the shackles? Or the one to find the silver pieces?"

"All of them. You know the outcome of Broderick coming down here. We have saved him from killing Angus so the prophecy can still be fulfilled. These, my dear," Malloren said, holding up the iron cuffs. "These will be needed to trap Broderick later and force his hand."

"But when will—"

"Cordelia." The prophetess sighed. "I seek just as many answers as you do. I only know what my visions have told me...and they are incomplete." She put the shackles inside the lamb-skin bag. "Remember, you must keep these in the satchel or handle them with the lamb-skin gloves."

"Yes, yes, I know. The lamb skin is the barrier against blessed items."

Malloren shook her head, but rose and offered her hand. "Come. We must now fulfill the second milestone of the prophecy."

Cordelia jumped to her feet and rushed to take Malloren's offered hand. Grabbing the lantern, the prophetess pointed at the far door and led Cordelia up the opposite stairs.

She padded after Malloren through the corridor leading to her private chambers. "You still have not told me what the second milestone is." Anticipation fluttered in Cordelia's stomach and she tugged Malloren's dark braid playfully.

Malloren pulled her hair away from Cordelia. "'One of God's chosen will become one of God's cursed so that the prophecy may be preserved.'"

Cordelia stopped in stunned silence as Malloren continued down the corridor. "She's going to become immortal," Cordelia whispered. Picking up her skirts, the enthusiasm surged through her limbs and she dashed after Malloren. "I am going to transform you!"

Malloren stood at the hearth, placed the lantern on the mantle and faced Cordelia with a smile. "Yes, my dear."

Cordelia rushed into Malloren's arms and spun her around, the two of them laughing. "But wait!" She held the prophetess at arm's length. "We cannot go before the Council. I have been banished. They'll kill me if—"

"No, child." Malloren ushered Cordelia to the chair by the hearth and sat in the adjacent seat. "The purpose of going before the Council is to ensure the one to be transformed is fully educated on their choice, so one is not made unwillingly. Nothing more. The Council started those lies about *sensing* whenever a rogue Vamsyrian is made to discourage anyone from doing so. I am a member of the *Tzava Ha'or*, so I am more than educated on the choice I am making. I am also more than willing to make such a choice. I must do this to fulfill the milestone of the prophecy and to continue to be the Keeper of Knowledge."

She touched Cordelia's cheek. "Remember, your grandmother prophesied I would be the last Prophetess of the Order. My womb is barren and you are the closest I will ever have to a daughter." A tear slipped down her cheek and Cordelia knelt before Malloren, laying her head in her lap. "The visions have shown me that since the bloodline of Keepers ends with me, immortality is the answer to preserving the prophecy. Even though God has granted me a longer life than anyone in this history of the *Tzava Ha'or*, I am still mortal and I can feel my death before me. It is time. This is God's will so that I might fulfill my destiny…and ensure yours."

Cordelia stood, anxious to begin. "Did you see your last sunrise?"

Malloren nodded with a tender smile as she stood. "I did. This morning."

The prophetess inhaled deeply and pulled her long, raven braid aside, baring her neck.

Cordelia eyed the rapid pulse at Malloren's throat. "At long last," she breathed. Stepping into the embrace of the prophetess, Cordelia sank her fangs into her flesh and drank deep to begin the transformation.

EPILOGUE

The sun sparkled across the waters in the port harbor of Leith, *Knightly's Refuge* swaying gently under Cailin's feet as she stood on the port side of its deck. A breeze lifted stray auburn locks from her cheeks and she smiled into the salty air.

"That be the last of it, Mistress Cailin."

She turned to their first mate, Joseph, and nodded with a grin. "Thank you, Joe. I'll tell James."

Joe tipped his hat and descended into the belly of the vessel. A man of habit, he would be about his routine preparations in his cabin before they set sail on their third voyage. The merchant trips were short and fairly local and Cailin always reveled in the freedom surging through her spirit as the ship cut through the open waters. Holding her palms open, she performed *her* routine, reciting the blessing incantation as she envisioned a bubble of protection around the entire ship—from bow to stern and from mast to belly. Satisfied her task was complete, she gripped the rail and enjoyed the view.

Mesmerized by the ocean beyond the marina, Cailin sighed when her husband's body pressed against her back. His warm hands smoothed over her rounded belly and the familiar nuzzle at her neck sent shivers of anticipation down her arms.

"How is our boy doing?" he murmured against her skin.

She giggled. "Our *girl* is doing just fine." She enjoyed this banter she had with her husband since they discovered she was with child four months or so ago. She honestly didn't care if she had a boy or girl. It wouldn't be their last and they had plenty of time to have a brood of male and female Knightlys.

James turned her in his arms and slanted his mouth over hers. He then planted a sweet kiss to the tip of her nose. "Are we ready?"

"Aye, Joe says everything is loaded."

"Good."

Cailin fingered the cross hanging around James's neck and touched the one between her breasts. Both had been blessed with the incantation as well. Added protection and with them wherever they went. *Never again to live in fear.* "And the barrier is up on the ship."

"Very good."

A stout man with a light-brown beard and severe eyes stalked down the dock.

"That's our final passenger," James whispered and patted her bottom before he meandered to the opposite side of the deck. He waved to the man, who grunted in response. Occasionally, *Knightly's Refuge* took paying passengers to local destinations. Many were friendly enough. Some liked to keep to themselves.

This may be one of those who likes to keep to himself, Cailin pondered as the scowling man approached the ship.

"The last of your cargo is loaded, sir," her husband greeted. "We're ready to set sail."

Another grunted response, the man stepped onto the gang plank and stopped. His frown deepened and he stepped back onto the dock, his eyes roaming over the length of the vessel.

Cailin stood at her husband's side as the man assessed their boat. He took another step back and leveled a stare at James and Cailin. She gasped when a yellow light flashed in his eyes. *Did he just growl?*

"I want my cargo off this ship immediately."

James glanced at Cailin, his brow furrowed. "Is there something amiss, sir?"

The bearded man narrowed his eyes. "I'll not travel with the likes of you," he snarled. "Get my cargo off your ship…now."

James shrugged and stepped to the cabin stairs. "Joseph, let's get Paddy and Keith up here. Mr. Stellar wants his cargo unloaded."

"He what?" the first mate bellowed from below. "But we just loaded it!"

James flashed Cailin a smile and skipped down the stairs into the ship. After some heated mumbling, Joe stalked up the stairs with a smirking James not far behind, Paddy and Keith in tow. Grumbling, the three men did as ordered, taking many opportunities to glare at their ex-passenger.

James grinned at Mr. Stellar, nodded and returned to Cailin's side. She also smiled at the scowling man and snuggled beside James to enjoy the warmth of his arms. *Aye, never again to live in fear. And neither will our children.*

The End

SNEAK PEAK AT BOOK 3

MIDNIGHT HUNT

CHAPTER ONE

Outside the Village of Kostbar, Germany—1636

Eighty years ago today, he killed her…

Broderick clenched his teeth as he held the frail body of his beloved Davina to his chest. "Please." He gashed his wrist with his fangs and offered his healing blood. She shook her head. His wound healed in moments.

"We have already discussed this." Davina pushed his wrist from her face then coughed and curled in his lap like a fetus. She pressed the kerchief to her mouth as she labored through another long spell of hacking and wheezing.

The scent of her blood wafted up to his senses and he savored the sweet essence of his wife as tears stung his eyes. "I will not lose you. Please let me heal you, just this once more." His plea would be useless.

Drawing shallow breaths and wiping the blood from her mouth, she gazed at him with sorrow in her eyes. "That is what you said the last two times. Darling, I cannot bear to live like this. You know the healing is only temporary. Your blood cannot purge this disease from my body and each time it returns worse." His wife gasped and coughed, crying out through the agony of her condition.

"Let me transform you, Davina!" He clung to her tiny body, so thin from the sickness, willing with all his spirit she would listen this time. "Then you will be healed and we can spend eternity together."

"And spend an eternity running from—" She gritted her teeth as a spasm wracked her body. "Running from the Vamsyrian Council. I want peace, my love." She heaved breaths and relaxed in his arms. "I want peace."

Broderick helped her lie back onto their bed and nestled under the covers beside her. She shivered in his arms. Her fingers feathered across his bare chest, trembling as she reached for his face. He grasped her hand and pressed his lips to her palm. Though gray streaks had dulled her hair with age and the wrinkles on her beautiful face bore testimony to her sixty years, the light of her spirit shining from within had never diminished. But in these last two weeks, that light faded. Davina grew weary.

"It is too late for me, Broderick. Even immortality cannot restore my youth." She chuckled and Rick's heart constricted. "We would forever receive the scathing looks thrown at us now…an old woman with such a young, handsome man. Scandalous."

"I care not what others think. I—"

She placed a finger on his lips. "Hush." She moaned and clung to him, coughing and bleeding from her mouth onto his chest. "End this now," she wheezed, when the fit had passed. "Feed from me one last time, my darling. Let my life give you sustenance and give me peace."

"Nay!" He gripped her shoulders and searched her eyes for reason. "You cannot ask this of me!"

"I plead for mercy, Rick." She sobbed and a wave of misery flooded him with such a force, it stole the breath from his lungs. His wife had been holding back all this time!

"My god! Why did you not let me—"

"Forgive me, my love, but I did not want you to worry so." She pressed her palms to his cheeks, wet from tears. "But now you know why I beg you to let me go."

"Nay, Davina," he whimpered into her hair and enveloped her in his embrace. Rocking her in his arms, he wept as she wracked through another fit of coughing and moaning. She held nothing back. Her anguish consumed him. Heart breaking, but knowing he could not let her endure this misery for his sake, he surrendered. "Aye, Blossom."

Broderick pushed the hair from her smiling face and tired eyes. She nodded and sighed. "Thank you, my love."

He pressed his forehead to hers and clenched his jaw. "How will I live eternity without you?"

Threading her tiny fingers into his hair, she gripped him with as much strength as her weakened form would allow, but her eyes bore into his with purpose. "Hear this now.

Nothing, not even death, will keep me from loving you. Though this body may wither and become a dry shell, my spirit will pursue you until the end of time. We will never be apart."

He covered her mouth with his and tasted her blood. Trailing tender kisses across her cheek and jawline, he nestled against her neck. "Eternally yours," he whispered.

She clutched his head and offered her throat. "Together forever," she responded.

Broderick hesitated, her erratic pulse beating against his tongue.

"Give me peace," she whispered in a tortured breath. "Do this for me."

"I will love you forever, Davina." His fangs pierced her cool skin and Broderick drank the life from his wife, granting her wish…and tormenting his already damned soul.

Broderick threw the empty earthen cup across the tavern and it shattered, raining pottery shards over the patrons at the far wall.

"Acht!" The innkeeper charged to Broderick's table and stuck a rigid finger in his face. "Another outburst like that and I'll toss you out on your rump!"

Rick scoffed and leaned forward. "Don't you have anything stronger than beer?" he demanded in German. "Bring me Scotch."

The owner threw his head back and let forth a hearty guffaw. "You're drunk enough, if you ask for that." He glanced around as a few others joined him in a chuckle, but Broderick frowned. The man sobered. "Beer and wine is all I have. You want *aqua vitae*, you'll have to travel down the river to Bremen."

Rick tossed a small sack of coins onto the table. "Then bring a cask of beer to my table. There's enough there to pay for ten of them."

The stocky man snatched the bag and examined the coins. Cocking an eyebrow, he hefted the sack then narrowed his eyes at Rick. The innkeeper disappeared through the door at the rear of the tavern and returned with a cask and a lead cup. "No more smashing my wares. It's no business of mine if you want to drink yourself into sin, but you've been peaceful until now. Let's keep it that way." With a nod, he stomped off to his post behind the wooden counter.

Broderick glared at the other patrons, who eyed him with a mixture of apprehension, anger and disgust. However, they were all wise enough to divert their attention elsewhere, leaving him to his drink. The small tavern he'd wandered into was dark and unassuming. He just needed a hole in which to hide and sort through his thoughts.

What in blazes am I doing in Germany?

The decades had been lonely without Davina, but he had managed. Seeing Cailin and James eased some of the grief. Though he mostly left Cailin in the capable hands of her husband, Broderick returned every few years to visit…and they grew older while he did not. They had five beautiful children, who also grew into adulthood. Broderick watched from afar as time stole them from him, one by one. None of their children or grandchildren pursued the shipping company so, when Cailin and James passed, Broderick reclaimed it, long forgotten by their offspring. The business kept him occupied enough to stave off the heartache of losing Davina. Though his bereavement had never disappeared, he *had* managed. And when her birthday arrived, he mourned as he always did on those special days. But this year, as he wept over her grave, grief swallowed him. The specter of his beloved Davina had penetrated his defenses and pierced through the numbness he'd forged over the near-century. A yearning had pulled him south, out of Scotland, through England, across the Channel and into France. Then the compelling desire to traverse along the war-torn, northern coast yanked his soul through the Netherlands and into Germania of the Holy Roman Empire. And here he sat, staring at the leaden mug waiting to be filled, just as he ached for his own heart to be filled.

Due to the rapid healing of his immortal blood, alcohol had no real effect on him. At one time, he'd had a generous portion of Scotch whiskey and started to feel the effects, but it passed quickly. He gulped down six mugs of beer from the cask and closed his eyes tight against the ache in his chest. The libation did nothing to drive the images of her from his mind. *I should savor them. Relive them again and again. Eight decades of silence…and then a precious, spectral encounter with her today.* He had only dreamt when Davina was near, whenever she thought of him while he slumbered during the day. But she was dead, so these new visions couldn't be her. Perhaps he had been so consumed with grief on the eightieth anniversary of her death, he had finally gone mad.

Davina had been in the woods, her ethereal form naked and waiting for him. Her cinnamon tresses spilled over her shoulders and hid the precious globes of her breasts, but blended with the thatch of curls at the juncture of her thighs. Young and breathtaking as when she'd entered his Gypsy tent as a voluptuous woman.

He fell to his knees before her and buried his face in her skin, inhaling the lavender scent of her hair and growing hard. "Davina!" He covered her belly with kisses and nibbles, his hands smoothing over her silken legs and bottom and back, not able to get enough of her.

She cradled his head against her breasts and wept. "How I've missed you!"

Davina straddled his thighs and Broderick claimed her lips. Tearing open his breeches, he slipped inside her wet heat. Surely he had died and gone to heaven! She clung to his back as she rode him to a swift and furious climax, taking Broderick with her.

Shuddering and panting, he pulled back to gaze at the rapture on her face and a raven-haired woman with olive skin rocked in his arms. "Blossom?"

She nodded, her sapphire eyes revealing the woman he would die for. Davina pressed her lips to his and wrapped her legs around his waist. "Together forever."

Aye, he *had* gone mad. Broderick opened his eyes, reached for the cask and jerked with a start.

Malloren Rune sat across the table from him. "Well met, Broderick MacDougal," she whispered in her British accent, concern in her gaze.

The Prophetess! "I cannot recall the last time I have been taken by surprise." He scowled at her. "Exactly how much does your position as the Keeper of Secrets prolong your life?" The last time he had seen her, over a century ago, she was more than one-hundred sixty years old. What was different about her? Her skin had the subtle luster only seen on… "You are a Vamsyrian?"

She nodded.

"But…you are a member of the Army of Light."

"It was necessary so I may continue my station. My transformation was the second milestone in the prophecy. It appears I will be the steward of this journey to redemption for Vamsyrians."

He tipped his head back and a sardonic chuckle rumbled through him at the irony. "The one who advises mortals against the very choice you made. Have you sacrificed your soul to save us all?"

Clearing her throat, she squared her shoulders and raised her chin with regal defiance. "There are many sacrifices I have made through the years in my service to God, though none quite as important as this. The prophecy is why I am here."

He grumbled. "Where were you when Davina died of consumption? You claimed she was the key to this damned prophecy and, when I needed answers, you were nowhere to be found. How is it I did not sense you approach me?"

She shifted in her chair and avoided his glare. "My talents for remaining unseen were magnified when I crossed over." She narrowed her eyes. "You will not find me if I do not wish to be found." She glanced at his cup, then the cask. Sadness shrouded her face and she sighed. "I truly regret the sorrow you have endured over her passing. But I have—"

Broderick jumped to his feet and snatched her throat in his hand. "Lies!" he hissed. "The prophecy. Her part in it. Don't pretend to show compassion toward either of us. If you had a care, you would have let me kill Angus and I could have made amends with the Council. She would be with me now."

In spite of the hold Rick had on her, she only encircled his wrist with her fingers and shook her head. "If you had killed Angus," she whispered. "Davina's soul would have been destroyed and you would have lost her forever."

"I *did* lose her!"

"Take your hands off the maiden, son."

Broderick glanced to his left and spied a half-dozen glowering men, ready to pounce with various blunt objects and clubs in their fists.

But Malloren put her palm out to stay the crowd. "I am not in danger, kind sirs," she rasped in German. "But *you* will be, if you take another step closer. I know this man and, in his present disposition, he will tear your beating hearts from your chests."

Broderick shoved Malloren back into her chair and snarled. "You know nothing about me, woman." He waved a dismissive hand at the intimidated men. "You have nothing to fear from me." He crossed his arms and scowled at the Prophetess.

The innkeeper narrowed his eyes. "Acht! Damned gentry and your sick games." He pointed his axe at Broderick. "I've had enough of you and your lady friend. Get out of my tavern."

As much as Broderick wanted to release his pent up anger and grief on everyone around him, rational thought won over his emotions. These men didn't deserve his wrath. He'd save that for

Malloren. He leveled his gaze on her. "Aye, let us take this outside, shall we?"

She rubbed her throat and nodded. Rick pivoted on his heel and stalked out of the tavern.

The damp, chilled August night haunted his form, surrounding him with heavy foreboding. Malloren scampered to catch up as he stomped down the road to the coastline. The North Sea lay quietly hidden on his left behind an oppressive fog bank. The stillness of the late night sucked the life out of his argument. He grumbled.

"We are far enough from the town. Let us speak."

He continued down the road at a determined pace. "So you can feed me more of your lies? I think not."

"You dreamt of her today, didn't you?"

He stopped and held his breath, squeezing his eyes shut against the dream and Davina's haunting presence.

"She lives, Broderick MacDougal."

He whirled to face the prophetess and she stepped back. "Why are you here! To torment me? Is my grief not enough to satisfy you?"

"I'm here to help you. Davina has been reborn. Have you not had a yearning to come here? Are you not drawn to this place by an unknown force?"

"Stop speaking to me in riddles! She is dead!" Broderick paced, doing his best to push down the rising tide of hope the Prophetess could bring back his wife…because believing was insane.

"Davina's soul resides in another body and is calling out to you now."

"What are you…? So she is a wee bairn? A child I am to…what, *raise*?" Broderick resisted the urge to slap the woman, who had obviously lost all her faculties.

"No, of course not. She is a full-grown woman."

He stood with his mouth agape. "Do you hear yourself?"

"I know this may sound…"

"Mad? That it does! And you contradict your teachings. The soul lives once and is destined for heaven or hell. Is it not why Vamsyrians were created…to trap the soul and condemn it to an eternity in hell? A choice, I might add, you have also made."

"As is my understanding of this *arrangement* with Satan, and yes…I am a part of those souls now. But if we can fulfill the prophecy, we will be saved. Davina is the key."

"If *we* can fulfill the prophecy?" Broderick placed his fists on his hips. "You speak as though we have a say in the matter."

Color mottled Malloren's cheeks. "*If* the prophecy can be fulfilled," she amended. "As for the soul's journey in death, there are some who are given the choice to return to earth. Thus is the purpose of Davina's soul, to return and fulfill the prophecy."

Broderick's mind twirled with confusion and he shook his head to clear it. "I have had enough of this." He stalked away from Malloren, the sea on his left once again, his figure bent forward to his destination.

"And you still walk toward her," Malloren confirmed. "She has raven-black hair, does she not?"

Broderick slowed his steps.

"But still has the dark-blue eyes of Davina, no?"

He stopped and, again, closed his eyes to resist becoming lost in the dream of her. "How do you know this?"

"I have seen her in visions and this is why I am here. Tell me the dream."

He breathed deep, his eyes still closed. "She was in the woods. We had a tearful reunion and spoke of our love." Broderick turned to Malloren. "When I pulled back from our embrace, I saw the dark-haired woman of whom you speak, yet she had the eyes of Davina."

The Prophetess treaded carefully to Broderick's side. "In my visions, she holds a wooden tome in her arms, a pentacle surrounded by vines burned into the cover."

"A pentacle?"

She nodded and knelt, drawing in the dirt with her finger a five-pointed star inside a circle with a continuous stroke of her hand, ending where she began.

Broderick's brows rose. "Aye, I saw this book, on the ground by her feet. A thick volume, bound with leather laces crisscrossed along the spine?"

"Yes, the very one."

"But the pentacle. 'Tis the symbol of witchcraft, is it not? The sign I've seen used against the accused, which are facing the endless inquisitions that rape these lands? I saw many such trials on my journey here."

She frowned. "Yes, but unfortunately, the Church has taken this symbol of life and protection against evil and turned it into a tool of hatred. Hypocrites." She tapped on each point of the star. "Water, fire, earth, air and spirit enclosed within the circle. All of the elements of life in a never-ending knot." Malloren snatched Broderick's hand, using him to help her rise, and she gasped, holding tight. He tried to free from her grasp, but she refused to release him until she opened her eyes and grinned. "I see you have made yourself a bit of a nuisance to the Inquisitors."

Broderick crossed his arms and stepped away from her. "I couldn't just let those innocent people burn. I heard their thoughts. The church is wrong…as usual." He glared down his nose at her. "What does all this have to do with Davina?"

"This book holds the next milestone in the prophecy. And she seeks a cure for Satan's weapon against the Vamsyrians."

"Now you're talking in circles, Prophetess. If Satan created the Vamsyrians, why would he need a weapon against them?" He cocked his eyebrow, skeptical of the forthcoming explanation.

"That is the deception of the Prince of Darkness. He lures God's children to willingly turn their back against their Father, and then slays them with another creature to ensure their souls belong to him. Satan's sure way to bypass the redemption of the prophecy."

"You speak of werewolves." Broderick rubbed his left shoulder, scarred over thirty years ago during his first encounter with *Satan's weapon.*

"Yes, and you are treading into their territory. There are many sightings and encounters in this area. I suggest you find aconite to guard your lair during the day. They are not harmed by the sun."

"Aconite? I've never heard of it."

"It is also known as monkshood, wolfsbane." She jerked her head in the direction of the road. "You will find Davina in the Village of Kostbar ahead. You are here to reunite with her and protect her."

Broderick turned his back on the Prophetess for fear he might strangle her again. "And why would she be looking for a cure for werewolves?"

The gentle waves lapping against the beach was his answer. Rick whirled to find the Prophetess gone. "Curse you, woman!"

He wiped his face and paced a few steps before sighing and studying the empty road to the village. The fog from the North Sea crept onto the land and wove through the trees bordering the path, obscuring his view. His wandering had led him here. He would see this through. If Davina wasn't there and if these were more lies, then he would put this damned prophecy and his grief behind him. But if the Prophetess was right… Broderick's heart hammered in his chest with a hope he'd not felt in almost a century. *Could it be? Will she know me? Will she remember our love?* He shook his head. "I am mad."

Nothing, not even death, will keep me from loving you…my spirit will pursue you until the end of time. Together forever.

"Eternally yours." Broderick stomped down the path toward Kostbar.

NOTE TO THE READER

Thank you for taking the time to read *Midnight Captive – Book 2 of the Bonded By Blood Vampire Chronicles*. I hope you enjoyed the story and you're looking forward to *Book 3 – Midnight Hunt*! If you did like the book, reviews are always appreciated at Amazon, GoodReads, LibraryThing or your favorite book review website. I invite you to visit my website at **www.ArialBurnz.com** for updates on my latest tales, appearances, contests, and writing tips. I love to hear from my readers, so be sure to leave a comment on my blog.

ABOUT THE AUTHOR

Arial Burnz has been an avid reader of both paranormal and fantasy fiction for over thirty years. With bedtime stories filled with unicorns, hobbits, dragons and elves, she had no choice but to craft her own tales, penning to life the many magical creatures roaming her mind and dreams. And with a romantic husband who's taught her the meaning of true love, she's helpless to weave romance into her tales. Now she shares them with the world. Arial Burnz lives in Rancho Cucamonga, California, with her husband (a.k.a. her romance novel hero)—who is also a descendent of Clan MacDougal—along with their dog and two cats.

Made in the USA
San Bernardino, CA
21 March 2014